Valley of Decision

The novels of Stanley Middleton

A Short Answer
Harris's Requiem
A Serious Woman
The Just Exchange
Two's Company
Him They Compelled
Terms of Reference
The Golden Evening
Wages of Virtue
Apple of the Eye
Brazen Prison
Cold Gradations
A Man Made of Smoke
Holiday
Distractions
Still Waters
Ends and Means
Two Brothers
In a Strange Land
The Other Side
Blind Understanding
Entry into Jerusalem
The Daysman

Valley of Decision

STANLEY MIDDLETON

Hutchinson

London Melbourne Sydney Auckland Johannesburg

Hutchinson & Co. (Publishers) Ltd

An imprint of the Hutchinson Publishing Group

17–21 Conway Street, London W1P 6JD

Hutchinson Publishing Group (Australia) Pty Ltd
16–22 Church Street, Hawthorn, Melbourne, Victoria 3122

Hutchinson Group (NZ) Ltd
32–34 View Road, PO Box 40–086, Glenfield, Auckland 10

Hutchinson Group (SA) Pty Ltd
PO Box 337, Bergvlei 2012, South Africa

First published 1985
© Stanley Middleton 1985

Set in Plantin by D. P. Media Limited,
Hitchin, Hertfordshire

Printed and bound in Great Britain by Anchor Brendon Ltd,
Tiptree, Essex

British Library Cataloguing in Publication Data
Middleton, Stanley
Valley of decision.
I. Title
823'. 914[F]   PR6063.125
ISBN 0 09 159430 8

For Chloe, Caroline, Matthew and Elizabeth,
with love

Multitudes, multitudes, in the valley of decision.

Joel, 3, 14

1

Voices trickled insistent but subdued in the open air. Lights from the portico and lines of windows of the great house touched, yellowed the foliage of lime trees, full-leaved still in October. In the distance of the park mist clung a yard deep to the ground, unmoving, thick as bonfire smoke.

On the drive a small bus, J. Salmon, Luxury Coaches, Beechnall, and a van nearly as large were parked. The footsteps of the players crunched satisfyingly on the gravel towards these.

'Not so cold as I thought it would be.'

'You'll cool off.'

'Aren't you waiting for Mary, then?'

'No. She'll come back by car, and I'll have the kettle on. I hope.'

They filed towards the van to hand over their instruments, three cellos and a double bass; a shadowy scarfed figure received them, stacked them into a flimsy, prepared framework; the upper strings had carried their cases with them to the bus.

'That's it, then.' The van doors slammed.

David Blackwall made for the bus, took a seat to himself, opened his overcoat, stretched his legs. He could not maintain the position for long, sat, scrubbed at the misted windows. Car lights streamed and flashed; engines crashed into noise.

'That's all of us, is it?'

The driver, not waiting for an answer, switched on with violence, dimming the coach lights. They left with a jerk; one minute under the superior glow of Rathe Hall, the next they were lurching through the blacknesses of the park, ground fog, trees, in an avenue under a cheesy slice of moon.

Seven musicians made their way back towards life. Three discussed football without animation, the rest held themselves in uncompanionable silence, dark, jerking figures, yawning.

7

David Blackwall pulled his coat round him again, buttoned it, straightened the tails, stared out. They had passed the lodge, the wrought-iron gates which were fastened back, and now bumped through a village, its one street incongruously garish under a short stretch of sodium lights.

'Remember me, but, ah, forget my fate.'

Blackwall smiled, removed a glove to wipe his dry lips with the back of his hand, re-dressed himself. Now they smoothly took the approach road to the motorway, headed south among darkness and headlights.

They were later than expected, at nearly half past eleven. *Dido and Aeneas* due to start at 9.30 had not begun until after ten and then to an audience garrulous with wine or groping their way in from the lavatories. Blackwall felt no affection for these people who had bought their way into Rathe Hall for a charity performance, had eaten and drunk and been seen, had sat down in snobbery to Purcell. They would have taken more of their money's worth humming to a selection of *Chu Chin Chow* or *Oklahoma*.

'You don't look pleased.' His neighbour, Guy Foulds, turned from the seat in front.

'I'm tired.'

'I was never tired at your age.' Foulds tucked his thick white wavy hair into the corner between window and seat, closing his eyes, expelling breath as one justified.

The driver belted along the motorway so that the whole bus shook and rattled, precluding consecutive thought. Blackwall was content at this rolling in his seat, not unprepared to end up in the gangway; the roughness of the bus lulled and symbolized his anger. Once they left the motorway the driver proceeded no more decorously, rounding corners with careless skill, raspingly determined to smash into the headlights of oncoming cars. Blackwall was amazed, as usual, at the number of vehicles on the road at this time of night.

'Right, David. Here y'are. Station Road. Home.'

Blackwall stood. In spite of the bus's headlong career, the instrument van had already arrived, back doors gaping.

'There she is.'

The cello was handed down. The bus rattled off; Victor

8

Houghton, next away, would have to wait, though not long, for his case. David Blackwall picked up his Amati, the most valuable object in the street, and let himself into the house.

By the time his wife arrived David had switched on the electric blankets, made coffee and toast, had poached an egg and had just opened yesterday morning's newspaper by one bar of the electric fire.

Mary slipped off her rain mac, looking as tired as he felt. He sprang up, buttered her bread, crowned it with the egg, placed it in front of her as she sat stiffly at the end of the table. She held her face cupped in her hands; he kissed the top of her head, and she uncovered to smile up at him. Her skin was sallow in this light, and traces of make-up remained in the roots of her hair above the forehead.

'Is the water hot?' she asked, when she had thanked him, picked up her knife and fork.

'I'll turn it on.'

'No. Don't bother. I'll wash my hair in the morning.'

She was beautiful as she ate, in spite of fatigue and the banality of cutting and chewing; but quite different from the dazzling creature on the stage two hours earlier. She had played Belinda, with her hair piled, pleated white garments catching, outlining in light the shape of her legs as she moved. Her arms had been bare; these hands deliberately expressive.

'Thy hand, Belinda, darkness shades me. On thy bosom I would rest.' Dido's huge eyes, black as cherries, had flashed; the imperious breasts had heaved under royal purple. 'More I would but death invades me. Death is now a welcome guest.' And already the vibrato was moving in Blackwall's fingers to introduce the ground bass of Purcell's chacony, to clear the wine fumes, to announce heavenly seriousness.

'Are the beds on?' she asked, mouth full.

'They are.'

She nodded, a prosaic gesture, not to be compared with the statuesque clarity of her persona on stage, but cheering. She acknowledged her husband's efficiency.

'It went well,' he told her.

'Once we started.'

'Yes. They took some prising from the gin bottles.'

'We'd be there still. Alfred was complaining. He said he'll speak to Tait or Sir Edward.'

Tonight, Wednesday, was the first performance; they had two more, on Friday and Saturday.

'It was crowded,' she said, finishing her egg.

'More toast?'

She shook her head. 'It'll do for the birds.'

He cleared her plate, taking it out to the kitchen, brought in the breakfast dishes, laid the spoons and knives.

'I'm knackered,' she said.

'You get to bed. It needs Samson to hold Fat Liza up for long.' He staggered through a brief, exaggerated caricature of Belinda supporting the expiring Dido.

'She was marvellous, though.' Mary stood, as if uncertain which way to turn.

'I'll give you that,' he admitted.

Mary extended her hand. He took it, pulled her to him, kissed her full on the mouth, but gently.

'Five and twenty to bloody one,' he said.

'Leave things.'

'No. I'll just straighten up. Won't take a minute. I'll be glad in the morning.'

She allowed it, drifted away towards the stairs. He bustled, removing crumbs from the tablecloth, checking window fastenings and locks. Satisfied he removed plugs from sockets, made for the bathroom where Mary had left the light on, whether by deliberation or not he did not know, to scrub his teeth.

His wife loved his teeth-cleaning, with mockery. 'It's a military operation,' she had said. 'It's more thorough than Mr Gladstone's mastication. It's a thirty-year war.' He admitted the truth of her exaggeration, carefully scouring his mouth with the brush, not once, but twice.

'Why don't you buy yourself an electric brush?' she had asked often enough.

'And let my right hand forget its cunning.'

Mary cleaned her teeth left-handed, quickly and lightly. They had been married now for just over twelve months and could still be surprised, delighted, caught up with some everyday action in the partner.

10

They had met at the Royal College where he had done a year with his cello after completing a history degree, and much music, at Cambridge. She had been in her second year, a talented student, but already certain that she would not make her career in singing, an amateur, an outsider. Her teacher praised her; she won a prize; she was outstandingly good at her second subject, the piano, but she seemed to stand apart, to lack large ambition. This is a dead end, she appeared to pronounce, attractive, glittering, but a corpse.

When David came back to his home town to teach music and history at the grammar school, Mary spent a last year at the college, which she completed with plaudits. They had written twice a week, and met as often as possible during the year of separation, but when he proposed marriage she had informed him that she had joined a small new touring company and was committed for at least twelve months. He was surprised, slightly fearful, as if all her impudences at the expense of a career in singing had been forgotten once an opportunity had presented itself.

'It's what I've been trained for.'

'But you always said . . .'

'I know, I know. That was no reason for you to believe me, was it, now?' She sounded affectionate. She loved him. She had said so.

They did not argue at length, but he continued to propose, by post during an extended tour of north Germany. It was thus by letter that he was accepted, while she similarly instructed him later to make arrangements for the wedding at a register office in London. He taught his classes the day before; she sang that Friday in *Così* in Paddington; they were man and wife by 11 a.m. and she was back in the theatre that evening. They spent Sunday together in a borrowed flat though he had to set off in the early hours to teach first period Monday. She came to the Midlands for Wednesday, Thursday and Friday, but left on that day for the first stage of another tour of Germany. It had all been haphazard, ill-arranged. He remembered coming back home on Friday afternoon, no schoolmaster is quite sane at that time, to the room they had shared in his parents' house. Nothing reminded him of her: no perfume, no discarded garment, only a row of untenanted coat hangers in the wardrobe.

11

Mary and his mother, he imagined them at it, had cleared the place between them so that it stood now in unusual tidiness, bed squared, carpets hoovered, aerosol in the high cornices ready for the onset of his bachelor squalor.

The first six months of their marriage were spent with only occasional meeting and frequent letters; he arranged his Easter vacation in Hamburg where the company performed *The Turn of the Screw*; this period now seemed a happy chaotic time, with the chatter of pedestrians in a German they could not exactly make out matching their pleasure, their body contacts, their delightful recognition of love. They acted like children, without responsibility except towards each other and in physical discovery. The dark world of houses and factories, of ships and container lorries blossomed, put out a new leaf, a greenness, a promise of fulfilment; sunlight shaped shadows, shifted cameos, warmed naked skin. Sparrows crowded the parks.

'They sing just like our birds,' he said.

'What do you expect?' She was pleased with him. 'German?'

'Wagner.' He stuck his chin into his collar and mimed a *Heldentenor* in full crow.

'Virginia Woolf's birds spoke Greek when she was mad.'

'How d'you know that?'

'I read it. I've plenty of time for reading.'

'Is that what the rest of them do?'

'Some.' Her voice rose, reflecting morning joy, the brightness of sky, the presence of a husband. 'Some not.' Truth prevailed, happily.

It was, oddly, from his father that he had learned the direction his wife's career was next to take. Horace Blackwall, not much of a talker at breakfast, a heavy-breathing reader of the *Daily Telegraph*, had lowered his paper that morning to announce, clearing the frog from his throat, that he had spoken to Mary and had offered her at any time she decided to leave opera a position in his firm's accounts department. David was surprised; his father, he knew, approved of the girl, courted her even in his dry, moustache-chewing fashion, would be only too glad to have her settled in with the family, but Mary herself said nothing to him.

12

'You mean you're holding a post open for her?' He liked to keep his father up to the mark.

'You could say so.' A shaking of creases out of the newspaper.

'And when will this start?'

'I should be asking you that.' His father frowned, clamping his lips, condemning the noncommunicative lives of young people. 'As far as I could ascertain,' his father loved on occasion such formality of lexis, 'she has not made up her mind. She is enjoying herself, and,' the copula heavily thumped, 'she doesn't feel it's too unfair on you yet. But we discussed the possibility.' The *Telegraph* was closed, with a brisk solemnity that still gave time for further comment, but as none was forthcoming, the old man coughed, brushing imaginary crumbs from his waistcoat, and attended by his wife made for bedroom, bathroom, hall closet and garage, all within five minutes, to join the crawl of traffic into town.

His father was shrewd; grandfather and great-uncle had hauled themselves by prodigious labour out of the working class into the ownership of two large furniture shops, a small factory and some scattered property acquired at knock-down prices during two wars. When Horace returned from the army in 1947, the uncle, David Daniel Blackwell, had died a bachelor, leaving his considerable estate between his younger brother and his nephew, Horace. The young captain, twenty-three years old but already confident, had taken the opportunity to expand, terrifying his father first with the extent of his borrowings and equally with the gigantic scale of his profits and holdings. He had twice sold off sections of his businesses to national concerns, and had then expanded elsewhere. When his father died in 1970 accountants had seen to it that the government did not seize too much. Horace George Blackwall was a successful man, and clearly, recessions and government changes notwithstanding, intended to remain so.

There was, however, no ostentation about him. He continued to live in the large, stone villa he had bought in 1954 on his marriage to Joan Blake. He had spent money on improvements, had added to the already considerable grounds by judicious purchase, but had not moved out to the manors,

13

houses, or old vicarages in the villages, the modern ranch styles with swimming pools and treble garages that people of not half his means had acquired. He gave moderately to charity, took no part in local or national politics, held no office in golf clubs, churches or societies, was reticent about his family affairs, sparing of advice, but considerably respected and feared. Those whom he employed were expected to work. He had experienced trouble with the unions, but paid well enough, and had sufficient shrewdness not to be intimidated. He could not be called well liked, but neither he nor his opponents saw much sense in popularity. He had lived in a period when expansion and success had been possible, and he had made the most of it.

By mentioning the possibility of Mary's joining the firm, Horace Blackwall had surprised his son. David, intrigued, slightly annoyed, had questioned his father the same evening and had been told that Mary had a good A-level in mathematics.

'I didn't know that,' the son confessed.

'No.' Irony of disbelief. 'You perhaps didn't need such information about a prospective partner in marriage.' The father slightly adjusted his dentures and, smiling, left David to think about the saw.

One never knew exactly how one stood with the senior Blackwall.

He had been pleased that his son had done well at school, and delighted by his scholarship to Cambridge. His wife had been responsible for his musical upbringing; her family, the Blakes, were accomplished amateurs, but Horace had attended the boy's performances when business commitments allowed, congratulated him, made odd, old-fashioned comments. When David had suggested first a year at the Royal College after university and then a job as a schoolmaster, his father had not demurred, to his son's surprise.

'I suppose it's not well paid,' David had said, feeling it his duty to ensure his family understood implications.

'What's the salary?'

David told him. His father touched his bristling moustache as if doing arithmetic.

'That's more than you'd get if you started with me,' he said.

14

'The big differences will come at the other end,' the son argued.

'Do they, then? Do they?' Glazing of eyes. 'Yes. Yes. If you get there.'

Horace had no ideas of founding a business dynasty. If David wished to become a schoolmaster, that would do; in time he would be rich compared with his colleagues, but that was no reason for largesse now.

Here the mother had intervened.

'All they'll be able to afford on David's salary,' she said, 'is a semi-detached.'

'What's wrong with that?' Horace went through the motions of opposition.

'I don't want my son in some poky little place when there's no need.'

'But if that's all they can afford?'

'What will people say?'

'That I'm mean,' Horace said. 'But I don't mind that. On the other hand, they may think the boy's too independent to accept my charity, and that will be much in his favour.'

'You talk to him,' she commanded, beautiful still at fifty, proud of her husband, quick to defend his dryness, adored in return.

When Mary's opera company finally found itself in financial trouble and disbanded, thus making up her mind for her, father Blackwall had offered them money for a house. Neither of the young people had made much fuss about acceptance, disappointing him, but had not chosen a house very much grander than they could afford on their joint salaries.

'It's quite pleasant,' Joan Blackwall had said to her husband.

'You mean it's not what you would have picked for them.'

'No. But it means we can buy Mary a grand piano.'

'You should have bought that first,' Horace, indulgently expansive, 'and built the house round it.'

'They could have ours for all the playing it gets.'

'Ah.' Horace lay back and invited his wife to perform. They moved upstairs, almost formally, as if observing some protocol.

'Let's have some favourites.' He loved patronage of this sort, knowing how assiduously his wife kept up her practice. The opening of Mozart's *Sonate Facile*, Chopin's E flat Nocturne, the three Brahms Intermezzi, op. 117, and finally, brilliantly, the last movement of Bach's 'Italian' Concerto. As she played he sat quite still, neither kicking nor shifting on his hams. She closed the lid with her usual comment: 'Too many wrong notes.'

He nodded, then shook his head, making no great play with denial. They put out the lights in the drawing room and went downstairs again, both satisfied by the recital. On such nights the television was left untouched.

As a boy David had sometimes listened to these performances from his room but had never sat in, though he knew he would be welcome, that his presence would have pleased his parents. Horace Blackwall loved his wife always, but when she played the Bechstein he seemed lifted out of himself. His son never grasped how this happened; his father was no musician, had to be bullied to attend a concert or opera, but regarded these perhaps once-weekly performances as not unlike the twice-yearly Eucharist he attended at St Jude's; these were numinous. They did not make him wish his life otherwise, but were of a different order from a glass of fine claret or even, rare-favoured delicacy, his wife's lardy cake.

The bedroom light was still on, but Mary lay fast asleep, face perfectly in repose. He drew the sheets up to her chin, but she did not stir. The dark hair, blue-back, seemed hardly disarranged by the pillow, and the shape of cheekbones, nose, mouth was utterly satisfying. Tired as he was, he wished she would open her light blue eyes, lifting the long lashes, but he knew that unlikely. He undressed at speed, wound the alarm, set the radio and slipped in beside her. She stirred, and immediately settled back.

The Blackwall men loved their wives.

2

At a quarter to eight the next evening the four Blackwalls occupied the table at the end of dinner. Horace issued his orders.

'David can help his mother carry the dishes out to the machine.'

'I'll do it,' Mary said.

'You'll stay with me. Perhaps later you can sing. Your mother thinks you should both be in bed early tonight, so we shall be sending you off at nine thirty.' He consulted his watch and the grandfather clock behind him, then blew out the candles. 'Don't like these things. Dangerous, and they stink.'

He led Mary to the drawing room where they sat side by side on the second settee.

'Must have you in good form for tomorrow and Saturday.' He continued in the grum-and-gruff vein he sometimes adopted with his daughter-in-law, telling her how his wife had inveigled him into parting with an immense cheque to pay for tickets for dinner and the Saturday performance at Rathe Hall.

'Even David said the Purcell was good.'

'But the food. The grub.' The word was plucked from some earlier vocabulary, perhaps that of the comics or library books he had read in his boyhood. 'Holkham Tait's no idea.'

'They're using an outside caterer.'

'Is that likely to be better? He'll just spread mushrooms in sauce over everything.'

Blackwall senior had little interest in *haute cuisine*; he had a healthy appetite which needed no cosseting, and preferred, as he said often, plain fare, but on these social occasions he enjoyed parading himself to his daughter-in-law as a man of the world.

'Colonel Tait's a bit of a recluse, isn't he?'

'Did he show up, then?'

'We were backstage. I didn't see him. Perhaps he did.'

'He's old now. Older than me, anyhow. Seventy. And spends a good part of the year abroad. Not that he's poverty-stricken. He farms in a big way. But he's not at everybody's beck and call, I'll give you that. I'm surprised he gave permission for this week's disruption.'

'Elizabeth Falconer's a persuasive woman.'

Horace Blackwall coughed, checking conversation, saying no more himself as if Mary had broken a taboo. David returned with his mother.

'Are you two tittle-tattling?' Joan asked.

'Of course.' Her husband.

'Colonel Tait's love for Lizzie Falconer,' Mary added, mischievously, not certain that her father-in-law would approve.

'It's over,' Joan Blackwall said, finding herself a brocaded chair to face her husband.

'How do you know that?' Horace.

'He told me so, himself.'

They all laughed, but nervously, as if not disputing the claim.

'How's she singing?' Horace asked. 'That's what I want to know about. I've paid good money.'

'Marvellously.'

'She's keeping her practice up?'

'Must be. She's due to go back to it. She'll have to lose a stone or two.'

'Can't have too much of a good thing.' Horace was pleased to be sitting with his daughter-in-law, pleased with himself, his wife, her cooking, the time of night.

'Was she a good teacher?' Joan Blackwall asked Mary.

'I hardly saw her at the RCM. The odd consultation lesson. She was in Bayreuth, or New York, or Sydney. But she was good. She bothered to listen.'

'She thought you would make it,' David said.

'She was kind to me. It was her recommendation to Will Broderick that got me into Omnium.'

'And now you're both retired up here?' Mrs Blackwall said.

'She won't stay long,' David prophesied. 'She's not sung out her old engagements, and she's been here three years. She'll be signing up again. Won't leave it there.'

'How old is she?'

18

'Thirty-eight, would you say, Mary? Thereabouts.'

'And what will her husband do about her setting off again?' Horace.

'There's a very great deal of money in it,' David said. 'Cash talks.'

'He's not short.' Mary.

'No. But she's had enough as the squire's wife.'

'Has she told you?' Mary, mocking.

'You know her better than I do,' he said sombrely. 'She's ambitious, a singer. She thinks of herself. Can hardly do otherwise in her position. Sir Edward has had her home now for some months each year. People did say she was just a bit frightened of singing herself out.'

'No sign of it,' Mary said.

'There must be,' Horace Blackwall sounded interested, 'quite a difference between Rathe Hall and Purcell and howling Wagner over immense distances and a full orchestra. It's nothing to do with music really.'

Nobody took him up. David had his eyes shut as if he were dropping asleep. When they had all refused alcohol Horace invited Mary to sing. She stood up.

'I know what I like,' he said, guying himself.

'Not more than two,' his wife warned, moving towards the piano. 'Mary's tired.'

He chose, immediately, without hesitation. 'Have you seen but a bright lily grow?'

'And?' Joan looking for music.

' "The Lass with the Delicate Air".' He smiled in anticipation, pleased that he could make such a demand. He conducted to himself, though one could not tell which song.

Mary sang, standing by the piano, one hand splayed on the lid. Her voice rang with no strain, no fatigue, soared about the big room, clipping the notes in the centre, taking the upward rising scale of the first song like a jewelled stairway. She smiled vaguely, impersonally in the direction of her father-in-law. 'Oh, so white', the tone exactly reflected the purity, the strength of her musicality and the transient, elusive beauty of whiteness in nature that resided permanently, 'oh, so white, oh so soft', in the lady, in Mary. Small lines furrowed at the

19

corners of her eyes, her mouth; her skin seemed, trick of the light, to have lost something of its bloom. She was tired, David decided, but it did not show in the voice. That sprang, leaped, couched, settled with creamy power.

Horace, David knew, was particularly fond of the high notes at the end of 'The Lass'. Under Mary's skill the simple device, the soaring and dropping, had about it an innocence, a freedom from the sensual yet based distantly, obliquely in sexuality, a richness of some golden, naked age that existed only out of the corner of the eye. David himself stretching, knowing exactly how his wife would perform, would bring the effect off, was yet moved by it. It was distilled, freed from impurity, but caught the light artlessly like burn water. His father's eyes brightened with tears; the old man did not mind who saw him draw out, shake loose his handkerchief to wipe them off, but the voice with which he thanked her was steady enough.

'One more,' almost peremptorily from Joan Blackwall. She had noticed her husband's joy, and would cover it with a different, livelier pleasure. She sorted through a small pile of music, held up a piece briefly, open, to Mary and then straightened it on her stand. David, staring, had no time to make out the title, but the first sharp chord, the pace now furious but steady, made him aware, and his father, of what happened. Purcell's 'Hark the Echoing Air', lively, brisk, trumpet-bright, echoed from the panels of the room, bounced, ran headlong into the ears, gold, speedy, a marvel. Each semiquaver she touched burst with the flash of a grenade, small, lilting, lifting, a-dance, sparking with young life's exuberance. 'And all around pleased Cupids clap their wings', and the accompaniment, needle-sharp, applauded the voice, little handclaps of musical appreciation, tripping, shifting perfumed air, clap, clap, clap, delicate in confidence, chasing, matching the racing voice so that when the second brilliance of the repeat ended with a touch, an off-handedness of allargando, the two men both sat upright, wanting the light, the run of tiny, life-giving explosions, again, again, again.

Mary smiled broadly. Her mother-in-law wiped nonexistent sweat from her brow. The men were smiling, sitting alert and radiant, wide awake, angels in bright daytime.

'Marvellous,' Horace said.

'Well done, both.' David.

'We married a couple of winners,' the father said. 'Don't let anyone tell you otherwise.'

The four sat for perhaps another ten minutes, completely content with the others, but immersed still in the music. They spoke, now and again, as if to disperse the solipsism of their pleasure; the longest passage between Joan and Mary concerned the breakdown of a washing machine, but that itself took the form of a text to be set by Purcell, a few incomplete statements needing music to match them to the hour.

'Come on,' David said, yawning again. 'It's time.' The others rose; he kissed his mother here, though he would kiss again by the door.

'That was a treat,' Horace touched his daughter-in-law on the arm, 'and a half.' He was fond of his childhood's phrases.

Mary seemed to expand as she put on her outdoor clothes. Now, hatted, she stood larger than life, a Valkyrie, formidably tall, not the slim girl who'd dazzled them with brightness of voice.

'Ready, my lord,' she informed her husband. She kissed the parents.

'Save something for Saturday,' Horace said.

'You'll get your money's worth.'

'In mushroom sauce.'

They laughed hoarsely in the hall and the heavy door clanged, dividing their harmony. Horace switched on the television with lacklustre eye, knowing he had to pass time until he went upstairs to bed. His wife pottered round in the kitchen; she could always find a chore to combat the bathetic, but he had no such art. David drove home quietly and saw Mary's eyes closed against undipped headlights. The road shone greasily; their house was cold and the electric blankets unwarming. On the wall the quartz clock ticked synthetically and louder than usual.

'Another day gone,' she said, plugging in the kettle.

'You're not making another drink?' he complained.

'We've got to give the blankets half a chance.' She seemed livelier. 'Enjoy it?'

'I'm always too tired, but, yes. You transform the old man. I wouldn't have said he was all that keen on music, but look at him tonight.'

'He was crying, David.'

'Yes.'

'Why was that?'

'Who am I to say?' He spoke sharply, as if annoyance had woken him from lethargy. 'He feels strongly, and that's how it shows itself. He's getting old.'

'He's fifty-eight, and young at that.'

David did not answer, but banged about the house closing up. Perhaps he felt betrayed by his father's overt emotionalism, she did not know, or perhaps he'd had an unsatisfactory day at school. She sipped her weak instant coffee, wishing him quiet and sitting by her.

'Liz Falconer rang me up at work,' she told him. He did not answer, waited for further information. Mary seemed unwilling to continue without his questions.

'Um?' he compromised, then capitulated. 'About tomorrow?'

'No. She was sounding me out about a singing job.' She used the flat words to pacify him. 'In America. She's singing for two seasons there, she says. In a year's time.'

'Wagner?'

'No, she's already committed to that in Bayreuth and Paris. This is Mozart, Meyerbeer and perhaps *Dido*, she hopes. And she says she can get me into the act.'

The steadiness of the tone belied the lightness of the words.

'Is she sure?' he asked.

'No. Not really. It depends if I want it, but then she'll use her influence. She couldn't promise anything. She made that clear.'

'And you said?'

'That I'd have to think about it, and consult you.'

They both sat at either end of a table laid for breakfast, awake, troubled for the other. Ten o'clock struck.

'Do you want to hear the news?' she asked.

'No.' He shook his head, sighing, like a dazed boxer. 'Well, what do you think then?'

22

'I don't know.'

A spurt of anger jangled in him.

'That means you'd like to go,' he said.

They did not stir, but she watched him as he idly but methodically moved spoons and plates about the tablecloth.

'I don't blame you,' he continued, but dully, as if he were hampered by a cold in the head. 'It's a great opportunity.'

'I'm not sure.' Mary spoke firmly now, as his father spoke about imports of Swedish furniture or the buying of shares in office blocks. 'There'll be some travelling because there'll be at least two companies, and I shall almost certainly be in the "B" if not lower. And that's not altogether comfortable. Digs,' she said laughing, 'and men. And women.'

'But you'll see the world.' It sounded feeble.

'It will only be worthwhile if I do well enough to go on. And you know what that means.'

'If you don't do it, you'll blame yourself for the rest of your life.'

'I wonder,' she said.

At the words love gushed in him, like the bursting of an artery, a warm, a killing comfort. It meant nothing; she would modify the meaning in the next sentence in all probability, but the three syllables spoke with a reasonableness that masked love, a mathematical equation, a quantifying of her affection for him.

'Are you bored with your work here?' he asked.

'No, I'm not. There's plenty to do, and I've got the hang of it. I like the people, and this house.' The blue eyes widened. 'Then there's you.'

'Yes,' he said.

'What do you think?'

'If you want to go, you grab the chance. "There is a tide in the affairs of men . . ." '

'I don't really know, David. I wish she hadn't said anything. I was quite settled yesterday, and enjoying the chance to sing the Purcell, and now. I don't want to change.'

'But you want to try it.'

She shook her head. Her bewilderment touched him, more deeply than his own anxiety, his self-interest. He held out his

23

hand and she took it; the contact of flesh on flesh meant nothing in that it did not allay foreboding. They sat there, hand in hand, as if in a charade, parading the action of love to themselves, ingraining the habit.

'I wonder why she rang up just this morning,' Mary asked. She could not, he thought, let it go.

'She wanted to hear you first.'

'Rehearsals. We've been at it for weeks.'

'In performance. And she'd have her friends here, and they'd perhaps say something. There'll be pieces in the Sundays, I tell you. She doesn't sing, even in a small concert like this, unnoticed. Her agents will have notified everybody.'

'I'm surprised,' she said, 'that she's been allowed to sing. She must be under contract to half the operatic managements in the world.'

He shrugged. 'Three nights. In an out-of-the-way place. Professional help to be hired. I wonder she did it at all. She could have given an equivalent to the profit they'll make and not notice it. Don't know. Can't fathom her.'

'She's a marvellous voice, hasn't she?'

'Sure. Even at half throttle. And personality.' He laughed, dropping her hand. 'She must think highly of you. There's no need for her to make moves on your behalf, is there? You must have impressed. Her or somebody else.' He laughed again, a chuckle in his throat, poor acting. 'She's not got the reputation of a wrecker, has she?'

'What do you mean?'

'Nothing.'

'Oh, come on.'

'She wouldn't want to do you and me one in the eye, split us apart, just out of mischief, would she?'

'Why would she want that?' Mary asked.

'Mischief, I suggested, or to get her own back on Edward. It is just possible, my sweet, that she envies you, with your little house and your little schoolteacher . . .'

She stared, then frowned before her face cleared. He was making fun of her.

'Let's go to bed.' He put his hand out again. She took it, but made a revolver with her other, pointing it at him.

3

The dressing rooms, formerly servants' quarters, for *Dido and Aeneas* were scattered; the men replaced jeans and pullovers by dinner jackets or sailors' kilts, courtly togas, hunting brown and green in a disused kitchen, while the ladies prepared themselves in bedrooms along a corridor two storeys above the hall itself. Elizabeth Falconer changed from twentieth-century flamboyance to a more restrained royal purple or white in some distant chamber, but already messages had been dispatched to the lower orders that she was displeased with Friday's performance. The conductor, an up-and-coming young man from Covent Garden, had been sent for during the day, when he had been handed a typed list of errors to be set right. He could not disagree, la Falconer had her musical wits about her, but with an amateur chorus, however good, a partly amateur orchestra, an unsuitable cramped stage, inadequate lighting, he hardly expected otherwise.

He ventured to say as much.

Elizabeth Falconer did not argue.

'Mr Silver,' she said. 'It will be right this evening.'

'There are no . . . I can't call another rehearsal.'

'You can let them know what you think. The performance was not a patch on Wednesday's.'

'With amateurs . . .'

'You are not an amateur. I may say with confidence that I am not an amateur.'

His attempts at argument were met with direct orders. 'It will be better tonight. As musical director it is your duty to see to it.'

She had influence, he knew. Her husband, Sir Edward Brook-Fane, escorting him from the presence, offered no comfort.

'Why's she so upset?' the conductor had asked.

'She has her standards.'

25

'That performance was no better and no worse than I expected. Given the . . .'

'Make it known to your people.' Sir Edward seemed almost biblical conveying his wife's tablets of stone.

'And have them flustered?'

Sir Edward opened a door, closed it behind the departing visitor and said not a word more.

Leonard Silver was no fool; he knew the value of a hate figure, and Elizabeth Falconer would do. He gathered male chorus with female and made the criticisms he would in any case have levelled, but associating them with the prima's anger. The orchestra he dealt with differently in that most of the violins were professionals, and his imports, so that his strictures were closely technical, and noted. To the other principals he offered a suggestion or two, mentioned la Falconer's dissatisfaction, and left them to it; he went down to his cubbyhole and cigarettes, congratulating himself on his diplomacy. A shrewd young man, he'd make his way in the world.

The performance began on time, again it was rumoured at Elizabeth Falconer's ukase. The hall was uncomfortably crowded, but the heat or hardness of chairs or lack of legroom or thoughts of the cost of tickets transformed the audience, who keenly attended, lifted performers, made themselves worthy of Purcell. These middle-class lay figures swooned with shy love, vigorously hunted, did not quite hiss the witches but frowned a displeasure across their ready faces, reeled with the boozy sailors, and in finality at Dido's lament were locked forward in their seats, held, mastered as Falconer's mellow pain-racked voice took on the steadiness of the falling ground bass, moved against it, over the bar lines in a frozen ecstasy of grief, that dissipated high living, gorgeous array and evening wear, unhurriedly but with immediacy spoke the sorrow that sooner or later cuts all humanity to the bare bone.

David Blackwall in the orchestral enclosure watched his colleagues; their faces did not reflect the rapt grief of stage or audience, but they were intent, responsive to the end of Silver's baton, which itself held emotion in check, in exact obedience to that golden plea of voice. 'Remember me, but, ah, forget my fate.' Purcell's heavenly invention soared, against logic, against

26

expectation with the, the complacency of achieved supremacy. Liz Falconer seemed outside, unlike herself; nothing of pride intervened; she became faultless, the channel of Purcell's genius, both plangent and restrained, in a laceration of grief that grew keener because of the order by which hurts were expressed. 'When I am laid in earth.' She begged them to forget her fate, the rejection of love, the lover's flight, but to recall her, her goodness or generosity to them in music that wrote her death across the heated air of the hall and into the spirits of a cramped and food-plumped audience.

The strings completed the chacony; the chorus gathered in a half-circle to sing their farewell in restraint, scattering roses on her and all tombs before the orchestra took on the repeat without voices as the lights were dimmed, the rosy twilight became bleaker, the statuesque figures held in stonily cold light for a time, faded, were visible, disappeared, were gone with her to the shades on the final bare fifth as the curtain fell.

The audience, released, cheered, stood, stamped, shouted, hardly aware of themselves, distracted by what they had heard, by each other. They sweated as they clapped. Someone forgot himself so far as to let rip a piercing yobbo's street whistle as the diva bowed low, taking with her Aeneas and Belinda, dominating witches and courtiers, dwarfing the Carthaginian pillars, the temples, the blue and cloudless North African sky. Silver, next to them, modestly incongruous in evening dress, beamed, stood his orchestra up; Elizabeth Falconer led their applause. There was no doubt of the triumph, either side of the footlights.

Word was given that the cast, the orchestral players, the backstage crews were to meet some chosen cognoscenti or affluent backers for a self-congratulatory glass of wine and sandwich in the dining room.

Sir Edward Brook-Fane, in evening dress with frilled shirt front, his few faded hairs exactly in place, appeared amongst the orchestra.

'Elizabeth would like to see you,' he said to David Blackwall.

'When?'

'Now.'

His cello was packed away and locked; his white shirt was

27

open at the throat over a woolly pullover, but he shrugged and followed the baronet up deeply red-carpeted stairs.

'Is your wife pleased?' David asked, trailing behind.

'You could say so.' Sir Edward's voice brayed; he was the descendant of squires and generals who bawled over hunting fields and barrack squares, of admirals blasting from the quarter deck. He stooped slightly, even decorously from his six feet five, as he ascended, and his hands and shoes moved prominently. He rapped at a door. A distant voice asked his business. He announced himself.

In the brilliantly lighted room a grey-haired woman dealt with Dido's dresses, smoothing them, spreading tissue, returning them to a wicker basket. She left that immediately the men entered the room and attacked a wig with a brush, motioning towards a closed door with her head.

'David Blackwall, darling,' Sir Edward howled. The woman pushed past him, still at work on the wig.

The inner door opened an inch or two.

'Sit him down, Thora.' The imperious Dido in prose. 'Go and make yourself pleasant, darling.'

'Anything you want?'

'A quarter of an hour. I'll be with you.'

Sir Edward pointed David to a chair, and wrapping the rags of authority about him, nodding at Thora as if giving some significant signal, left them to it. The grey-haired dresser chased about her chores, with speed, deftly, as Blackwall was left to watch her. She said nothing to him, hummed and now and then whispered some caution to herself or the costumes she tidied away.

The door of the inner room was opened, and the diva appeared, in a man's silken dressing gown. She seated herself immediately at a mirror and consulted her features, touching eyes or cheekbones with her fingers as if she needed further evidence of her obvious and gigantic beauty.

'I'm glad you're here.'

She did something to her mouth which necessitated the champing of teeth and thus inauspiciously grimacing spoke her sentence. He muttered a reply, but was forced to wait while she made up, however slightly, eyes and face, a process which

28

required the withdrawal of her magnificent head a metre back from the mirror and then, as she leaned forward, returning it to within six inches. The operation, though intense, was silent and occupied five minutes, which seemed interminable.

'You know why I've asked you to come?' She spoke at last not to him but to the looking glass.

'I can guess.'

Elizabeth Falconer suddenly stood, swept off her golden dressing gown, dropping it on to the chair she had left. She was not naked, she wore white bra and panties, but the effect was almost as startling as nudity. Her shoulders, her limbs were munificently large, marvellously shapely, shining. The brassière was a considerable construction, the word 'outworks' suggested itself, to control the fullness of her breasts, lifting them, the cleft reduced, no gorge now, no deep valley, but a controlled and shapely division. She stretched her arms to reveal the shaven armpits and her head was perfectly pitched, balanced on the pillared length and strength of her neck. The whole body matched, supported the grandiloquence of features under her short curls. The cheekbones were high, mounts of Venus, her eyes almond-shaped and large with thin brows, the mouth capacious and full-lipped, nostrils haughty under an imperious nose. She smiled, perhaps noticing his expression, and her teeth were perfection, larger than life, on her scale.

Thora silently handed her a pair of tights which she drew on, sitting again for seconds on the dressing gown.

'It's about Mary,' she said, taking a white shift to cover herself except for head, high chest and the naked gleaming power of her arms. 'She's spoken to you?'

Thora passed her mistress a dress, multicoloured, a kaleidoscope of dazzling but matching lozenges which flowed, spun, flashed silkily even when she belted it at her shapely waist. She lifted her feet high, he noticed, athletically, to ease on her shoes; high-heeled, these shone, dwarfed.

'Yes.'

'And what do you think?'

'I want to know what's in it for her.'

'Of course. That's sensible. But if that side were right, how would you feel?'

29

'I should want her to take her chance.'

'Want?'

'That's what I said.'

Elizabeth Falconer was seated again in front of her mirror, inspecting her flawless features, testing the skin with long, scarlet nails.

'You're angry with me, aren't you?'

Her voice had nothing of theatrical power, was delivered with a sweet clarity at the glass, modestly, like a nervous swimmer dipping a toe into cold water.

'No. Not really.'

'But I don't realize what I'm doing?'

'Yes. Something like that. It's a temptation to Mary; you'd call it a challenge. If it comes to nothing, or she doesn't make a success of it, she'll be in trouble.'

'And if she does, there's danger there?' She looked at him, the great eyes open wide, devouring him. 'For you? Your marriage?'

He did not reply.

'But,' steadily, 'you are still willing to let her go.'

'I don't think I could stop her. But certainly when she takes off from Heathrow she won't see the smoke from my funeral pyre. No.'

She rose; Thora, prepared for the movement, draped a shawl over her shoulders. Elizabeth looked now into distance.

'Do you know I never connected the two things. I am stupid. But it's changed round. She's off to found an empire, and he's left behind.' She conveyed her enormous pleasure at the comparison with these straightforward sentences. As she made her way towards the door she put out her left hand, blind, to lay on Thora's wrist denoting thanks. The gesture was operatic and utterly successful. The dresser stood at transformed attention. Blackwall himself dashed doorwards to open it, to expedite the progress, to offer her to the world.

As they descended the stairs she turned her head back to him.

'I just wanted to speak to you,' she said. 'To hear what you felt. There's no hurry for a week or two, but after that she'll have to commit herself one way or the other. Will she talk to your father about it? Edward says he's got his head screwed on the right way.'

'It's a bit outside his orbit. But they get on well, and she can have a word with him.'

'That's good.'

'Will she make it, do you think?' he asked desperately.

'Nobody can say that. It doesn't depend entirely on talent. Luck or opportunity are important. I don't think she'll ever be top of the operatic tree, because her voice isn't big enough for one thing, but I was impressed by her when she was a student, she shaped well with Omnium in Germany, and learned. She's been very good in these last,' a hand flew out, 'performances,' and then a sudden stop, a turn so that the full-frontal power of the woman, perfume, shape, colour, mien slapped him down. 'I did think, good as she was, that she hadn't been doing enough practice. It's now or never.' She said the last quietly, sedately, almost as if apologizing or asking him to question the judgement. 'She has a voice and a musicianship and a personality strong enough to make her a career in singing. But it won't wait.' Now she swept on. 'It won't wait for ever.'

'You're sure you can get her work in America?'

'As sure as one can be at this distance in space and time. My agent and hers will put it together.'

'Why do you do it?'

'There are some people too valuable to be lost.' She had no hesitation or difficulty with the answer. 'Even minor characters.'

These last sentences were spoken as she stood back to let him open a door on to a wide, picture-hung corridor; it was as though one had stepped from the servants' humdrum to the lordly. There was about this place an aristocratic darkness; the stairs they had descended though substantial might have been, in suitable reduction, found in a suburban house, with bright bourgeois lights, a comforting carpet. Now the pair walked, voices clashed at a distance, amongst ancestors, walls meant for arras, a place where blood had stained the floor. Immediately he had seen her through the pair of doors, caught out in that he had not expected the second much heavier barrier, they were joined by people who must have been waiting for them. These figures,

31

men, they had the appearance of footmen, inclined heads, signalled silently as if la Falconer might suddenly divagate from the thirty yards' straight, scuttle into side rooms.

They emerged into brightness through high doors into a brilliance of chandeliers, tables, chattering people all of whom ceased talking, lifted heads to greet her coming. A footman appeared with a tray of wine; she paid no attention. Her husband brought the correct offering, a tumbler of iced water, was received smilingly, and allowed a few seconds' private consultation before a crowd knotted round her.

David Blackwall looked for Mary, could not find her.

A yard or so away some young man with rimless glasses and long thin hair was quizzing Leonard Silver, now in a denim suit ready for his drive back to London. Blackwall listened, could not make out what they were saying because both talked fast, one interrupting the other, yoked in running duet. He heard 'Janáček' and wondered; 'Ligeti, Penderecki' and was satisfied. The conversation grew animated and softer, hands pointed. Suddenly he noticed that Silver was watching him, coldly, forgetting the companion, the exchange; the careful intensity of the stare seemed unwarranted, as if he had been a solicitor about to announce large but uncertain legacies.

He stared back, then nodded companionably, demotically. Silver disregarded the overture, as if the power of his stare brought no result, as if he looked because he could not see. Blackwall, experimenting, raised his glass. Nothing came of the gesture.

'Where's Mary?'

Now he was caught out, the voice at his back jolting him.

'Hello, Anna.'

He had no need to turn round; he recognized her. When he did swivel he noticed she wore a light blue coat, belted tight at the waist, dragging the material into attractive pleats. She carried an untouched glass of red wine in her right hand, and in her left she swung across her leg a wide-brimmed hat, round-crowned, black, black-ribboned.

'Hi. Isn't Mary down?'

'Can't see her.' He went through the motions. 'James?'

'He's about somewhere. I thought I'd better show my face.'

She'd sung, fair-haired and white-shouldered, a Carthaginian lady-in-waiting. 'Lizzie's pleased. She made us a little speech behind the curtain. I felt personally gratified.'

He pulled a face.

'Honestly,' she said. 'You won't believe it, but it was as if she singled me out for congratulation. There's something about that woman.'

'Ah, but what?'

'I don't like her.' She looked anxiously about for spies. 'I wouldn't trust her as far as I could throw her, but put her into the public eye and she's marvellous. She's like a cat jumping; she exerts exactly the right amount of effort, not a touch more, and yet there we are, people like me who think she's an old fraud, eating out of her hand.' Anna Talbot nodded in the direction of Liz Falconer, who was surrounded to such effect that outside her crushing bunch of courtiers there was left a whole circular strip of untenanted floor. Silver, David noticed, had joined the group, leaving lank-locks sitting disconsolately with his legs stretched long.

'And why is it?' he asked, not seriously.

'She just happens to be good. That's the top and bottom of it. And most of us aren't.'

'Isn't that sad?'

'You can say that again.' She flipped her hat against her legs, but did not cease looking over towards Falconer. 'What's next?' she asked.

'For whom?'

'You, charmer. Or Mary.'

'Concert next week for me. In the city, Wednesday, South-well, Thursday.'

'You take your punishment like a man.'

She dipped her head. Her hair, shoulder-length, was blonde, but with an odd green and yellowish tinge both unnatural and attractive. He looked around for his wife, but as she was nowhere yet, he refocused his attention on Anna. There was pleasure to be taken merely looking at her; she was always smart, stood pertly, spoke with a freshness. They had been lovers in what now seemed a hectic few weeks in London at the college, had parted violently when he had opted for Mary; he

33

remembered Anna's beating fists, drumming feet, the sobbing, her panting oath-racked appeals. He had, he decided, made an enemy for life, but she had gone off to live with James Talbot, there must have been something between them before, and had married him a few months later on his appointment as county music adviser at a much reported church ceremony with ostentatious white, six bridesmaids and half the county present. Towards David she now presented herself as content, a lively and valued friend who could pull his leg, chivvy him about his treatment of his wife, invite and be invited to an evening meal, speak to him in the street and become fascinating inside five minutes, with no mention of regret, no recrimination. She could touch him asexually, rib him, look him in the eye as if she had forgotten her jealousy; become his friend. Certainly he did not understand this and felt mild masculine disappointment, but Anna acted cheerfully, took Mary's side against him when it seemed proper, was the perfect foil.

'Yes,' he said, 'I think sometimes I'm doing too much of it.'

'Doesn't Mary mind?' The two women must have discussed it, and often enough.

'She has things to do.'

'She's well in with Madame, isn't she?'

'Seems so.'

Mary appeared; David took three steps to collect her a glass of white wine. She looked tired out.

'Where's your cello?' she asked.

'By the front door somewhere. Tom Todd put it with his.'

She yawned, only covering the gaping mouth at the last minute.

'Worn out?' he said. She nodded. 'It was good tonight. Even Anna thinks so.'

Mary smiled companionably at Mrs Talbot.

'Madame was pleased,' David told her.

'Yes. She's not too difficult.'

The other two pulled faces of delighted and incredulous disagreement.

'There speaks the queen's favourite,' Anna said. 'Anything exciting on the cards?'

Mary stayed silent about the American project, but the three

34

kept together, found chairs, were approached by notables who made a fuss of the women. For a brief time they seemed to be holding a smaller court in rivalry with Elizabeth Falconer. Colonel Tait himself made a stop. A tall man, with short grey hair and the appearance of a groomed scarecrow, he swayed on his large feet in front of them.

'Very good,' he said, the words barely escaping his lips. 'Very good.'

'It's a superb place to sing,' Mary said.

'You'll have to ask us again.' Anna simultaneously.

'Yes.' He seemed trying to catch a train of disappearing thought, painfully. 'Yes. The, the . . .' He put out a hand, pink like his face, well scrubbed, half finished. 'It's a . . .'

He passed on, a reed shaken by the wind.

'There's a zombie,' Anna said. 'Don't know what Liza saw in him.'

'He saw it in her,' David answered.

'Is he married? With a family? Or what?' Mary.

Anna dug David in the ribs as he was on the point of reply. Elizabeth Falconer had broken away from her entourage, had made straight for them, but no sooner had she taken her stand than the courtiers began to re-form round her.

'Your good health,' David said, raising his glass to her.

She acknowledged the toast with an inclination of her head, but did not lift her glass.

'I've spoken to your husband,' she said to Mary, who looked abashed. The diva turned her attention on Anna, found nothing of interest, shifted her front. Relenting, she refaced Anna, smiling, nodding. 'It was very good.' She consulted a minute golden wristwatch. 'I mustn't be too late. I like to take my exercise in the morning.'

'Some of us work,' David said.

'It's Sunday.' Anna defended the Falconer.

'I shall be up at exactly the same time.' It was not a rebuke, but a taking into the confidence which put the objectors into their places. She moved off and the crowd melted with her.

'She didn't say what time that was.' Anna had recovered. 'Come on, David. Let's go. I'm whacked.'

'You're certainly in with All-highest,' Anna tried, but the

35

Blackwalls had put down their glasses, were on the way to search out David's cello then make for home and bed before Sunday.

4

Mary consulted her parents-in-law one evening when David was out of the way. They listened with serious faces.

'What does David think?' Horace Blackwall asked. 'I take it you've talked this over with him.'

'Yes. He told me to ask you.'

'But what was his opinion?'

'That I should take my chance if I wanted to.'

The three then sat silent, Horace fidgeting unusually. His wife passed him a bowl of fruit, a plate and a knife, and he looked at her affronted. Joan seemed amused, superior, as if she had the answer ready if they called on her. He waved the dessert away, changed his mind, pared an apple, trying to remove the peel in one strip, failing. Now he quartered it, cut out the core.

'I don't know what to say,' he told Mary provisionally, baring his false teeth for a first bite.

The girl was prepared to wait.

'Do you want to go?' Joan asked suddenly.

'I'm torn.'

'That means you do,' Joan pronounced.

'Not of necessity,' said Horace, apple to lips.

'No dear.' Sweet sarcasm.

The women tittered, and Horace relaxed, waving the bitten fruit to indicate that once he had cleared his mouth, he'd sound off again.

'Tell us,' he began. Immediately his wife whistled the witches' duet from *Dido*: 'Tell us, tell us, how shall this be done?' The tone had impudent clarity, though Horace did not recognize the reference. Joan and Mary smiled at each other; he frowned. 'I don't know what you two are giggling about.'

Mary, now straight-faced, explained that she did not want to leave David, that she was enjoying her job, her house, her spare time.

'All that will have to go,' he said. 'I see that. But what about the other hand?'

Again, soberly, Mary expounded Elizabeth Falconer's scheme. They listened intently, but Horace's right leg, cocked over the left, was kicking.

'I know nothing about these things,' he said, 'but it all sounds rather vague.'

'So it is,' she admitted. 'And until I give my agents the go-ahead, it will remain so.'

'Remain so.' He repeated the two words softly, criticizing the phraseology, which raised the matter from sense to specious debate.

'Nobody can tell me anything, or promise me anything specific. Not as yet.'

'That sounds as if you commit yourself, and then leave the terms to them.'

'I needn't sign the contracts.' She glanced at her father-in-law. 'You don't like the look of it, do you?'

'I know nothing about it, Mary. But don't get it into your head that I'm writing it off as unbusinesslike. Even in my line, one has to put feelers out sometimes, expose oneself to danger before anything can happen. I understand that well enough. But one has to be sure that if there's half a chance of a deal, one wants it, one's ready to exert oneself and that the signed agreement will be checked.'

Joan made wordless noises, of doubt or disparagement. Her husband pulled his half-glasses even farther down his nose.

'It must be exciting,' the mother said.

'In a way. Yes.'

'I should go, then.'

Mary, suspicious, did not immediately answer.

'I thought,' she began, 'that you would say I shouldn't leave David, that my place was with him.'

'Not these days. The woman's career is as important as the man's. A good number of young people live apart.'

'But is that marriage?'

37

'Goodness knows what marriage is, or means,' Joan answered. 'But if it stops you doing something important for yourself, then I don't approve of it.'

Horace spluttered.

They discussed the few facts they had, skirmished round the effect on David's character, before both parents agreed that if the American venture was what she wanted, then she should go.

'Don't you want to talk to David first?' she asked them.

'By no means.' Horace, benign. 'You do the talking with him.'

She reported this to her husband, and at her insistence they tramped over the grounds of argument again.

'That's it,' he decided an hour and a half later. 'You must go.' He jumped up to open a bottle of dry sherry. 'To success,' he toasted her.

'I don't know, David. I don't know.'

They made love to rescue them from fright, and next day Mary rang Liz Falconer.

In fact, it took three days to reach the singer, who heard the decision calmly, instructing her to inform her agent. She showed not much concern, and no understanding of Mary's dilemma. Rather sharply she advised her protégée to get back to serious practice, and at once.

'There are no decent teachers about here. Start taking consultation lessons with Peter Reddaway. You could go up to London each Saturday.'

Mary, quite dashed, told her husband she'd a good mind to pack it all in.

'She'd no idea,' she complained, 'how I felt.'

'Why should she have? You've got out of the habit of taking risks.'

Furious, she turned on him, snarled her fear. He was so unresponsive that she burst into tears. He took her in his arms.

'There'll be as many rotten things as good. You know that. You'll have to get used to it.' He kissed her. 'The hard nut.' She smiled, gushed again into tears, clung madly round his neck.

Mark Wentmeyer, her agent, rang after a week and arranged to see her in London. She could combine this with her first lesson at Reddaway's studios. Mark had talked to Liz Falconer's agent, and they had cobbled a scheme together that was worth looking over.

'Cobbled?' she asked.

Mary was to go over to the States in the middle of January where she would join an ad hoc opera company for a two months' universities' tour as a trial for employment when Falconer arrived in April.

'And the advantages?'

'You'll be there. You'll be known. You'll be in full practice in case they want to audition you again. This whole thing of Falconer's is a mystery. She won't stay for long, because she'll be in Bayreuth all summer. It's a short season, mainly Mozart, some chance of Purcell. She's taking the opportunity to get you in on the circuit, Harold says. After that, it's up to you.'

'And what do you think?'

'Two things. It's a marvellous chance for you, if it comes off. This university opera's a new affair, but strongly backed. Ulrich Fenster's chief conductor the two months you'll be engaged, and he's on the up and up, if anybody is. And the producer they hope for is a real notable. Redvers Gage. If they get him. The payment's nothing to write home about, but I'm working on that.'

'You'd advise me to go?'

'Yes. Provisionally. But I'll know more about it by the time you come up to see me.'

David did not accompany her on the first trip to London, where Peter Reddaway heard her sing and suggested that she would need a fuller voice if she were to make a success of the American trip. He outlined a set of exercises, all of which she had heard before, ran through a song or two with her, and dismissed her on the hour. Disappointed that she had not discerned in him one iota of enthusiasm for her talents, her performance or her personality, she suspected that he had other pupils better than she who lacked the influential connections to put them on the American circuit. He even appeared loath to give her a lesson each week.

At her agent's office, she voiced these doubts to Mark Wentmeyer.

'Peter's a good teacher,' he said, 'but he might not suit you. Work as hard as you can for him, and . . .'

'But he was so dull.'

'He's had too much success. He was only very moderate himself as a singer, but a good musician. I thought he'd do better as a conductor. But in the past fifteen years he's had some marvellous pupils.'

'Did he teach Elizabeth?'

'He did. She still goes to him. Or that's the story.' Wentmeyer patted her arm. 'He's now of the opinion that one needs only to stand in his presence and improvement begins. But he can teach once he puts his mind to it.'

Mark looked pleased, expansive. He proposed that he'd tell her what he knew about the American company and that they would then discuss the plan of campaign over lunch. He must be enthusiastic, she concluded, in that she'd never eaten before at his expense.

An American tycoon had left money, a great deal, to be spent for the betterment of opera and opera singing. 'Now, you know what opera's like,' Mark's eyes twinkled; 'you can spend a fortune just looking for a suitable theatre, never mind putting one singer unaccompanied on stage. So the trustees, lawyers, an impresario and academic musicians, five all told, decided to set up this company, to perform short seasons of early operas over the next six years, *Dido*, *Venus and Adonis*, *Semele*, Locke's *Cupid and Death*, perhaps the *Incoronazione di Poppea*, round university campuses and towns. It'll cost a bomb, but even if it doesn't show much success commercially, they hope to raise funds, and it'll provide employment for orchestral musicians and promising young singers. The scenery's some simple marvel to be made by the plastic arts department at NYS, and the Met and the professional theatre have lent some costumes, a sure sign they're not threatened. The conductor'll mainly be this young man called Fenster, who's said to be good. They haven't nobbled Gage yet.'

'And where do I come in?' she asked after further long explanations.

'That's it really. That's the baffler. Lizzie's leaned on somebody. There are always wheels within wheels, even in a charitable concern like this, people doing themselves a bit of good, and I guess Lizzie Falconer's short season across there was always touch and go, and so she could demand your inclusion. That's how it is.'

'You don't say a word about merit,' she objected.

'There's plenty of that about. If that were the only criterion we could mount a dozen times the number of operas and still leave good singers unemployed.'

'So it's nepotism or nothing.'

'Don't get that into your head. They'll slide you out quick enough if they don't think much of you.'

'Don't you think,' she asked, 'I'm taking a risk? Putting my head on the block?'

'No doubt of it.' He roared with good-natured laughter.

'What should I prepare?' she asked.

'Get yourself copies of the things they're doing and be ready to sing any part that lies between middle C and C in alt.'

'That's not sensible.'

'I know. I know. But you're in with this, and . . .'

'Isn't it possible that they're waiting for me to arrive and then they'll find some excuse to push me out, or make me resign? Since I've been foisted on them?'

'Three-quarters of the singers have been foisted, as you call it,' Wentmeyer argued. 'It does no good to think about it in that way. Ulrich Fenster will listen to what he's got when he starts his preparation. Time's going to be short, I guess. He'll want you to pick up parts in a hurry. That's why I say, "Be ready". You've plenty going for you: looks, a good voice, an English accent, and, not least, Lizzie Falconer's backing. Come on, girl. God knows where this may lead you.'

'Away from my husband.'

'If you get into the big league you'll be able to afford to tote him around with you, and get tax-relief on him as your consultant for historical research.'

Mary enjoyed the lunch because she realized that Wentmeyer saw advantage in his contact with the Falconer agents and the American end; he'd take something out of this for himself in any case, but it would do him no harm if she made a good showing. They laughed; he was excellent company; the wine

41

calmed her trepidation and he covered his lack of information by bursts of praise.

'You've actually sung with Falconer,' he said, 'and so well that she's recommending you about the world. There won't be too many of them in that position.'

'If not her, somebody else.'

'There aren't too many Falconers, I'll tell you. And they don't fall over themselves to give a lift up to rivals.'

'You think over what you've just said,' Mary answered him. 'She only praises those who are no good, and won't stand in her way.'

'You won't be a Falconer. Ever, ever.' He laughed, his small beard flashing, his hair bouncing about his ears. 'And to the best of my knowledge you're the only one she's done anything for. Or taken the initiative over. "Oh, Mary, this London's a wonderful sight".'

She returned in euphoria, but the mood changed swiftly, darkly enough.

'I don't want to go, David,' she wailed, clinging.

'You do.'

'It's ridiculous. I've a job and a home and a husband I love. When I get over there I'll make a hash of it, and come back with my tail between my legs. I'm a fool, David. Don't let me go.'

He hugged her.

'If I stopped you from going,' he told her in her calmer moments, 'you'd never forgive me.'

She eyed him then.

'Sometimes you're a wise man,' she said.

'Yes, but not often.'

They laughed, embraced, with more than a month to go.

Mary worked hard at voice production and her study of the operas. Twice a week they had dinner with the senior Blackwalls so she could practise for an hour or two with Joan as accompanist. The men were not allowed to listen.

'Go and puff your cigars,' she ordered them. Neither man smoked. 'This is work in progress, not fit to be heard.'

'I'd listen to you gargling,' Horace told her.

She fell into a tête-à-tête with her father-in-law quite often, at work and at the weekends. He supported her powerfully.

42

'I shouldn't want you to go,' he said. 'Splitting up the partners of a new marriage is dangerous, but it has to be done in my sort of world. I know that. Neither shall I see much of you myself, and we shall miss you. Joan and I really like you.'

The voice ground out its sentences, impressing her.

At Christmas the departure seemed close enough to warrant a fervid gaiety in the festivities. David played in a concert or two, conducted a makeshift *Messiah*, and the pair attended parties, where she deliberately stayed sober.

'I'm going to drive you back,' she told her husband, who had drunk sufficiently to stroke her buttocks in public. She did not care; she needed all the reassurance she could find. 'I didn't know it would knock me about like this,' she would confess, 'or I wouldn't have taken it on.'

'You'll be as right as rain once you're there.'

'And you?'

'I shall have to grin and abide.'

'Does that appeal then?'

'It does not.'

'Where's your puritan ethic?' she mocked.

Her own unease was demonstrated by her complaints about the lessons with Peter Reddaway.

'He's an egomaniac,' she told her husband. 'Everlastingly demonstrating what he can do. I hate wasting the whole of a Saturday going to London just to hear him boast. I learn as much from your mother in ten minutes as I do from my hour with him.'

'Give it up, then.'

'I may need him later. And it does keep me singing.'

'Joan would do that.'

'I know. But he's the outside world. I pit my arrogance against his. I've got to learn to be the sort of bighead he is.'

'Oh, dear.'

David dreaded the tension in his wife's lips, the dark round her eyes.

No word came from the agent; whenever they rang he'd heard nothing, not even the place to which she had to report for rehearsals.

43

'Really,' Mary argued, 'they must know by now.'

'I'm not sure about that. This is the initial shot at a one-off, experimental affair, and though I guess that the first few ports of call are fixed, in fact, I'm certain they are, the venue for the preliminary rehearsals will be a matter for negotiation. They'll rehearse in some school hall or barn or something.'

'You make it sound very attractive, I must say.'

'This is something out of the ordinary run of things.'

'So I shall be living in a tent?'

'Oh, no. But they'll be collecting their wits. Honestly. There'll be a fortnight's intensive chaos after which you'll be fit to sing at Bayreuth. This boy Gage is terror, they tell me, but he won't mind if you rehearse in the street.'

'Find something out, will you?'

'I'll ring my New York end and instigate inquiries.' His jokey choice and stress of words did nothing to allay anxiety, any more than the blank silence which followed.

A week before her departure she sang Schumann's *Frauenliebe und -leben* at a charity gathering with Joan Blackwall as her accompanist. This had been half-arranged for six months, then seemingly forgotten and revived just before Christmas. Mary complained bitterly, but she knew the songs well enough; David remembered her singing them at the Royal College, and she had looked them through carefully enough once this performance had been mooted.

Joan, out of character, was uncertain even of the place at which they were to appear.

'This is the story of my life,' Mary said in public, laughing. 'Plenty to sing, but no idea where,' and to David, 'I can't understand your mother. She must be off her head.' He understood the desperation of the statement.

The chosen venue turned out to be an Edwardian mansion in the park, the town house of a business magnate. The event was for cancer research; Mary sang and a violinist played a Tartini sonata. For the rest, drinks were served, raffle tickets and donated gifts sold, one or two competitive paper games were played and for this people paid good money, and promised more. The uncertainty about this happening was due to an enormous sale of expensive tickets by an energetic couple who

44

had access to radio and newspaper publicity, and who found that they could not cram in the expected crowd and had to look at short notice for a larger space. They were never despondent, because they knew exactly what it was that they were after: a huge private house, preferably owned by somebody of note. Through friends they worked on Sir Harold Fitch, the managing director of a pharmaceutical complex, who opened his grandee's palace, Kenilworth, for the evening.

David bought a ticket, five pounds for admission only and the opportunity to purchase expensive alcohol. A television announcer auctioned toys, and then pretty trinkets. People talked at the tops of their voices, drank and seemed pleased with themselves. Many of the men wore evening dress as they wandered about the four large reception rooms and the foyer at their disposal; wives sounded as satisfied, as flashbulbs registered promised appearances in future issues of the local snob magazines if not the national. Nothing happened quickly; it took an age to dragoon an audience into the right place for the fiddler, and even as he played the voices at bars in the distance interrupted his powerful flow.

Mary did not sing until after ten o'clock; David thought that by that time the drink-happy audience would never assemble itself, but by 10.10 the concert hall was packed, more standing than sitting as the television personality silenced all clamour, David admired the man's iron charm, to announce Miss Mary Stiles, who next week was to make her American debut in opera, and whom they were lucky to have persuaded here tonight, but who out of her magnificently large generosity had put aside other commitments to sing these eight songs which he would paraphrase. They must offer her a fit welcome. They did. And her accompanist, Miss Joan Blake, formerly of the Royal Academy of Music, London. The announcer straightened his face.

Mary's entrance stunned her husband, though earlier he had watched her dress.

She had chosen white, which she wore with stately beauty, enhanced by the pallor of her face, the dark short shining curls. As she bowed, she smiled diffidently, but to them all, on the rows of chairs or behind a pillar, glass in hand. Her mother-in-

45

law, trailing her, looked what she was, a well-to-do provincial lady in her best dress, who had been wrongly convinced by some back-street coiffeuse that a confection of grey waves would add to her attraction. Her turn would come, at least for the few listening to Schumann rather than Mary, when her fingers touched the keyboard.

In the earlier songs Mary Blackwall stood radiantly, her voice vivid with delighted love, the freshness of attraction, the brilliancy. The practice of the last weeks had provided power, and Schumann's melody compelled the audience, enlivening bodies to the fingertips, setting them on the edge of expectation in 'Er, der Herrlichste von allen'. The room, jammed tight, with heads at all angles, the colours of dresses clashing or blending with the darkness of men's suits or the blackness of tall windows, seethed with excitement, David thought, so that people lost themselves in the genius of new love, marriage, childbirth and finally in the sustained sorrow of death. He said as much to his father later, and the old man nodded, at this mystery, life's passing, its bright fixing by this young man under womanly guise and voice, but David noted that as the audience walked out they spoke of gin, raffle tickets, chiropodists. That perhaps did not matter, he decided, in that for some minutes ordinary people had been allowed to climb, levitate above everyday concerns.

Mary herself, swamped with congratulation, surrounded by admirers, had lost the supple beauty she commanded on stage, had replaced it by a stiller, more composed version. She shook hands, said the right thing, charmed but stood away. For the first time she convinced her husband that her success in America was assured, that she had the social strengths to complement the musical. This sudden confidence warmed him, stiffened him, made it clear that he had done right in encouraging her to go. And yet in this paradigm he barely recognized the wife he had married.

'Are you tired?' he asked. 'Do you want to go home?' He had finally got near enough to speak.

'No, not yet.'

She enjoyed every second of her triumph, grew larger with it, picturesque.

'Well, what do you think of than, then?' Horace Blackwall had taken his son aside.

'She sang beautifully. She really did. She's a different woman from what she was three months ago.'

'Oh? How?'

'Her voice has come on since she started practising *Dido*. I didn't think it possible. The change is extraordinary.'

'You said "a different woman".'

'That's right. It, musical enlargement, can't help altering the personality.'

'So if she becomes a big star . . . ?'

'I don't think that's possible. She'll never have Liz Falconer's tremendous vocal equipment. Or, at least, I don't think so. She'll improve, but not in that . . .'

'You're not sure, are you?' Horace snapped his false teeth together.

'Tolerably.'

'Tolerably.' Horace mocked his intonation. 'Are you frightened she will?'

'Not frightened, no.' He answered the fool according to his folly. 'I hardly consider that. I don't like the idea of her leaving me.'

'I see.'

His father patted his shoulder in comfort, an awkward, dry movement, though David, once he was able to dissociate it from the dark-coated stick figure, saw it for what it was, and felt warmed.

'Joan played absolutely beautifully,' he said in return.

'Yes.' Horace brushed his chin. 'She could have made her way as a professional.'

'Did she want to?'

'I don't know. She played a great deal after we were married, in good amateur circles. At least until you were born. Even then she kept her practice up.'

'Do you think . . . ?'

'Go on.' Horace rebuked his son's hesitation. Truth bettered tact in his view.

'Has she regretted it?'

'I'd think so. Sometimes. She doesn't say much. She's a

remarkable woman, your mother. There'll be days when she's sorry she didn't take her chance. Just as she might have envied those with stable family lives and comfort if she'd been flitting about the world. Nobody's ever satisfied.'

'And has Mary's trip opened it up again?' David pursued.

'It hasn't crossed my mind, but then I'm a selfish devil, as well you know.'

Joan Blackwall crossed towards them.

'Now, then, you two.' She smiled, lifted out of herself by the occasion, younger than her years. 'What are you so serious about?'

'David's wondering if you ever regret not having a professional career in music.'

A stab of anger reddened the son's face. Joan pursed her lips, lifted her eyes to a large Victorian painting of *The Eve of the Flood*. The sky stretched blood-streaked as an illustration in a textbook of anatomy over a diminutive ark and Noah's dwarfed family. She seemed faintly amused.

'You played marvellously well tonight,' David said.

'We've done quite a bit together these last few weeks. It helps.'

'You have the hands,' he answered.

'Thanks.' Now she touched him, but more lightly than her husband, more prosaically, as if she were about to straighten his jacket. 'I enjoyed it. She really has come on. I have to open up to keep with her.' She had returned to her scrutiny of Linnell's liverish clouds. 'She was superb.' An ecstatic whisper now changed to mundane power. 'This other thing. Because Mary's going to America, you think . . . ? You think . . . ?' Another trailing away as if sense could not be exactly conveyed or attempted.

'He wonders,' Horace's voice croaked, 'if it's made you regret you never took your chance.'

She considered that, much at ease.

'No. Not really. A professional life's awful. You know that, David. All the air travel and hotel rooms and being pleasant to the world. And that's when you're outstandingly good. Otherwise you're sitting at home fretting yourself to death that no engagements are coming your way. No. I did the best thing by letting your father make the money.'

48

Her son looked over to where a group of men surrounded his wife, whose face seemed alight.

'But you played like an angel,' David said.

'There'll be five or six hundred people in this country who'd do it as well given the practice I had. Oh, I did it respectably, I grant you. But I'm in no way unique.'

'I married an honest woman,' Horace said.

'Is that good?'

'I do think he's beginning to learn,' Joan gibed.

'But what?' Horace.

They all laughed, insecurely, but joined the social round, chattered until the early hours, imagining they enjoyed themselves.

5

The day before Mary left for America David met Anna Talbot in the street. He was returning from school, on foot, because his wife had borrowed the car.

'Hello. You're in a hurry,' she greeted him.

'It's cold, dawdling about. Besides, I want my tea.'

'Husbands.' She grimaced. 'When's Mary due to go? Can't be too long now?'

He was surprised, again, that friends, who had been told often enough, still could not remember this date. To them its interest was peripheral. It was like reading of the death of an acquaintance in the newspaper: what stopped the heart for one was for another an item of casual conversation.

Now he told Anna.

'God,' she said. 'You shouldn't be hanging about the streets talking to me. Are you going down with her?'

'Yes.'

'The school's given you the day off, have they? Good for them.'

That tore his breath for him when he remembered how he'd had to ask Kenneth Reeve, the head, for the time off.

Reeve had frowned, tapped his desk, picked up a packet of cigarettes and put it down.

'Well. I can't, er, can't, er . . .' The man sat locked in some trance, will-less, aphasic.

'It's Wednesday,' David said. 'I can easily organize my absence from games. In the morning I've two sixth forms and a string group. I'll set work. They'll get on.'

'Yes. I'm sure.'

'So?' One felt always that one pushed this distinguished and silver-haired figurehead into a position he hated to occupy.

'You see, it's an inconvenient time of the year. January. There are always people absent with colds and flu. Classes, junior classes, have to be minded.'

'I can't have it, you mean?' Anger, reddening cheeks.

'I can't give it to you. The governing body would have to countenance the decision, and they have been known to be awkward. No. Take the day off. Make what arrangements you will about your commitments here, I think I can trust you, and then have, oh, a convenient bronchial catarrh.'

'Thank you.'

'You did not hear me say anything.' Reeve fiddled again with the golden cigarette packet, twisting it in his fingers with extra-ordinary dexterity. 'What was it your wife was going to sing? Opera?' The headmaster frowned again, willing recalcitrant fact from his memory, acting it out like a schoolboy on the front desk pleasing his masters with assumed puzzlement.

David offered a few sentences of explanation to which Reeve gave the appearance of listening keenly, as if to catch the speaker out. Though there was probably nothing in the attitude, David knew that he would leave the room feeling not only that he had been judged and found wanting but that he owed the headmaster a favour. None of the staff liked Reeve, but then the man did not look for warmth from his subordi-nates.

When he left the room as quickly as politeness allowed, for the headmaster did not encourage social conversation, David Blackwall felt himself smirched, diminished.

Now Anna Talbot walked alongside him.

'I'll go this way,' she said cheerfully. 'I've got a call to make.'

Her step was sprightly. 'Has Mary got everything ready?'

'I think so. She's good at that sort of . . .'

'Living out of a suitcase?'

'Packing, I meant. But, yes. They flitted about in Germany.'

'It must be exciting,' Anna said, gushing.

He did not know, guessing that his wife would have been at least momentarily delighted by a cancellation or postponement. Her anxieties had caused her to be more silent than usual, and only from her gestures or glances could he determine how she felt, and there he might merely be interpreting his own reactions.

'Where's she going first?' The woman needed no answers.

'New York State. The music department there has offered rehearsal facilities, and their first performances are there.'

'When?'

'In three weeks' time. Handel's *Semele*.'

'I've never seen it performed.'

'She was a woman with ideas above her station. Thought she could equal the goddesses.'

'And could she?'

'No.'

'Will Mary sing the title role, then?'

'Nobody knows. They audition and rehearse at the same time.'

'Won't that cause trouble?'

She continued with her catechism without slackening her pace. Conductor, parts, orchestra, itinerary, everything except payment.

'I'll tell you what,' she said as they stopped at the crossroad where he was to turn off. 'I wish it was me.' She comically blew out her lips. 'But it isn't. Always the same. Give her my regards.'

'Just come in.'

'No. No time. No inclination. I'll comfort the grass widower if he needs it.'

She laughed, touched his hand, strode away, her boots flashing in the electric lamps, reflecting from the puddles. Anna would have forgotten him before she'd covered a hundred yards.

51

Mary and the evening meal waited for him. The delicious smell of cooking spiced the house. As she served a meat pie she told him that there was another ready which he could take from the refrigerator on Thursday, that there was a fruit cake, scones, buns, a sponge.

'I don't want you starving,' she said.

Sourly he thought he'd see the fancy buns with their layer of icing, when she, a lively, bodied presence serving him now, had disappeared. On Thursday he'd be seated at this table with the second meat pie and no wife.

'You ought to do something,' he said as they were eating, 'to mark your departure.'

'Such as what?'

'Put your fingerprints on that wall.' He indicated the white stretch above the fireplace. 'To remind me.' There were three photographs of her already on the mantelpiece.

'You don't mean it, do you?'

'I don't know.' His body ached. 'Have you sung today?'

'Not a note.' She laughed, too loudly for comfort. 'Last day as a housewife. The parents want us to go there for an hour.'

'What do you think?'

'Suits me. Are you ready and willing?'

'Oh, yes.'

They ate, washed the dishes together and he spruced himself up. They stood together, passed each other, but failed to touch, perhaps out of fear. It was raining but comparatively mild as they drove out.

In the car they were silent until he made an effort.

'You won't see this again for a bit?' he said.

They were passing a piece of suburbia, closed shops with unlighted windows, a road of black glass, small trees in the pavement between the crooks of concrete lamp standards. Not much traffic obstructed them. Buses ran almost empty.

Horace and Joan Blackwall received them in one of the small back rooms downstairs. In the brightness a chintzy three-piece suite seemed cheerfully to clog the room; a signed Lowry print dotted its shadowless factories, men, dogs, above the gas fire. The other walls were bare, but looped with faint shadows from a pair of standard lamps, shades matching the furniture.

52

'Thought we'd come in here, and save money,' Horace said. He'd already inquired about Mary's preparations for the journey, and now offered drinks. Mary asked for a small sherry, David and his mother orange juice. 'Abstemious. I like to see it.' Horace looked to his wife for encouragement, did not receive it.

They settled to glum talk of the weather, and Horace outlined his holiday plans. He and Joan were considering a short Caribbean cruise.

'How will you find time?' David asked, not pleasantly.

'If things turn out as I hope I shall have plenty of that commodity.' Horace put his finger ends together.

'You're going to retire?' Mary.

'I've heard that before,' David said.

His father did not argue with him; his mother received the remark, it seemed, with approval.

'You and I are sticking our necks out,' Mary told her father-in-law, bringing the unspeakable into the open. 'How will you put up with him at home all day?'

'As your old man,' said Horace, 'will put up with you away.'

'Mine's only for three months; six at most if this Falconer scheme comes off.'

'You hope for more than that,' Horace countered. 'At least, I hope you do. It's no use going away on some bit of a jaunt. You might just as well stay back here.'

'Is that so, David?' his mother asked very quietly.

His right leg across his left was kicking.

'Yes.' The word flew out like blocking phlegm. 'Yes, that's about it. She must try for a career.'

Now, it had been said, they were silenced.

'If you've retired, there'll be no job for me to come back to,' Mary said, making a joke of it.

'That's as may be. You sing loud,' Horace said. 'You show them.' Then clearing his throat, 'I tell you this, though, I shall miss you, never mind our David.'

'Thank you.' The voice was beautiful.

'You're going to have so much time on your hands,' his wife warned, 'you'll be able to take a plane and go off to hear her sing whenever you like.'

'If there's any money left.'

'Or inclination,' Mary said.

They talked a miserable hour, never quite openly, always skirting the deepest anxieties. At the end, they kissed perfunctorily, in an embarrassment so desperate that David found himself shaking hands with his father.

'Don't forget,' Horace told his daughter-in-law, 'if you want anything, if you run short of money, let us know. We'll do our best.'

'Poor as we are,' Joan said, laughing.

Mary hugged Horace, Joan, Horace again. The parents came out to the drive to wave their goodbyes. A wet wind rustled the laurel bushes. In the car Mary dabbed at her eyes.

'I think sometimes I'm a fool,' she said, recovering.

'Bear up.'

They drank coffee together back at home and small glasses of Drambuie, looking about for an inspired word, not finding it. He carried the pots away into the kitchen, barked his shins on a stool, swore. Both laughed uncomfortably, and as he stood at the sink he heard Mary singing, not loud, but richly, 'Summer time, an' the livin' is easy,' lazily, putting the fingermark of her voice on the house.

They bundled themselves upstairs and made love but without forgetting imminent separation. Their naked union parted them; they were uneasily aware of otherness.

Next morning breakfast was leisurely, but breathless they punctuated silences with small controlled gusts of laughter. Joan rang from home; Horace from work; Mary cried, but meanly. When the time came they were glad to pile cases into the car and make a start. Very briefly Mary stood at the front gate, looked back at the house, but ventured no remark, her face set. As they drove along the main road near his school David noticed one or two latecomers hurrying in to begin an ordinary day, as usual, behind the time.

The journey was easier than they expected; they found their way through Heathrow without delay but had not too much time left for dawdling about in the lounges. They sipped scalding coffee, ate an iced bun, tensely, not saying much, barely trusting their lips, trying to keep still and sober as they observed the small dramas of an airport, the marshalling of children, the misplacement of hand luggage, the argument over next moves, the leaps upward after a public announcement, the handshakes, the watchfulness.

Mary's flight was called, exactly on time. The pair rose, kissed, held one another, and then she darted down for her bag.

'Bye,' she said. 'Take care of yourself.'

'And you.'

They kissed again and she was marching straight-backed away. At the glass doors she turned, raised her free hand, smiled, walked on. He looked at his mud-spattered shoes, buttoned his coat, made for the car park, drove back into gathering darkness, unsure how to contain his unease.

By the time he entered his home, he had prepared himself. He would not be disturbed by the cups and saucers on the draining board placed as Mary had left them in the last joint domestic chore. Oddly they were not as he remembered them, and this jolted him. Either he had not known what he was about, or he had casually observed when he ought to have been meticulous; he felt a pang of disappointment in himself, but set about cutting the loaf they had shared not ten hours before.

At eight his mother telephoned with a string of questions. He answered these easily, but she was not to be reassured.

'Do you want to come round?'

'No, thanks. I'm fine.'

'Shall we slip into the car and see you?'

'Please yourself.'

'Are you busy?'

'I can always find something to do.'

'Such as?'

'Marking history essays.'

Joan was not pleased, but left it at that. He ought to have produced some sign, some heavenly dove descending, to suit the occasion, but he could not. His wife had stepped firmly on to a plane, and at any time now would walk off it with as much resolution, and that was that. He summoned up his energies to swear, and beat a tattoo with clenched fists above the mantelpiece where she had not left her fingermarks.

He took his cello from the case, and a copy of the Bach

unaccompanied suites from the cabinet, and sat before the stand, without expectation. He turned and began quickly on the C major, boldly down, but was well into the movement before he realized how badly he played. Smoothing the copy with the end of his bow, he tried again and, failing, forced himself to continue, stumbling to the end of the Prelude, and breaking down in the Allemande. Omitting the Courante, he struck a few notes of the Sarabande and abandoned the project, taking his time as he unscrewed the bow, casing the cello, folding up the metal stand, something he never did. End of an era.

True to his word, he marked some lower sixth essays on Napoleon; they were conscientiously prepared, written with some style and energy, but they bored him. He awarded grades with equity, he thought, generously encouraging the highly intelligent, indulging in mild sarcasm in the manner of the school at the expense of misspellers or the slapdash. It was now half eleven and Mary would have been met, conducted to wherever she was going, and would be trying to prop her eyes open at 6.30 p.m. She had sense; possibly she'd demanded bath and bed; how could he know now they were on opposite sides of the Atlantic? He wound his alarm, set his radio and fell asleep immediately.

The next few days were barren.

No one at work asked about his day's absence; it had gone unremarked. At the Friday orchestral practice there were no inquiries about his wife or her travels, not even in the pub afterwards; his parents did not telephone; the postman delivered nothing interesting. The temperature dropped, and it rained harshly. These were evenings he ought to have enjoyed indoors, in the warmth, listening to the wind rattling panes or cracking raindrops bulletlike into the windows, but he was lonely.

The solitude carried no physical pain, rather a mental disorientation so that he could not concentrate for long. Twice he found himself upstairs on an errand he could not remember. He would lift down a book from his shelves and only by the most violent mental effort recall why he needed to consult it. He taught as he played sometimes in orchestral rehearsals, absentmindedly, on automatic pilot, but nobody complained, nobody noticed. The nearest he came to intellectual occupation was on the Saturday morning shopping expedition, when he needed to buy for his weekend meals, a new experience. He thought his mother might invite him for Sunday lunch, but she did not. Perhaps he had annoyed her, but he did not know how. When he rang his parents' house, Saturday at teatime, later that evening, Sunday at eleven, they did not answer the phone. He racked his brain, consulted his notepad, but there had been no prior intimation of their absence.

Lunch in the oven, two large potatoes; cold meat and salad in the fridge, he walked across to the Horace Blackwalls'. In the park he stood for a few dull minutes watching a football match, a ruthless encounter on a wet, sloping pitch. The players gasped and coughed; the thud of boot on ball had the uncouth roughness of the general strategy. With heavy kicks, furious shoulder charges, menacing shouts or appeals, muscly thighs bunched without resultant skill, men ran, sweated, blew out visible breath, steamed in the cold air, clogged their boots with mud. The referee's whistle screamed; athletic bolsheviks protested, reluctantly obeyed; the sodden ball flopped blackly skyward to no purpose.

David reached his parents' house, rang the bell, roused no one. He walked round to the back and sheltered for five minutes as a shower scudded from the northeast, whipping shrubs, bending branches. An attempt to peer into the garage failed; the sky cleared from blackish to mottled grey. His parents had gone out without informing him or he had forgotten.

At the end of the street the congregation from the parish church buttoned overcoats, held down hats, hurried for the line of cars parked along the gutter. In the park the footballers, redder in face and thigh, slogged on. Two biting showers caught, soaked him before he reached home.

After lunch, unusually, he fell asleep in his armchair over the Sunday papers. Middle age was setting in, he concluded, when he woke dazed and refreshed. It would be sensible to start a letter to Mary and slip it into an envelope for posting as soon as he had her address. He did nothing about it, deciding he would reply to her letter when it arrived. It surprised him that he did

57

not know how long it took for mail to cross the Atlantic. Two days? A week? Longer? Sluggishly he pulled a section of a newspaper towards him, read an article on women and unilateral disarmament, discovered he had not taken in a word. Staring towards the ceiling he considered action and decided after ten minutes to make a cup of instant coffee. He turned on his radio; an unknown nineteenth-century opera screeched at his boredom, so that he had switched it off before he could identify work or composer. Wind and cold rain devilled away outside.

It was dark before he left the chair. The telephone lay dumb. As he stood for some minutes at the front window the street seemed deserted. He considered a quick descent on the pub, saw no advantage in it. At this rate he'd be better off at school, with somebody to help him pass time. He looked at his cello case, but did no more than that, and fell asleep again over the early evening television news. At nine the phone shrilled and he ran towards it. His mother inquired how he progressed. When he had described his expedition to her house and she said, not sympathetically, 'You knew months ago that we were going to Annesley Hall last night. I was accompanying Christopher Mount. We did the *Dichterliebe*. We've been practising for weeks. In fact I offered you a ticket, but you said you weren't sure how you'd be fixed.'

Memory stirred vaguely in him as he bleated inanities down the mouthpiece. He asked how her concert had gone, and she softened. The Dyson Quartet had played Mozart's 'Hunt' and Janáček's First; she and Mount had performed between, and their audience had applauded generously.

'Good, good. You just did the Schumann.'

'Not all of that.'

'Oh. What was it in aid of?'

'David, David.' Again she explained to him, with the implication that he ought to have known. His mother appeared depressed, perhaps because she had little to occupy her now the recital was over. He inquired about American mail, and though she offered information she could not, would not be precise as he wished. She dismally arranged for him to dine with them on Thursday.

'You may have heard by then,' Joan said without enthusiasm. 'She'll be all right. There's a lot to that girl.'

On Wednesday, a week away from her departure, and with no word yet, he walked out from the gates of the school playing fields. It was cold, though the pitches were unfrozen, and flakes of snow drifted. He had not brought his car.

'Too cold for snow.'

A tall man blocked his path.

'That's something.'

'You one of the teachers at the high school, then?' The man nodded a cloth-capped hand in the direction of the pavilion.

'Yes.' 'Teacher' was not a popular term with the staff there.

'I've seen you before. I live just down there, Sunrise Road.'

The man wore a long, navy blue overcoat, frayed at the cuffs, brown knitted mittens, an ill-tied scarf; his collar and tie were none too clean. His boots were heavy, ex-army, the laces not tight.

'Yes.' David glanced at his watch.

'I watch the games, sometimes. Through the fence, y'know. I like the cricket better. Don't understand this rugby. Up and under. And it's a bit nippy standing about here in the winter.' The man's face was pale, unshaven, though his growth of beard was not strong, so that individual hairs stood shining. He needed a haircut, a nailfile. 'I have a walk out every afternoon, wet or fine. At my time of life you need the exercise, don't you?'

'I suppose you do.'

The man's brown eyes opened more widely, suspiciously at the answer.

'Housework and shopping and cooking in the morning. Out and about in the afternoon. That's the programme.' David said nothing. 'My wife died two years ago. I'm on my own.'

'I'm sorry.'

'I don't know how I put up with it, at first. I don't really. It affected me that bad. My children are grown-up, married. One in Frimley, the other, the girl, up north in Gateshead.'

'Do they visit you?'

The man opened his mouth, revealing brown, uneven teeth. He rubbed the end of his nose with the back of his hand. A gust of wind deposited wet snowflakes on the blue coat.

'They've got families of their own. Don't come often. Don't write much.'

'A pity.'

'Send cheques at Christmas. Good job in a bank, the daughter's husband. My son's in car repair. I'd like to see the children, but they don't come. Not that I blame them. Just look at me. I'm not much of an oil painting, am I? And this is an improvement. When my wife died, I went to pot. I did. Didn't look after myself. Well, there didn't seem much point in it.' He blew out breath grotesquely. 'I see now that was wrong. You've got to soldier on. I mean, if I don't look after myself, somebody else will have to, the council or the social services, and I don't want that. I want my independence while I'm capable. That's sensible, in't it?'

'Yes.'

'They send women in to bath you.' He eyed David narrowly. 'One poor old man down our street. How old do you think I am?'

'I've no idea.'

'Sixty-seven. She died just as I was retiring.'

'Was it unexpected?'

'She'd been bad for a year. More, perhaps. She wasn't the sort to moan.'

Pupils from the field, sportsgear in bags over their shoulders, passed, turning their heads to stare at Blackwall talking to a tramp. The man, perhaps out of deference, did not speak until the road was clear of boys.

'Are you married?'

David nodded.

'Make the most of it. We were married forty years, and it's all done now, gone, as if it never had been.'

'You've memories,' David checked him, 'surely.'

'That's thin gruel.'

The man laughed, spittle ugly at the corners of his mouth. David pushed back his sleeve to consult his watch, said he had a bus to catch. No attempt was made to detain him and when he looked back, he noted that the man walked, swinging his arms, smartly up the hill.

Snowflakes landed, melted.

6

On Thursday morning, the day he'd arranged to visit his parents, Mary's first letters arrived, two long envelopes. As he opened them he checked the dates, a day apart, to make sure he read them in the right order.

She was well. She had been met at the airport, fed and put early into a comfortable bed by a decent well-to-do couple who had some connection with the operatic venture. Next day, the woman, Muriel Winckler, had driven her to the university and left her. There she learned that they had three weeks to prepare *Semele*, the only opera they were doing. The administrator had shown her their schedule and later in the afternoon she had sung to Redvers Gage and Ulrich Fenster, who had talked to her in an interesting way about the songs, and had made some suggestions, said they would hear her again next day when she was less tired. Gage was a dark, taciturn young man, balding with curls, who stared you out, and then smiled.

She had met the rest of the company, who seemed pleasant. One or two had been very nice to her. She was temporarily in a hostel for overseas students, as far as she could make out, not far from the practice hall in the music school. There had never been any idea of producing more than one opera, and that had been known from the beginning. The producer man Gage, who was very lively indeed, seemed in sole charge. She'd let him know further about developments. She still felt tired and dazed, but she missed him. All her love.

The second letter sketched a second audition. Ulrich had listened to her again that morning, for twenty minutes, a couple of songs, again had made one or two suggestions about recitatives and said they'd both hear her again after lunch. In the afternoon, she, Ulrich, Red Gage, a pianist called Eddie and another man, Si Somebody, had piled into a car, dashed elsewhere on the campus into some large assembly hall and there she'd sung again. Gage had asked her to do one or two things, operatic poses, walking across the place diagonally, falling to her knees and then they'd asked her to sing again. She went through 'Ah me, too late I now repent my pride and impious vanity', while the three men sat at the back, talking loudly, paying no attention to her. When she'd finished they'd continued their discussion, leaving her standing there. She had felt frightened, she said, and angry, and after a bit had walked over to the accompanist, who spoke with an American accent so thick she could barely understand him, to ask what they were on with. He was noncommittal at first, but said in the end that it was all chaos, and always would be, until they could make up their minds. Gage had then come forward and asked if she would mind singing the first part of the song again, right back to the far wall, just standing there, fortissimo. The pianist had asked if he should wheel his piano nearer to her, but had been told it didn't matter.

'I'm twen'y-five medres away,' he had protested.

'Play louder, then,' Gage had said, serious in his misunderstanding. 'I've heard you.' He'd then laughed, blackly, bleakly.

She'd sung and Fenster had waved a hand in thanks or dismissal as he turned to his colleagues again. Gage straddled a chair, grasping the back as if he'd shake it off. The third personage, Simon, had talked in a deep voice. From where she stood she could not make out a word, but noted that on occasion all three yammered away together. She had just found a seat, parked there trembling, when a fourth man joined the group. Almost immediately Gage detached himself, walked easily towards her, wobbling slightly as if his shoes needed heeling, and said, 'That was beautiful, beautiful. We loved it. But I shall have to ask you to do it again. I'm sorry, honey, but . . .'

She had shrugged, she said, kept mum. Gage instructed Ed who had been quietly improvising jazz. Mary sang again, but not well. The quartet at the far end of the hall rudely chattered. She could have kicked somebody, but immediately the newcomer had walked towards her; it took him an hour.

'Robert Harnack,' he announced. 'Superb, Miss Blackwall, superb. We're lucky, and I don't say that often. Not in my nature.' He had shaken her hand, his was large and dry, and

62

nodded, smiling, muttered more congratulatory phrases and stalked off, past the other three without a word.

She, seeing nothing further happened, Gage and colleagues at least were standing, made for Eddie, asked him who Harnack was.

'Search me,' he had answered. 'Some professor, I guess.'

Suddenly, this was described in a later letter, she raked over this first day or two in reply to the many questions David scribbled at her, she began to whistle. Ever since childhood she had been competent with a powerful, sweet sound, and she, standing at the back of the upright piano, let herself into Gershwin's 'Summer time, and the livin' is easy'. She had not finished the first line before Eddie had joined her with the piano, straight into key, rhythmically powerful but quiet, creative, finding his way into variation but supporting in a brilliance of subdued opposition the liquid line of the air above. Mary finished, Ed continued, chirping in the top register of his piano as if to mock the clarity, the lazy insouciance of the solo. He looked at her, pursing his lips, inviting her to another burst, but she turned away. 'I hadn't come three thousand miles to do music-hall turns,' she'd written.

The whistling, unlike her singing, had silenced the three men at the back. Eddie, registering a comical dismay at her refusal, signed off with a large, splayed, unfinished, sustained arpeggio. Fenster came across; he hurried now, and hauled his glasses off as if they irritated his prominent nose. All American musicians have large conks, she had comforted herself, big beaks. He was smiling with real pleasure, at the *Porgy and Bess*, she imagined.

'We'd like you to sing the part of Semele for us,' he had said, without preamble. She had not answered. 'You will, I know.'

Eddie was beaming; she noticed that. Gage and Si had joined Ulrich. Still she said not a word, near weeping. Her silence disconcerted the men; they'd expected an outburst of joy, kissings, hugs, screams perhaps, and this pale beauty, standing with her back now to the piano, defending it, keeping their world at arm's length puzzled them.

'Sorry we were so long,' Gage said, coming forward, taking both her hands. 'We knew, but we didn't believe it.'

That made no sense to her.

'I was touched,' Si said. He looked younger from this distance in spite of baldness, and his voice sounded resonantly deep. 'As I did not expect.'

A tear forced itself out of the corner of her left eye, trickled, seemed enormous. Si nodded approval.

Then the hand-shaking and kisses began. Gage disappeared.

Fenster, returning to his normal fidgeting, issued instructions. She could have Eddie and a studio the whole of the next day; he'd give her an hour on Saturday afternoon, Sunday was her own unless Red had different ideas, and on Monday they'd start putting it on stage. The first performance would be mounted, here, a fortnight on Saturday.

'We haven't much time,' Fenster said. 'Red asks a great deal of us.'

The men led her triumphantly back to the car.

Much of this David learned later, but from the first two sketchy letters he caught something of his wife's apprehension and excitement, and, he suspected, her stubborn habits, her failure to understand exaggeration. She would sing her heart out for her mentors, he knew, but would remain unconvinced that her performance changed the world, even minutely. What these men made of that he'd learn, in time, perhaps he feared only when they had broken her. To him, striding his streets or carpets, rereading the thin sheets, success appeared now more a question of character than musical ability. And Mary lacked pliability. Thus far, and no farther was her motto. Fool's gold shone prettily, and none the worse for that, but lacked market value. Operatic performance, even at a high level, fell short of the dimensions of life. She, he, both knew it; in the world of art nobody did, or nobody admitted it.

He carried the letters to his parents' house in a flush of ambivalence, questioning his motives. The parents read the letters carefully, his father shifting his glasses up and down his nose.

'Is that the leading part?' Horace asked his wife. He handed the envelope back to his son; his perusal had been slower than Joan's, with his eyes half-narrowed. 'Well?' Suddenly to his son.

David voiced his doubts; Horace looked towards his wife; Joan did not speak.

'She's made her mark by the sound of it,' Horace pronounced. 'Yes. I'm glad.'

'She'll be bemused,' Joan told them. 'Won't know what she's about, but she's still able to give a good performance. That's the test. When you're half dead with jetlag or headache or a cold or homesickness you can stand up and sing as if you're on top of the world.'

David enjoyed the evening. His father talked about his American trips, ventured a few generalizations about people. Joan was quieter than usual, left the room to make lemonade for her son.

'Is Ma all right?' David asked. He was never sure these days what to call his mother.

'Why?'

'She's not saying much.'

'She's living that life with Mary. I'm not joking. I rang up some friends last night in New York, and made inquiries about nipping across to hear Mary sing once she starts. The Feinsteins will put us up.'

'Does Ma know you've done this?'

'She suggested it.'

'And you've got the time?'

'I'm nearly retired. Or I shall be when I've finished with lawyers and accountants. Even so, I can take a week off now without noticing it.'

'And you'll fly to America just to hear one performance?'

'To see Mary. Yes. If I have a bob or two, I might as well spend it.' He picked a boxed set from a cabinet. 'Your mother brought it in this morning. Been on order. So we shall get to know it.' He displayed the title: *Semele*. 'She was pretty certain Mary would do well.'

'More than I was.'

'She's confidence . . .'

'There's so much luck . . .'

'Fortune favours the brave.' Horace's foxy grin neither displeased nor comforted his son. 'We'll let you know how she is.'

As he left Joan kissed him, she did not always, saying, 'Write some good long letters, now, David, all about the weather, and

65

the school, and the orchestra. It's important.' He left the house cheered.

For the next week transatlantic silence rankled, and though David warned himself that Mary was busy, tired out, waiting for his first letters, the nondelivery disheartened him each morning.

On the Saturday morning, having waited for the postman, who brought bills and appeals, he did his shopping, called in at the library. The sun shone coldly bright; windows misted; he was in no hurry though the afternoon and evening would be taken up by rehearsal and performance in Newark. He walked home circuitously.

This way he had to pass a factory once owned by a friend of his father's. The office premises on the front were deserted, panes dirty or holed. As a sixth former he had glanced in the place, certain that well-dressed young women, with fashionable bright hairstyles, would mince round with folders, cock their heads to take phone calls, frown fetchingly at typewriters under a brilliancy of bar lights. Now dirt, and darkness, as he peered in, not a stick of furniture, rubble about the floor, electrical fittings all disconnected. The golden letters of the name Thomas Bliss and Son Ltd, which had stretched block length, were dismantled, leaving only black boltmarks in the brick. The main gates, grandly double, bright with carved and polished panels in their heyday, had gone, leaving the walls gashed, molested as if the doors had been wrenched off, elaborate craftmanship firewood from that moment.

He stood staring in through the gap by a board with a roughly chalked legend: Reclaimed Timber for Sale. Apply within. At the other side of the courtyard and loading bays, an enormous earth-shifting machine towered ready to clear debris. Two men lounged, talking; one bonfire sent up a pillar of smoke, another flamed but darkly; there was no activity. The main block of the factory was being demolished, beginning with the left corner where the outside walls had been battered into hillocks of bricks but where the first floor hung tottering, at a crazy angle, still holding its shape, but hirsute with spikes of broken laths or floorboards. Presumably it would sag thus until work began on Monday, unless it collapsed. The yard was littered with lengths of wood, rubble, concrete nuggets; every surface was dulled with dust.

Hooting behind him startled David. A mini, driven by a young woman, darted in.

'They're getting on with it,' a passer-by opined.

'What's going to happen?'

'Flats.'

'They're going to pull it all down, then?'

'They are. Every brick. My, some jobs went west when they shut down.'

'How long ago is that?'

'Been standin' derelict a twelvemonth, if not more.'

The man lifted his cloth cap to scratch his head, moved on without another word. David was utterly surprised by the information for he felt certain that he and Mary had stood here watching the lorries, enjoying the ordered bustle, less than a year ago. He remembered telling her of the golden-haired beauties in the office, and while they were still laughing she had slipped back to glance in.

'Nothing to write home about,' she reported. 'All your fevered imagination.'

'Don't ruin it,' he begged, mocking himself, and they had marched off, arm in arm, pleased with the exchange.

Yet at that time, whenever it was, negotiations must have been completed. The overalled workmen, the lorry drivers, the representatives and administrators with their line of smart cars along the right of the court, the golden girls, the managing director were proscribed, marked down for redundancy.

Shouldering his bag, he read a notice warning children and their parents that while demolition was going on, trespass was dangerous. The solidity of the wall on which the bill was stuck, the beauty of the bricklaying would soon disappear like the already fading chalk and black felt tip or aerosol spray graffiti. He consoled himself that people had to have somewhere to live.

Back home, he drank his coffee gloomily, and cursed out loud the phone call he was pleased to hear.

Anna Talbot, first inquiring about Mary's progress, his health, then said she had a proposition to put to him.

'Go on.'

'Would you like to join a string quartet?'

'Depends.' He showed no enthusiasm. 'Who are the others for a start?'

'The Trent,' she said.

'Where's Jon Mahon?' The cellist.

'Found himself a job in Australia. Can I come and see you?'

Anna's connections were many: her husband James was senior musical adviser for the county; she sang in three choirs; her father taught counterpoint at the university. She enjoyed power, and interference. She and David had of course briefly been lovers when they were students at the Royal College. Without much enthusiasm he arranged to see her on Sunday evening.

Beautifully dressed, carefully made up, Anna Talbot arrived half an hour late, because she had been looking after her demanding mother-in-law, who had Sunday lunch with them each week. James had promised to drop in on some orchestral rehearsal and had thus left 'the old biddy' to be cared for. David spoke sympathetically as Anna gracefully fumed.

'She's not old, for one thing. Sixty-six, but acts as if she's eighty. She's a widow, and her husband carried her about for forty years. Now she expects Jim to do the same.'

'Is she a musician?'

'She thinks so. She'd tell you so.' Anna accepted a martini and lemon, much iced. 'I need that.' Her tongue played snakily along her lips.

'Is James the only child?'

'No. There are three. He's the only one who does anything for her.'

'He's the youngest?'

'No, he isn't. He's the soft-hearted one. And even he goes out and leaves me to cope.'

David looked over this fashionable woman, now much at ease, from her neat head to her polished and buckled boots. She moved elegantly manicured hands with restraint; she smiled with effect, like the breaking through of the sun on a cloudy day; her silver earrings played with the light. She might well have just been photographed in the green, plain, neck-high dress for the glossy magazines. All was simple, admirable, artificial. Phrases like 'bath-fresh', 'jewel-clear', 'true love' scrambled into his head from advertisements. No one could be as perfect as she looked.

For five minutes she was distantly amusing about old Mrs Talbot, who had spent the afternoon in inquiring how her son wasted his time, why they had no children, and when the house was to be properly furnished. Bright-eyed Anna reported that the old hag had accused her of hardness of heart, slovenly habits and infertility.

'And you said?'

'Nothing for a while, and then, when she wouldn't stop, "You're not enjoying yourself here, are you? You know where the front door is. I'll fetch your coat." '

'And?'

'She burst into tears. Like a child. Really loud. Then she calms down, for the next half-hour just sits there and lets out gulps and sobs at strategic intervals.'

'Is she unhappy?'

'Must be, to act as she does. But I'm not giving in to her. I hide behind the Sunday papers.'

'And James?'

'Oh, he's like his father. He lets the old harpy sink her talons in, but at least he's learned some sense now. He keeps out of her way.'

'Leaves you to it.'

'No.' Anna raised her glass. 'This afternoon was unusual. But he won't put himself at her bidding quite as he used to.' She laughed, drank. 'For Christ's sake – I don't know why I'm giving you all this. Tell me about Mary, now.

She listened to his account, sitting motionless, without questions until he had finished.

'They're just doing the *Semele*?' she asked, thoughtfully.

'So it seems.'

'James says it's very good, but static. He reckons we went to a performance, Sadlers Wells, but I can't remember a thing about it. He might be right. He usually is.' She drained her drink, accepted a refill. 'Yes, super. Same again. Exactly right.' Now she gently pinched her upper lip between the thumb and forefinger of her left hand, quick, regular move-

69

ments. He guessed she was more disturbed by the afternoon's collision with her mother-in-law than she'd admit.

She described a trip she and James had made to the States during the summer, and said she would like to live there. This surprised him.

'This country's finished,' she said, 'done.'

He waited but she made no additions.

'And James, what does he say?'

'Nothing. The matter hasn't been raised. I'm telling you what I think. But if a good job came up there, he'd be off smartly.'

'And leave his mother?'

'And leave his mother.'

She liked the people they had met in the States; there was plenty going on; the cultural spectrum was very much broader. She admitted the low standards of television and journalism, but said their best people were better than England's, even James thought so. 'There are signs of life.'

'Are you serious?' David asked.

Anna nodded her head, thoughts elsewhere. He found no comfort in her silence, but she brightened again, signalled the change by tapping with her nails on the arm of the chair.

'My proposition, now,' she began.

She had been talking to Frederick Payne, the leader of the Trent Quartet, a friend and protégé of her husband's. The Trent had been doing particularly well, with plenty of engagements, had begun to attract notice in the right places when Jonathan Mahon, their cellist, had applied for a job in Australia, his wife's country. This was not, Anna said, altogether a tragedy in that they were not satisfied with Mahon's attitude; he was too casual by half. Quite likely they would have turned him out, and his replacement, Robert Knight, had already been chosen. James had fixed Knight up with a job as a peripatetic string teacher, but he could not start until September. That left the quartet with a dozen concerts to cancel. Worse, they had been considering turning professional in a year's time, and this would now have to be put back if not altogether abandoned.

'Why is there so little notice?' he asked.

70

'Wheels within wheels. Jon has been secretive about his new job; he just sprang it on them. They've not been hitting it off, and he thought he owed them nothing.'

'Rightly?'

'Probably. But they're in serious trouble. They've been looking around. And James has. Things didn't work out. Yours was the only serious name to come up locally. Jim said I knew you better than he did, and Freddy got on to me to ask you.'

'Why didn't he ask me himself?'

'You're a bit of a nob, you know. Cambridge and high school. And your father's who he is.'

'If they were in such dire straits, they'd ring me if I was Gregor Piatigorsky.'

'I don't know about that. It's just a stand-in. You'll be dropped in the summer. And it'll mean one hell of a lot of hard graft.'

'Why me?' David asked.

'Fred says you're a good enough player and a good musician. You might have some ideas while you're with 'em. If they can't get you they'll have to bring a scratch player up from London or the College or the Academy for concerts, and that's goodbye to continuity or practice. And expensive.'

'Supposing I'm not up to standard? I've hardly done any chamber music since I've been up here.'

'Never crossed anybody's mind. But then it'll be the substitute players. Nothing else for it. What do you say now?' She waited equably. 'They're good. You'll enjoy it.'

'I'm not so sure of that. When do they practise?'

'Tuesdays, Thursdays, though they'll change that to suit you. The concerts are all Saturdays and Sundays except one, that's a Wednesday, I think. If they're not giving a concert, they rehearse Sunday mornings as well.'

'Where?'

'At Cyril Barton's. But they'll come here, if that's any easier. I've brought a list, a programme and Jon's scores. They'll simplify programmes, not play so much, I mean, if you want that. Shall I fetch the music in? It's in the car.'

He said nothing; he wanted to be left alone. She seemed in no hurry.

71

'Shall I?'

'You just hold your horses. I shall have to think about this.'

'Go on, then.'

'Why can't this Knight man come up for the concerts?'

'He's busy, and he lives too far away. He's somewhere in Scotland. He's said to be outstandingly good.'

'Where's he from?'

'He's Scottish, but he was at the Royal Northern with Fred. Won no end of prizes.'

'But hasn't got anywhere?'

'I wouldn't say that.' She stopped him with a finger. 'They genuinely look forward to his coming, but they dread it. He's a terror, and they think they might have got slack while Mahon messed them about.'

'Have they?'

'I doubt it, but that's why they don't want ad hoc performances. They need three hard sessions a week. Another thing, Fred thinks you'll be good for them. You're not just a scraper. You've had professional teaching, but you're a musician, a cultured man. You'll keep 'em on their toes.'

'Counting my wrong notes.'

'No, David,' Anna said. 'It might sound flattering, but it's somewhere near the truth.'

'What's in all this for you?' he asked.

'I like to throw my weight about. Two, I'm interested in them. I'm quite interested in you, believe it or not. I'd like to see if they can make a go of it full time. It's likely, even in these hard days. Jim thinks so. And here you are, with a big gap in your life at the right moment, and plenty to offer. It's what you need.'

'I've hardly time to turn round now.'

'That's the sort of man to ask, I think.'

They sat silently; she knew when she had said enough.

'It's tempting,' he said. 'Let's look at your list and see if there are any immovable clashes with the dates in my diary.'

'Good.' She sipped, rose slowly. He let her out of the front door, where he waited. She returned with a battered music case, the leather scarred, one strap broken so that the metal bar dangled loose. 'Here you are.'

The first two concerts were strictly classical, Haydn, Mozart, Beethoven, he'd played them at some time, but then Debussy, Bartók, Shostakovich, Britten.

'No Elliott Carter,' he said. He sat silently again, picking at his chin. 'I'd like to have a rehearsal with them, and see then what I think about it.'

'That's what I would have suggested. How about Tuesday?'

'Right. They realize I shan't have had any practice?'

'I expect so.' She straightened up. 'That's it, then. You'll go to Cy Barton's, will you? His address is on the programme.'

'Cup of coffee?' he asked.

'Yes, that'll be great. I can't tell you how pleased I am, David. You'll be good for them.'

'I'm not so sure.'

'If they're going professional, they've got to offer something out of the ordinary. You can help.'

As they drank their coffee he felt lassitude as if he'd been out walking all day, but at the same time a certain satisfaction in that he was about to parallel Mary's venture in New York. He'd have to abandon serious schoolmastering for a few weeks, as she'd abandoned husband, home, country, but now he fiercely wanted to do it. If he could come up to scratch, so could his wife. Superstitiously he felt he helped her by taking on this burden.

Anna was chattering; he barely listened. She refused more coffee, said she must go.

'Will James be home?'

'He was there when I came out.'

'Doing what?'

'Reading something. Planning something. Drinking. He'll be pleased you've decided as you have.'

She kissed him, and made off into the night.

73

7

On the morning of David's first rehearsal with the Trent Quartet, he received a letter from Mary, as did his mother.

The letters, identical in content, varied in tone. Rehearsals were long and tiring; the director, unassertive one minute, suddenly became arbitrary and inflexible the next. Talent abounded, but nobody seemed quite sure what to make of the opera so that one day would be spent in detailed rehearsal of movements which were modified on the next. They knew the music, certainly, but, but. David's letter, written the day after Joan's, seemed edgy, bad-tempered, while the one to his mother was sharp, witty, in high good humour.

Joan rang her son before he left for school, invited him round for lunch so they could exchange letters.

'I oughtn't to come. I've marking by the pile.' He explained about his trial that evening with the Trent.

'All the more reason to get out of the place for an hour. It'll save you preparing anything this evening. Dad's away again, so I'll be pleased to see you.'

He enjoyed the meal and his mother's conversation.

'I'll write to her this afternoon,' she promised. 'That'll set your conscience at rest. You can dash her a few lines tomorrow. You can tell she's tired.'

'I wish to God she'd never gone.'

'No, you don't. She's young, and she's strong. As soon as they begin to perform she'll be right as rain. Especially as she's only doing the one opera.'

'The whole thing baffles me.'

'I don't think it should. They always work like this, these theatre people. They seem incapable of sitting down before rehearsals and thinking out what they want.'

'But wasn't this Gage man an academic?'

'They're least able to make their minds up. That's why

74

they're so violent defending their ideas once they've been forced into saying what they are. She'll be right as ninepence.'

He left his parents' house much cheered, replete and re-assured. As he was on the point of driving off his mother tapped on the window of his car. He wound it down.

'Do you know,' Joan said, brightly still, 'I think your Dad is looking forward to retirement. I was dreading it.'

'When's the fatal day?'

'He keeps hinting he'll need some months to tie his loose ends. But we're freer now than we ever have been.'

'How will he occupy himself?'

'I'm not sure. I think we're going to travel.'

'Don't you have any say in the matter?'

'I'm only a poor, weak woman.' She laughed heartily, with irony. 'Mary will be pleased about this Trent thing. But don't go knocking yourself up.'

'No fear of that.'

'You're too like your father. Once he's got the bit between his teeth, there's no stopping him.'

He noticed as he turned the corner of the street she was still out there on the pavement.

The afternoon's lessons went by habit, but seemed none the worse for that. After he'd picked at his tea, he tried to practise, but found himself lacking in willpower. When he had played a difficult passage, he'd little idea whether or not he'd done it well, only that he had not performed it badly. He tried to force his whole attention on the music, but failed, and turned dismally to the television. If he'd anything about him, he instructed himself, he'd write to Mary, or use the spare hour marking essays, but he attempted neither, and was unreasonably glad when he could lock up and go out.

He arrived five minutes early, but the other three were already assembled. They shook hands, and Frederick Payne mumbled through the expected welcome. David knew them all, if not intimately. The room in which they practised was upstairs, a square, thirteen by thirteen feet, without carpets, with four chairs, four stands, an upright piano and a large standard lamp the only furniture. The floorboards shone varnished, and the whole room gave the impression of a recent

75

spring cleaning. Though the radiators were hot, David touched one, Cyril Barton, the violist, whose house this was, brought in a two-bar fire, 'Just in case.'

'We'll do the Mozart first,' Payne said, mildly enough. In B flat, Köchel 458. 'We thought a quick runthrough tonight would be in order. To give you some idea.' They were all intent on their instruments, tuning, rubbing rosin on the bows, raising lowering, shifting stands, making sure they could see their books or turn the leaves. 'Let's get the rhythm right if we can.' He was not speaking directly to David. 'Forte.' He glanced over at Walter Wilkinson, the second fiddle, who was having trouble with final tuning. Wilkinson beamed back at him, alert.

'New strings,' he said. He seemed not to be excusing himself.

Payne, now satisfied they were ready, lifted his head and lilted away on the anacrusis. In no time David found himself, lifted himself with them, was one with three. He held his breath, or it was constricted in his chest; tense, bound, he still managed to keep up with his colleagues.

Where he did not match them was in volume. His instrument, he knew, was superior to any of theirs, capable of a larger sound, but the others outsoared him. It was as if the whole of their bodyweight were concentrated on to their fiddles, so that these spoke with a large, steely tone, not only powerfully broad, but with a cutting edge, each note strong from the initial impact of bow on the string. This magnificent forte had nothing laboured or brutal about it; it was loud because the composer demanded it, but lucid, inherently musical. They were playing in readiness for a large hall where variations had to be made sharply. David leaned into his cello.

At the first double bar line Payne stopped them.

'All right?' he asked David. The man seemed to be smiling. He made no mention of the cellist's slight fluff as he had moved into the C clef. Wilkinson was leaning back, testing his tuning with left hand only, his bow held out swordlike in front of him. A grin, a sneer of satisfaction was set on his bearded face. 'We'll do all repeats,' Payne ordered. 'Good for us. Right. Second time.'

They played without reserve, only stopping when someone asked for a repetition; Payne was immediately ready, naming the bar to which they were to return. David noticed that Cyril Barton sniffed loudly, at climaxes, whereas Payne's face was inscrutable, narrow-eyed, unmoved as if the energy of his playing came from the wide shoulders, the flexible wrists. They did not talk much about interpretation, but when they repeated a passage they built each other up, learned, taught, combined, refined in concert, in keeping.

Oddly, they had more difficulty with the Minuet than with the following Adagio which they raised so that David found fingers singing in necessary eloquence above their supportive semiquaver accompaniment. Payne's runs were free as birdflight, as perfectly controlled; his colleagues were no less technically graceful, emotionally alert. At the end of the movement the leader nodded towards his cellist.

'Impressive,' he said. Warmth of praise clashed with a phlegmy sarcasm, and he dashed off into the Allegro assai.

No sooner had they finished the Mozart than the order was given: 'Beethoven.' David wanted to pause, to savour the experience, to rest, to expand, but they'd dropped Mozart to the floor and were turning up op. 18, no. 2. Wilkinson, scratching his beard, he'd laid his violin for the moment in his case, raised some question of speed in the abandoned B flat, but Payne, who was frowning at the Beethoven, poking the page down with the tip of his bow, crossly surprised, David thought comically, that the composer had given the leader so full a first bar compared with the bland lengths allotted to the rest of them, wearily demurred.

'We'll do it in detail next time,' he said, clearing his throat. 'Mark your copies if there are snags. I've not much faith in talk, anyway,' he muttered in David's direction.

'Strong and silent,' Cyril Barton offered.

'This bloody fiddle.' Wilkinson was vigorously tuning again. 'Worse than a lute.'

'Piano,' Payne commanded, and they were away.

When they had completed the Beethoven, with very few breaks and a little discussion, Barton went downstairs to put the kettle on. Wilkinson practised an awkward passage as if the other two were not there.

'How did it seem?' Payne asked David.

77

'Reasonably comfortable. Did I suit you?'

'Excellent, for a first time.'

'Am I making enough row?'

'No, but you'll come to it. When you know your part as well as the rest of us.'

Payne stood, stretching and yawning, crossed to the uncurtained window to stare out. Wilkinson concentrated on his violin bowing lightly, so that David was left, instrument alongside, to lounge in his chair. He felt he had not let them down, but recognized his faults clearly enough. Barton arrived with large steaming mugs and a tin of biscuits.

'The only part I enjoy,' Wilkinson said, shovelling in piled spoonfuls of sugar.

'We hardly drink alcohol,' Payne had returned. 'God knows how we shall get on when Knighty comes. He can knock it back.'

'You think he'll have you out at the pub?' David asked. The coffee had scalded his tongue.

'I don't think so.' Barton, very quiet, very confident.

They inquired what David's wife thought about his turning out three extra times a week, whether she had complained, and when he informed them about her American trip they seemed not to have heard of it. This surprised him. Hadn't Anna Talbot mentioned it? Payne pursed his lips as if he ought to have known something. Wilkinson and Barton talked about proposed cuts in school music and both praised James, Anna's husband, for his support, but the conversation was dull, made as if to ease Blackwall into their company, to show the newcomer they could talk in front of him, but at the same time suggesting they found his eavesdropping slightly threatening. No remarks were directed towards him, and they were all relieved to put down their mugs and begin on the Haydn, op. 17, no. 3.

'I like this,' Barton told David, beaming, before they began, 'this is my style.'

Again they spoke little beyond curt, polite demands for repetitions of unsatisfactory passages. Once, in the slow movement, when Payne stopped them, the newcomer ventured to interfere.

78

'What was wrong?' David asked.

The rest looked up, Payne puzzled, Wilkinson mildly taken aback and Barton with approval.

'My fingering,' Payne answered.

'It sounded marvellous.'

'It felt uncomfortable.'

They lifted their instruments.

The rehearsal finished at half past ten. David, fagged out, could barely summon energy to push himself up from his seat.

'Is it possible to start at seven o'clock on Thursday?' Payne queried, uncertainly. Now they were all on their feet. Agreement.

'Thanks very much, David.' Barton smiled. 'That was very good. You played that Haydn beautifully, really beautifully.'

David locked his case.

'Thanks.' Payne. 'Mark up any tricky passages. Is there anything now that strikes you? Before we leave?'

'No.'

'That's it, then. We don't talk much, but if you can't tell what the three of us want from our playing, we aren't making much of a job of it. Quartet playing's a bastard. I got an offer once when I was at college to join the Toledo. I should have accepted.'

'The result is,' Barton said, 'we're all being driven raving mad to make up for it.'

Wilkinson cadged a lift back and David was glad of his company.

'Barton seems a nice chap,' Blackwall suggested.

'There are ten thousand ways a quartet can up-end itself,' Wilkinson answered, 'but the quickest and first and least obvious is to have a viola who's no bloody use. We're lucky in Cy.'

Just as Wilkinson was about to leave the car, David asked him, 'Would you like to go professional?'

Wilkinson thumped back into his seat as though the question needed leisure and stillness to answer.

'I'm a married man,' he said, 'with two kids. Fred and Cy, and Knighty for that matter, are bachelors. It makes me expendable.' He scratched his beard. 'Don't get me wrong. They'd like to keep me if they could, but there'll be no half-measures. Fred Payne's determined to make it if he has to wreck the Atlantic Alliance to do it.'

'And he's good enough?'

'You could see that for yourself, couldn't you?' He was up and out. 'Thanks for the lift. No, I s'll have my own back for Thursday. And I need it.'

David, wearied, did not leave his armchair until after midnight and then could not sleep. The ferocity of the practice jolted phrases into his head until he wished he had his instrument to hand so that he could exorcize them. He recalled snatches of conversation, the laconic, exact words with which they had asked for a repetition, Payne's immediate command as he'd named the bar. Wilkinson's rebuke. 'You could see that for yourself, couldn't you?' He could see, if nothing else, that he had spent three hours in the company of his superiors, and this did not please. He did not hate them, but self-concern rankled so that inability to equal their technical standard seemed a moral fault.

He spent the whole of Wednesday evening on the music, as on solo parts. Not quite sure whether this made sense, he persevered, drove himself to be ready. Thursday's rehearsal seemed less satisfactory than the first, more bitty, and once some argument from Wilkinson over a descending phrase marked crescendo for the lower instruments against a piano in the first violin. Nobody else could see what the man was getting at; he himself seemed uncertain.

'We'll do it again.' Payne.

'Better?' when they had tried.

'It doesn't sound right.'

'Outside parts crescendo earlier, piano earlier; inner, well you know. Again.'

They set to.

'No,' Wilkinson cried sharply.

David could see little wrong.

'Same spot then. Again.'

They did the offending bars and stopped.

'Well?'

'Perhaps it's me,' Wilkinson admitted. 'But it doesn't sound right.'

80

'Is it the balance?'

'I don't know what the hell it is. Let's do it again and go on.'

That seemed typical of the evening's work. The beautiful playing, and there was much, would be interrupted unreasonably, so that they repeated a passage, were forced apart into variation for variation's sake. Perhaps this was what quartet work entailed, the practising and final discarding of unacceptable interpretations, but the whole lay fragmented, in meaningless pieces. At five to ten they called it a day, and Wilkinson immediately left.

'How did you find that?' Payne asked David. They sat downstairs.

'I didn't feel so comfortable.'

'No. Walter had it on him tonight.'

'Is he often like this?'

'Well. It's his wife. She doesn't want him to turn to professional quartet playing. When he was in the BBC Symphony, she wasn't happy until she had him out. I don't blame her. She had full responsibility for the children, and he had to be away often. It's a pity. He's a marvellous player. He keeps me on my toes.'

'Will he go with you?' David asked.

'Yes, I think he will.'

'It'll be a loss if he doesn't,' Cy Barton said. 'It's this awkwardness of his that makes us. He rubs us up the wrong way. That makes us better, because he's such a good player. Not like Jon.'

'He just annoyed us.'

'He wasn't anything but a good sight-reader,' Cyril said. 'You give us more after two rehearsals than he gave us after two hundred. I think that's why Walter's on edge. He thought this might put the evil day off.'

They laughed.

'What's his wife like?' David asked.

'We're bachelors. She's an attractive girl. Met her in the music library here. Like your wife. A singer. In the local choirs. Or was, till the family started. Trouble with Walter is that he thinks she hasn't had the opportunities he has. And she hasn't.

81

He feels guilty. Walter's what you'd call a good man. He bothers about being fair.'

'And that will never do,' Payne added.

'Not in this game.'

8

Mary's one letter in the next week said she had been unwell.

She did not write at length about her illness, just that she felt off colour, and took up the rest of the letter with a satirical outline of preparations for the first performance and sourly with the constantly changed proposals about the itinerary. Simple as the scenery was, it took some moving, as anyone in his right mind could have foreseen, and yet this college, that theatre was allowed to cry off performances or demand more or call for alterations. Getting the show on the road made lunatics of the most sensible; she had had one desperate day in bed away from it all. People had been most kind. They were to spend an extra three days in New York, she added in a PS, before they made for Boston and their next longest stay. Redvers Gage was now superb.

Her first performance took place on the same day as his, but he worked it out that the Trent's concert would be finished by the time *Semele* began.

David consulted his mother, who had heard nothing from her daughter-in-law, but who had been in touch with their friends in New York. On Saturday the senior Blackwalls would listen to the quartet's concert, would drive down at leisure to London on Sunday, stay the night with a cousin, fly to New York on Monday morning and attend performances on Tuesday and Thursday. A letter to this effect had been dispatched to Mary.

'I hope you're writing regularly,' his mother warned.

'I add a bit every day and send it off every third.'

'It could be worse.'

'The playing takes up such a time. I've started on the Shostakovich, no. 8, C minor. It's tricky, especially as I've never seen it before. It's for the third concert.'

'Have you done it together yet?'

'No. That's part of the trouble. It doesn't make sense to me.'

'I've got a record.'

It would be reasonable to listen, even if the performance misled, but he felt bound to refuse, to be awkward, to do a Wilkinson and cite moral grounds, musical integrity. Joan laughed at him.

'They'll make you as bad as they are,' she told him.

'I've not far to go.'

When he asked what she thought about Mary's illness, she refused to be dogmatic.

'It could be a chill or something of the kind.'

'You don't think she's fed up with it all?'

'I don't see why I should think that, but by a week on Monday evening we'll be back with an eyewitness account.'

' "How pleasant it is to have money",' he said, grudgingly.

'I hope so.'

Kenneth Reeve stopped him in the corridor to inquire about Mary's progress. Taken by surprise, David explained that the first performance had yet to take place.

'Keep me informed,' Reeve said. 'My wife is always worrying me about it.'

'That's kind of her.'

'It's her nature.' Reeve coughed drily and stalked quietly off, on his toes.

On the Saturday of the concert, David rose early, completed the weekend shopping by 9.30 and did an hour's playing, not at the quartets, before coffee. He had decided to lunch out, and then make his way to Newark for their rehearsal at three o'clock. Without haste he decided on a walk in the park; the air stung crisp, small pockets of frozen, sooty snow piled in shadowed hollows; middle-aged women walking their dogs were muffled up to the eyebrows. He met no one he knew; such a morning ought to have exhilarated him, but though he walked smartly only children seemed cheerful among the black trees. The concert nagged at his nerves, but he could do nothing to settle himself; his breath came short and, he reminded himself gloomily as he emerged through the cast-iron gates into the main road, he had not once thought of Mary and *Semele*.

He chewed his way through a boring expensive steak and, deciding against alcohol or coffee, sipped mineral water. The meal was not enjoyable, but he comforted himself that he would not be hungry again that day. Back at home, he checked that he had spare strings, that his music was complete, that he had three bows packed. To fill in time, he rang his mother to make sure she knew the venue of the concert; she went there, it appeared, quite often. The hall was shabby, an ex-cinema, but magnificent for chamber music, and she was looking forward to the evening. She sounded cheerful and confident, unperturbed by the imminent flight to America, more concerned, he guessed, that he looked smart than that he played well.

'We'll see you in the interval or afterwards, I expect.'

He wished time would melt as he kicked around the house from room to room, finding nothing to occupy him.

At five minutes to three when he parked his car outside the Fine Arts Centre in Newark he found Cyril Barton stamping about, slapping his overcoat. The sun had gone; an east wind harried every corner. Cyril tapped his window, slipped in alongside.

'I hope it's warm in there,' David began.

'That's one thing about this place. They do know what they're about.'

'What was it? A cinema?'

'Combined cinema–theatre. The stage is still there, though we shan't use it. But it's been an arts centre for ten years, more, now. It's a nice size, good high ceiling and no draughty windows. It's big enough for a small orchestral concert. Haven't you ever played there with the Symphonia?'

Payne and Wilkinson had arrived in the same car and seemed in no hurry to disembark. A hatless man, with beard and glasses, in a navy anorak, waved hard from the small door above six brick steps and an iron rail.

'Oh, Harry's here,' Barton said. 'We can get the kit out.'

Inside in a yellow corridor, streakily discoloured, dampish, they were led into a room with four canvas chairs, two deal trestle tables and a hat rack. Harry led them, then Wilkinson, David, Barton, Payne last.

'By God, it's cold,' Wilkinson said.

'Not in here.' Harry filled a pipe, with fingers too large for the task, but made no attempt to light it, after he had shaken hands with David. 'We've got a full house for you tonight.'

'Why's that?' Wilkinson again.

'The programme for one thing. And a bit of cooperation between two music societies. For once.'

The hall was large, barn-bare, its walls a faded orange decorated with swirls and knobs of lifted plaster. The stage stood curtainless and in front of it a raised platform, four rostra with chairs and a shaded lamp, which Harry immediately tested out.

'No trouble seeing with that,' he said, pulling at the switch. He and Payne wandered towards the auditorium, which sloped upwards. The cinema seats had been removed, replaced by modern metallic chairs. The two men perched with their backs to the others, heads down in earnest consultation.

'Good place to play in,' Barton told David.

'It's warm.'

'It's bloody ugly, but the sound's superb – really bounces off the walls.'

'Why's that?'

'Pure chance. It always seemed too loud and too blurred for me in the old picture palaces. Let's go and hang our glad rags up. Fred'll be gassing to Harry for twenty minutes.'

'Who's Harry?' David asked once they were outside in the corridors.

'Harry Owen. A solicitor. President of this place. Runs culture, but he keeps the books and turns the heating on. I don't know whether he likes music or just dragooning his fellow citizens. Wouldn't be the only one.' He let David into the changing room, closed the door behind him. 'I've got something to tell you. There's an agent coming to listen. Fred said not to say anything to you.'

'Why not?'

'Not fair on you. We argued. He said you'd give your best whether you knew or not, but it might knock you off your cool, that it was our concern, not yours.'

'I don't know that I like that.'

'Don't say anything. You've not heard a word.' Barton laughed, open and sunny, losing something of his diffidence, as he stroked his suit straight on its hanger. 'We're divided as it is. Wilko's got this wife, and I'm too comfortable. We shall play well, in spite.' He now picked up a top programme from a pile, perused it. 'At least they've spelt us properly.' He handed it over. 'There you are, in print.'

Looking round this stripped place, David wondered how Mary felt at 10.30 in the morning, in the bright American snow. A depression nagged, because he could do nothing for her, she for him. He wanted to risk a prayer, dared not for self-scorn.

'Well, let's get back,' Barton warned, 'before Fred flogs your cello.'

'How long shall we practise?'

'Dunno. That's one thing Fred won't make up his mind about. He's a marvellous leader, but he can't be sure whether we take the edge off things scratching away all afternoon. And you worry him.'

'Why?'

'Because you're new. If you were Rostropovich he'd be wondering. But it makes him play better. You wait till you hear him tonight. He's like an angel.'

'You terrify me,' David said, only half laughing.

'Wait till you catch Wilko doing his yoga.'

Wilkinson was fiddling hard, bow elbow energetic, whiskers bristling, but Payne turned from Harry Owen, they both stood watching the second violin, immediately the others entered.

'Right,' he said. 'Let's see what we can do.'

'I shall have to go,' Owen said.

'You just hold your horses. You've time to hear a bar or three.' He took out his violin and tuning fork, which he banged. 'You're spot on, Wilk.'

'I know where bloody A is.' Wilkinson rosined away at his bow.

'Make sure that your seat's rock solid,' Payne told David, standing over him. 'You can't play on a seesaw.' He circled the platform, blowing like a grampus, the violin he was carrying dwarfed. 'Can you see, Cy? Wilk's not hogged the light again?'

He took his chair, shifted it about as if to show David what was necessary. 'Right we'll tune. In order.' The three sat silenced until he had satisfied himself, then Wilkinson, Barton and finally David took their turn. 'Check your scores.' He turned his own pages, then eyed his troops, lifted fiddle to chin, bow arm up, and they had started.

'What's that like?' he shouted to Owen. They'd done half a dozen lines, stopped without reason.

'Beautiful, beautiful.'

'I hope you're right. Again.'

They worked through the Haydn, without breaks. David Blackwall, breath crushed inside his lungs, played uncomfortably, but not badly, and without show. He had practised carefully, and the superb instrument served him well. Payne asked for a repetition on one or two bars, expressed gratification, scratched his face, practised furiously a run he managed with easy limpidity and said, interrupting the others who were fluently fingering awkward passages, that they'd have the Beethoven.

'That's second,' he told David. 'Mozart after the interval.'

Owen noisily left his seat, came down, congratulating them.

'You've got the dressing-room key?' he asked.

'Cyril has.'

'Fear not.' Barton, socially. Wilkinson in some world of his own dashed away at Beethoven as if he grudged time off from the music. Owen banged the door; somewhere in the recesses of the building a telephone trilled. The four became one.

After the Beethoven, during which Payne stopped them several times with a show of ill-temper, as if Owen's departure had opened his lips, and they repeated the unsatisfactory sections, never more than a half-dozen bars, the order was given.

'Walk round and a pee.'

David three or four times played the solo opening of the last movement, Allegro molto quasi presto.

'Perfect,' Barton said. 'Couldn't do it better myself.'

'You have a walk round,' Payne commanded. David laid his cello down, replacing the bow in its case.

'How's it going?' he asked.

'Good enough. As long as you've a decent chair and your

instrument's not on the wobble. Harry knows that. You've plenty of light?'

'Yes.'

That Payne should bother himself about details of comfort rather than interpretation seemed improper, but he himself was in no mood to judge. He had lost fear, but with it his exhilaration, was locked inside himself in a mild insensitivity, as if he were beginning a cold.

'Walk to the back,' Payne ordered. They stood by the main doors, watching, hearing Wilkinson play, hunched over his fiddle, with powerful clarity, repeating passages already polished. David whispered a compliment and the leader nodded succinct agreement. 'He can't trust himself. But if somebody pinched the scores he'd be the one who could play it through. Whole programme. No bother. And there he sits, worrying himself to death.' They had walked into the foyer. 'He'll be here till the concert starts, you know. Lying on the floor doing his exercises. I want you to go out with Cy for a bit of tea. When we come here I go to visit an aunt. Cy'll look after you. He's the nearest to a human being we've got. I think he'll get married.' He showed yellow teeth.

Now they stood shoulder to shoulder in front of a crowded, neat notice board.

'Harry Owen's a marvel, really. Gets some first-rate concerts and audiences for them. Isn't easy, but he does it. And why? Why? I can't answer. He wants us to do a whole Shostakovich evening, three quartets, in June.

'Is he keen on Shostakovich?'

'I shouldn't think so. No more than the next man. But he thinks that's what they ought to have.'

'Ought?' David felt a stir of delight.

'Somebody's convinced him. Somehow. And not only shall we play them, but he'll have people here to listen.' Payne tapped at the mosaic floor with his toe. 'We shall be packed out tonight.'

'Does that suit you?'

'Oh, yes. I long enough ago gave up playing to myself.'

They returned after a tour of the building to Mozart. Payne was more critical than ever, but not sarcastic now, placid. 'Let's

88

do that again,' he invited them, sternly calm. Once or twice he played a phrase over, elegantly with emphasis, muttering, 'Something like that.' At the end of the rehearsal David now understood with certainty who led the group.

'Twenty past five,' Payne said. 'You're not going out, Walter?'

'No. I've brought a flask.'

'Give him the dressing-room key, Cy. And don't go wandering off, for God's sake. We'll meet at just after seven. Five past at the latest. On time. I don't want heart failure.' They cased instruments, stacked them on a table. Payne dragged on an overcoat and a flat cap David had not seen before, and sloped off, a pale man, frozen, looking older than his years. Barton explained to Wilkinson where he and David were going, and how long they would be out.

'Do you want to come?' he asked.

'No. I've got to get myself ready.'

As the two left they heard Wilkinson fasten lock and bolt behind them. Barton grinned.

'He'll do his exercises now, lying on the floor. It's funny; he's very good at it, twists himself into knots. He goes through a routine every day, morning and night, but on concert days it's an orgy.'

They walked into the main road, peered into antique shops most of which displayed notices of their concert, and watched people pass on a cold evening. In a café Barton ordered two pots of tea, honey and toast. 'Make it thick slices,' he said at the counter. 'Hunks.'

The cook disappeared round the back to comply.

'You're lucky,' he told them, reappearing, 'I thought we'd only got this thin-sliced muck.'

'You're a friend,' Barton said.

'To everybody except myself,' the man replied, dabbing sloppy margarine on to the sides of their plates.

The place was not crowded, but overpoweringly hot so that the windows were steamy, ran with moisture. The two men ate silently, before deciding against cream buns.

'I don't like to play on an empty stomach,' Barton said, pouring himself a fourth large cup from David's pot. 'On the other hand . . .' He seemed to be guying himself, and his lips shone unnaturally red, greasy from the toast. David thought his companion was encouraging confession, but had no idea how to satisfy him. He mentioned Mary's *Semele*, but neither man raised much enthusiasm. He dredged up a reminiscence about the difficulties of a series of lunchtime recitals he had arranged as a student in Cambridge. Barton countered with an orchestral concert he had played under Britten, but now both were immersed in themselves, vaguely waving from parallel lines.

'Quarter past six,' Barton said. A youth plonked down his plate on the next table, and without loosening his scarf wolfed into his sausage, beans and chips. 'It'll give us time to cool off and warm up again. Wilko will have done. I don't like to hurry.' They watched the youth's demolition act.

Outside the cold attacked them, suddenly ferocious. Barton found a confectionery shop still open, went in for cough sweets, left David in the bitterness of the east wind.

For some reason Barton circled the hall so that they entered by the main door which was open. One or two people, presumably officials, darted about in the foyer. 'Just under an hour,' Barton grunted, consulting his watch. 'By God, it was cold out there.' They heard a clashing of cups and saucers; Barton held out his hands in front of a radiator before pushing into the hall, which was thinly lighted. A young woman carrying a pile of programmes up the central aisle looked them over without much interest. Barton prowled over their rostra, tested his chair, picking it up, then sitting on it and inviting his companion with a left-handed flourish to do likewise. There they sat, uncomfortably, men with nothing to do.

'Will you know anybody here?' Cy asked.

'My parents are coming.' David explained about the jaunt to America and Barton smiled, pleased to hear this, human again.

'Tell you what,' he confided, 'I wouldn't mind being able to nip off to the States for a week. If I could afford it.'

Payne and Owen came down the aisle together, Harry talking still, not yet out of his anorak. They took up a position halfway down to halt, to stop talking before making sedately for the front.

'Ready, then?' Payne asked.

90

'Don't make so many mistakes this way.' Barton mimed performance.

'Walter all set?'

'Haven't been round yet. Don't want to interrupt.'

The young woman reappeared calling for Owen, who stormed off.

'Is your stand firm?' Payne asked David. 'And tight? You get it just right in the afternoon and some caretaker comes in swopping 'em or unscrewing the things. These are good, aren't they?' He approached Barton, grasped and shook the upright.

'Compared with some we've seen.'

'I'm surprised you don't bring your own,' David said.

'We do. Cy's back seat. But these are good. Let's go and put Walt out of his misery.'

Wilkinson was sitting easily, plastic cup of milkless tea in hand, feet up on one of the deal tables. He raised his drink.

'All present and correct.' He shouted confidently, out of character.

They hung up their overcoats.

'We'll spruce up, then get changed and have a tune,' Payne ordered. 'Washrooms, mirrors and loos through there.' He disappeared in that direction.

'He puts water on his hair,' Wilkinson informed David, who sat miserably by a table, one hand on his cello case, searching for confidence.

They washed, changed, combed hair a second, a third time, hindering one another, apologizing, grinning weakly. At quarter past, Payne said they'd tune, slapped his fork on the table. This over, they immediately began to play, famished for their instruments. Wilkinson raced with schoolboy zest into the Allegro of Fiocco; Barton improvised broad chords; Payne with earpiercing tone mastered the preludio of the E major Partita while David turned to the comfortable difficulty of his Bach in C major. For a few minutes they lost each other in brilliant discord, forgetful of everything except the relearning of trust in instrument and fingers, running counter to each other as they prepared by the violence of individualism for the supreme combined rationality they were to demonstrate within a few minutes. David felt better; he knew his capability.

91

The torrent had eased when Harry Owen pushed in, penguin-stout.

'We shall be a bit late starting,' he said, squinting down to silken lapels. 'They're coming in by the thousand.'

'What time is it?' Wilkinson, not lowering his fiddle.

'Seven twenty-seven.' One glance at his wristwatch; absolute certainty of statement. 'He's here,' in a low voice to Payne, who paid no attention ostentatiously. That would be the agent.

'How long, then?' Payne asked.

'Five minutes, perhaps. We're still selling tickets. Fiddled another row of chairs in, and God bless the fire precautions. Can't keep 'em out. Don't know why. They must have heard of your new cellist.' He pulled a face at David. 'And they say there's no audience for chamber music. I'll be back to fetch you.'

'Keep your eyes on me when we're making our bow. No need to do it like drill, though. And don't forget, somebody, to look at the clients in the side blocks and the gallery. They've paid. Carry your cello in with you if they call us back. It looks better.'

At 7.36 Owen summoned them. They stood, shook their trousers straight, breathed deeply.

'Forward, the Light Brigade.' Barton.

They walked in line down the corridor behind Owen, who opened the door, closed it after them. The crowded hall smelled of the audience, crackled with their talk; applause jumped, inordinately amplified. Barton signalled his partner back and the quartet bowed, two either side of the platform, before they took to their chairs. David, glad to be seated, bending with bow and cello in one hand, copy in the other had been awkward, arranged his instrument, opened his music, tried his first turn-over. Now he felt neither fear nor pleasure, a mere indifference to himself, a wish to make a start, complete the job. He tuned, as if it had been at home. Payne seemed in no hurry. Cyril Barton leaned towards David, face serious, man on the threshold of communion with the great.

'There's always some woman wearing a fancy hat,' he said. David nodded, but could not crack his face into a smile.

The audience grew still, in seconds, as if to order. Payne

92

looked round his men, eyebrows raised in question, then lifted his violin. Easily, broadly they embraced Haydn.

David, in relief, unaware of his audience, found he could concentrate, that his instrument spoke back to him, allowed him to take his rightful place amongst the others, without showing off. He knew his role, and keeping to it excelled himself. Payne set precisely the pace they had practised; the marks on Blackwall's copy could be seen, were obeyed. Sometimes he lacked breath, but once they were beyond the first movement, the constriction vanished and he was the player he had prepared himself to be. He paid no attention to the actions of his colleagues, their becks, posturings, head jerks, Cyril's sniffs, only to the sounds they made, his cues, their magnificent reassurance.

When they had finished Haydn, he felt sorry, slightly abashed by the strength of the applause, modestly waiting to repay the noisy, expressed gratitude by a repeat which would set right the few flaws. As the four bowed, clapping gained in ferocity.

'That'll do. On your way, brother.' Barton again, guide and counsellor.

David led them smartly out.

'Whoa,' Payne said in the corridor. 'They want to see us again. We won't cross the platform this time. Just from this side.' Back they trotted to renewed delight.

In the dressing room, Payne gave them two minutes to themselves, he said, and publicly congratulated his cellist.

'That's the way to do it,' he called, Punch-happy. He mopped his brow. 'Never does to drink at this game. Sweat too much. If your mouth's dry, swill it out and spit it out.' When it was time to return, he straightened himself, said unemphatically, 'They've had time to wriggle,' played the first four bars of the Beethoven, picked up his copy with 'Let's get it over and done with,' led them forward.

This time David could make out individuals in the audience, though he recognized nobody he knew, not his parents, not Barton's lady with hat. The settling process on the platform was over more quickly, but Payne, violin held balanced and straight up on his knee, sat back, thumb to lips as if waiting for some

93

signal. Finally, he leaned wickedly to Wilkinson, muttered what looked like a sardonic aside, winning a gawp, and then upped his fiddle and Beethoven had begun.

Again David did not find his ease until the opening Allegro neared its end. To his great joy he began the last movement at Payne's friendly nod with incisive verve, with a precision in confident piano that lifted his colleagues. No doubt, there; only certainty certainly expressed. The audience leaped into enthusiasm, recalling the quartet four times.

Payne and Owen congratulated them.

'Put your instrument away,' the leader warned David. 'It'll be Piccadilly Circus in here in a minute.'

'They seemed to like that,' David suggested to Barton as they locked their cases.

'Early Beethoven's perfect for these. A great composer before he's too complicated. But, I'll say this, we made a good job of it.'

Raps at the door announced friends and admirers, crowding into the corner where Frederick Payne held court in his shirt-sleeves. He wore, David noticed, elastic armbands and, like Wilkinson, highly polished dancing shoes. A young couple, man and wife in anoraks, hand in hand, engaged Blackwall in talk about gut strings and pitch in Beethoven's time; he felt trapped, unwilling to argue, was glad when his parents rescued him.

'Marvellous,' Joan told him. 'It really is.'

Horace stood back, smiling, pink-cheeked, the picture of healthy maturity. He still wore his raincoat.

'That Haydn's superb,' she said.

'Did you know it?'

'We have a record.'

Barton edged across, was introduced.

'It's exciting in here,' Joan said. Certainly chatter hurtled, broken by laughs, once by a spasm of coughing. 'Wouldn't you prefer quiet?'

'I'm not sociable,' Cy answered, 'but I like to see all this.' He looked at the tall figure of Wilkinson draped back over a table, besieged by three matrons. 'We shall come to the Mozart all the fresher.' He asked about their trip to America, coaxed a sentence or two out of Horace to which he solemnly listened and slid away.

'He seems nice.' Joan.

'Very. He looks after me.'

'Not the leader?' His father, voice hoarse, forced up.

'Fred's a remarkable man, and he's wasted up here and he knows it. He talks with his fiddle. You can't help being impressed.'

'Hero worship,' Horace said, out of the blue, as if surprising himself.

'I wonder how Mary's feeling?' Joan asked.

'It'll be the middle of the afternoon, now. I hope she's fit.'

'She's very strong, physically.' Joan scraped her bottom lip with her front teeth. Anna Talbot came across, dressed in a short fur coat and wide, electric-green trousers. She wore a hat, a green half-walnutshell shape with red jewels and a dyed feather. Cyril's lady? David began to introduce them.

'I know your parents,' Anna smiled powerfully. 'James and your mother are practising together. St Anthony Variations for good causes.' She congratulated David, asked after Mary, ribbed Horace about gentlemen of leisure. 'I got your son into this outfit.'

'Have it mentioned on the programme next time.' David's father, expansive.

They talked easily together, enjoying themselves, until Owen clapped his hands, announcing that the second half wasn't too far away and that he'd like them to clear the room to give the players a couple of minutes. People, surprisingly to David, obeyed. Joan said she would give him a ring as soon as they returned from America, kissed him, and led Horace out. The father gave a stiff nod of approval. Anna, who had been brilliantly there one minute, had vanished. James her husband raised a hand to David as he left the room.

Owen removed the last few, laying a large right hand across shoulderblades to speed the departure.

'Five minutes,' he fog-horned to the quartet. 'I'll be back to fetch you. I'll drop the catch.'

The ugly room hung heavy with quiet, with perfume, with

disappearance. Payne stood near the middle, still in his shirt-sleeves, his thin hair rumpled.

'Can we do the Shostakovich tomorrow morning?' he asked.

'Bloody hell,' Wilkinson.

'Can you, though?'

'Suppose so.'

'David?'

'Yes.'

'Anstey seems to think we might do. He's offered us three dates this year, cancellations. Must have old Shosto for the second half. All mid-week. Tell you tomorrow.' He tucked his chin in apologetically towards David. 'He's an agent, who came up to listen to us.'

The Mozart went without hitch, was well received, but by this time David Blackwall was blind to the outside world, beaten by concentration, fatigue, his forced attention to colleagues, score and instrument; as he thought about it later, even Mozart, the essence of the composer, had vanished, in that the player no longer created, merely repeated what he had practised. Perhaps he did that well, but he felt nothing of the joy of cooperation with a musical genius; he was an efficient tape, going over its one track. Payne and his mother told him later how beautifully he had played, and this led him to wonder whether his height of performance could only be reached by a series of creative rehearsals and a lack of energy sufficient to hamper even minor experiments. This seemed unsatisfactory, but one, he, was as one was.

Again the congratulatory session took up half an hour. He shook hands, signed three autograph books, heard breathlessly, succinctly from Wilkinson that they hadn't played so well for the past two years, was questioned gently by Barton, touched on the shoulder by Payne, kissed by Anna, who said that now this part of the Blackwall family had covered itself in glory, it was to be hoped that the other wouldn't come short. He glanced at his watch; Mary would be on stage within three hours. He felt sentimentally towards her, a weakness that did not lack power, but could do nothing for her, not even detain his thoughts on her ordeal. Tiredness pained his shoulder-blades, even as he blamed himself.

He changed, checked on the time of the morning rehearsal, and went out into a yard that was dark, lit in one corner by a high, oddly placed lamp, and by the yellow of the distant streets. The east wind ripped clouds into rags; people had not lingered and the park lay almost empty; the top of his car showed a thin grey rug of snow, ugly and unsymmetrical.

His engine started reluctantly, on the fifth try. A man quite different from the cello player of an hour before drove home.

9

Mary telephoned on Sunday night.

She sounded elated, the first evening's performance had been superb. Though she in no way praised herself, but chattered with feverish speed about the quality of the orchestral playing, the brilliance of the scenery, the almost frightening enthusiasm of the audience, Red Gage's unalloyed pleasure, the speech made to Fenster by a most influential critic, the delight of the university bigwigs, it was clear to David that she had done herself proud.

'How did you sing?' he asked.

'Quite nicely.'

'Were you satisfied with it?'

'I'm not grumbling.'

Redvers Gage, the producer, had been walking on air; there had been nothing to touch this; the money had been spent to marvellous advantage; it was possible that they might be taken up commercially, but there was another two months to do on circuit. They were here for an extra week, she had explained in a letter, and then they were off to Boston, to Cambridge for their next run.

'Is that far?'

'I've no idea. A hundred, two hundred miles, is it?'

He asked if she had learned anything about Elizabeth Falconer's tour. She had not. She had heard nothing from anybody. She had been busy twenty-four hours a day. Excitement and defiance crackled in her voice across the transatlantic telephone wires.

'And are you any better?' he asked.

'I'm still a bit off.'

'What's that mean?' It seemed a shame to blot her copybook happiness.

'I just feel run down, especially in the mornings. No appetite. Backache. By the evening I'm normal again. I don't know. Strange food or hard work or a combination.'

'It doesn't stop you singing?'

'Not so far, touch wood.'

Comforted, he took instant pleasure in her enthusiasm, encouraging her to expand. It was the first time since she had left that he had heard her voice, which sounded as clear as if she had rung from the next room. After they had finished, he recollected that they had mentioned neither his parents' visit to the States nor his joining the Trent Quartet. It did not matter. He had listened to her in her delight, and with his last words he had promised to toast her health. Fetching out the gin and tonic, icing it, he had strutted about the room, twice the man he had been; he lifted her photographs from the mantelpiece and his drink to them. He was not himself, but grew glad about it.

When he had finished the gin, he knew he had to settle to dull piles of exercise books which would occupy him till midnight or beyond, but the chore no longer daunted. By 10.30 the glow would have disappeared, but now, beside himself, he kissed the cold glass of the photograph of newly-weds in the porch of St Saviour's. *Prosit.*

During the week he received two long, out-of-date letters from her. The Shostakovich, his classes occupied him to the full; sometimes he was tired, he could barely drag himself from one lesson to the next, but his energy revived, and he took pride in these little resurrections, trusting their recurrence, certain of his own vitality.

On the Friday morning as he was teaching the lower history sixth, the real historians, the medievalists, the headmaster knocked at his classroom door, sidled in, waited for the group to scramble to their feet.

'I'm sorry to interrupt,' Reeve began, signalling the class to be seated, 'but could I have a word with you?' He waited, to David's puzzlement. 'Outside?'

Reeve rarely disturbed people at their teaching; even then he sent for them. He looked up and down the corridor suspiciously and spoke in a whisper.

'Have you noticed Dick Wilson?'

'No. What about him?'

'He hasn't seemed, well, urrm, strange?'

'No. Not really.'

'I see.' Reeve marched three or four long steps away, rubbing his mouth with the flat of his hand, holding back eruption of speech. There he stood, six yards away, with his back to his subordinate, the grey hair haloed.

'Yes. Yes.' He loosed the two words lengthily, breathily upwards, towards the top of the high window lighting the end of the corridor. He did not turn, but thrust his clenched hands into his jacket pockets.

David was nonplussed, mildly amused at the headmaster's antics. Presumably he was about to say something he did not consider concerned his function in the school, and feared the consequences. The man of timetables, requisitions, factual notes, marks, lists, statistics was about to venture beyond his safe territory. The Richard Wilson he had mentioned was David's immediate superior, the head of history, a bright, nervous, aggressive, posh character, looking nothing like his thirty-eight years.

'He's not made,' Reeve had turned about, locked his fingers behind slim buttocks, bounced on his toes, 'untoward demands on you? Has not acted unreasonably?'

'No.'

'I see. You don't mind my asking this?'

'Not at all.'

'Good, good. I thought I'd inquire.'

'Is there anything wrong?' David pressed him. 'He wasn't in assembly this morning.'

'No, he wasn't.' Reeve made a convulsive movement as if to flex every muscle in his body, or dislocate each joint. 'His father is dying. Last night he went off to see him.'

99

'I thought his father was still at work?' A master at Manchester Grammar School.

'He was until recently. It is all very sudden.'

'How long has Dick known?'

'I've no idea.' Reeve looked affronted. 'Anyhow, he's gone. I'd be grateful if you didn't mention this conversation. Thank you very much.'

And he stepped away almost at a run.

David returned to the economic consequences of the Black Death puzzled. He had no idea how close Wilson's relationship stood with his father, and had heard nothing of any illness. Wilson certainly let his department know, in his unhurried far-back voice, just what it was he wanted from them, and made it clear when they did not come up to scratch. He was never impolite, could argue a case with plausibility and weight, but did not suffer the unreasonable or the fool gladly. At present he had annoyed a young colleague who had taught a fourth form carelessly.

'It's at this stage we catch our sixth form historians,' he had said. 'I don't like to see you queering our pitch. We have enough competition from other departments for bright individuals, without your help. As well you know.'

Seddon, the rebuked master, had reported this to David and one other friend in a corner of the common room.

'What did you say?'

'Oh, I made it clear that to start specializing at that age was lunacy.'

'And?'

'While he was running the department he would remain the judge of that.'

Seddon was, David thought, idle if clever, and had not done his job properly. Next year, and the man could complain or rant as he liked, he would not be allocated 3A or 4A.

Yet Dick Wilson making, as Reeve hinted, untoward demands had seemed out of character. The man said what he wanted, not cheerfully but plainly; he knew, moreover, what it was he required, and in that his strength resided. 'Untoward' did not enter into it.

On the other hand, the headmaster was quite devoid of

imagination, so that his breaking of routine set in itself a poser. Why should he consider it important enough to cross the courtyard, when a note asking for his junior's presence would have been as effective? If it was that Reeve merely wanted to make a foray into the sixth form block to check on smoking or alcohol or damage, then why had he asked this baffling question? David grimaced. It was as if the old man had barged into his classroom to ask if David believed that the world was flat or about to end inside the next quarter of an hour. Perhaps Reeve was socially so uncertain that he had drummed up these unlikely questions about Wilson merely to cover some other pretext for the interruption, a check on David himself, on the presence of some as yet unnamed delinquent in the class or the state of the cupboards or shelves. That seemed improbable, for however gauchely the head acted in his dealings with pupils and colleagues, he had a sharp eye for his own peace of mind and would by no means put himself at a disadvantage.

Perhaps Reeve himself was going round the twist.

On Monday morning, after disappointing silence from his parents the previous evening, he sought out Wilson during break.

'All well?' David began.

'Yes. Why do you ask?'

'You were away Friday. I thought you might be ill.' Duplicity in innocence.

'No, I went to visit my father. He's in hospital.'

'I'm sorry. Is it serious?'

'I shouldn't think so. He's the worrying type. And a bad patient. But he'll recover. And it gives my mother a rest.'

Wilson straightened his pile of books, picked them up, smiled as if the exchange had eased him and made off for his next class, terminal illness unmentioned. David, not knowing where he stood, sat down, quashed.

On the same evening his mother telephoned.

She spoke with enthusiasm of Mary's performance and of the production, which had been brilliantly successful because it seemed designed to demonstrate the powerful beauty of Handel's music. She and Horace had been twice, and only on the second occasion had she understood how much of the success was due to the stage direction of Redvers Gage. At the first performance singers appeared merely to deliver their recitatives and arias, which they did with touching skill, though nobody matched Mary's consummate, delicate art, and it was not until Joan had watched it again, had known what to expect, that she realized how great a part movement, lighting, unobtrusive grouping or shifting, use of dress, gesture, even facial expression had played in this effect. Simplicity had been achieved by considerable art and, she guessed, unremitting discipline and practice.

'And Mary?'

'She was superb. They all think so. The newspaper critics have been very flattering. I'm not telling you that I think it's set the whole of America on fire; it's a campus event, but it's attracting full houses and quite a bit of outside publicity. She's been on one breakfast show already.'

'Will it lead anywhere?'

'Commercially? Mary didn't think so, though Red Gage is going to be a somebody. They still haven't quite got the itinerary settled, and it is possible that the schedule will be extended for another period. But that will be that, it seems. I mean, the fund is still there, and there'll be something next year, and they all said they must have Mary back, but you know what some of these theatrical people are like.'

Joan had been surprised by the strength of the performance, and suggested that if anybody knew his way about the operatic circuit, he could make something of this production and certainly of Mary's talent.

'But it won't happen?'

'Mary thinks not. It's only in films that the great impresario's car breaks down outside the barn where the heroine . . .' Joan broke off to laugh. 'They're all working five, ten years ahead.'

'And not looking for replacements?'

'Yes. But from their own contacts. This is a new, fringe thing. If it's as good for the next two years, somebody'll take notice.'

'And Liz Falconer's appearance?'

'Not mentioned.'

Mary had appeared well, as far as she could make out, but

tired, perhaps. Joan fumbled round with her words, unforth-coming, evasive.

'Are you all right?' he asked.

'Yes. We only arrived back about four. We spent the night at the airport hotel and I didn't sleep well. Are you busy? Can you come round? Your father's out. He's had to see Timothy Langham about something.'

He agreed, though it meant another late night's marking. He listened now to his mother's account of Mary's voice, which had enriched itself beyond all telling. Joan seemed glad to rhap-sodize. David promised to appear at eight o'clock.

His father answered the door.

'I thought you were out.'

'You know what thought did. And anybody would think from your face that you're not pleased to see me back.' Horace led the way, grimly smiling at his wordplay.

Joan sat at her writing desk, dressed as if to continue the expensive formality of the American outings. She closed a folder, ordered her husband to pour David a cup of freshly made coffee, began to answer questions with voluble zest. Again, Mary had been marvellous, the production outstanding; everyone in university circles talked of nothing else.

'It's not the sort of thing you'd expect for a spectacular success. They all said it was a dressed-up secular oratorio where people sang pretty arias like 'O Sleep, why dost thou leave me?' or 'Where'er you walk', but it's nothing of the kind. It's drama-tic.' Joan attempted explanations three or four times, but broke off without convincing herself. It had been magnificently sung and the direction had enhanced this musical excellence, but then she found it entrancing, magic intervened, the marmoreal pulsated as living, godlike flesh. Joan's speed but hesitancy of delivery went some way to excuse the extravagance of her metaphors; she had seen and heard what she had not expected. Moreover, the miracle had been repeated.

David listened to his mother with interest; he had never regarded her as volatile; her sensibility pursued, verbally at least, its middle way. Now she launched herself into this new style of communication, not without difficulty, and the change intrigued her son, who plied her hard with questions.

103

The conductor was good, a perfect ear, Mary claimed, but the presiding genius was this Redvers, Red Gage, the marvel, the leaper over high hedges. He was astounding, clever, he'd been a don at Harvard, but the life there was too flat and he'd taken to the theatre. First he'd written a play, *Jehovah's Witness*, which had had considerable commercial success, still had, then he'd directed Tennessee Williams, Albee, Stoppard, Ibsen, Büchner, Frisch and had laid claim to large mastership with his Brecht. David vaguely remembered encomia in the Sunday columns about this American *Threepenny Opera* which had convinced critics they'd neither seen nor heard the piece before. He'd set up *Mother Courage* on the West Coast, attracting the film and television moguls, was to direct *Tosca* and *Lulu* in two years' time at the Metropolitan, and had taken these three weeks off on *Semele* as a working holiday. 'I guess,' he'd told Joan, in his quiet voice, which dodged behind you so that you looked over your shoulder to see who else was speaking to you as you were held by the great, watery eyes, the delicate beaky nose, the nicotine-stained lips, 'I always wanted to impress academics. I couldn't do it with scholarship. Or not quickly enough. I'm a restless spirit. So I do it this way. God help me and the devil take them.'

'How old's this paragon?' David asked.

'Thirties.'

'And he's impressive.'

'He's a genius.' No mistake. Joan described the dark velvet jacket, the subfusc trousers, boots, the sober cravat, the pale, dry skin, his thinning black curls brushed and flattened but not quite covering a colourless pate, the high cold forehead over the violet eyes, the mouth adrift with new truths.

'What's Mary say about him?'

'Didn't take to him at first. He smokes. But he was always kind to her, she thought, but quiet, not assertive enough. He was making his mind up, she thinks, deciding how her qualities could be employed, or changed. But once he'd decided and rehearsals started, he assaulted the cast. He's frightening. His standards are sky-high. He'd go raving wild at the conductor, and he's no nonentity, over a few bars of introduction.'

'Didn't this put them at loggerheads?'

'Fenster crumbled', she said. 'He'd met his match. Red can be satanic. And yet he speaks so quietly. He's striking to look at, well, at second glance, but he doesn't rail. But if once you get across some principle, he's a tiger. His face sets.'

Joan attempted to explain, not successfully, why the opera gripped with dramatic power. It was as if the essence of Handel's music had been transfused into formalized action so that the one sharpened, deepened the other. The listener was embroiled, musically. The original code had been broken, or employed contemporaneously for the first time, shatteringly. Yes, they decorated repeats. No, they did not use authentic instruments or pitch, but Fenster obviously had studied eighteenth-century techniques.

While his wife enthused, Horace sat with pinched lips, intervening once in the half-hour to ask for more coffee. He did not support her account, and his prim mouth suggested reservations.

'And Mary herself?' David asked. 'How did she seem?' His mother had already told him that the girl said she was well.

'Ah, that's it,' Horace snapped.

David jerked his head; the unexpected remark struck abruptly for all its dryness. His father's lips were wet, red, his mouth slightly open under the bristle of moustache. Silence met, spoilt the tick of the coffee-heater, the creak of woodwork, a sniffle of draught; three human beings sat motionless, the mother with chin to chest.

'What do you mean?' David forced himself to clothe anxiety with the humdrum.

They did not answer, but Horace twisted in his chair.

'Are you saying, then, that she isn't very well?'

Again, nothing. His father rapped the arm of his leather chair with a tattoo from the middle finger.

Joan spoke first, having blown breath out.

'We've talked about this,' she said, and stopped. Her eyes were wide; she was a different woman from the one who had struggled to express Handel's genius. Before, conviction underlay her hesitation; like a mystic she had lacked exactitude of words, not experience. Now she was about to fumble again, but without trust in herself. 'I don't know whether we ought to

105

mention it. It may be us.' She looked across at Horace, who avoided the glance.

David waited, not shortly.

'She didn't seem pleased to see us,' Joan said at length.

All looked glum.

'We saw her on the Tuesday night after the performance. She was tired, then. We didn't stay too long, but we took her to lunch on Wednesday, and we spent three hours with her. On Thursday, the fifth performance was that night, our second, she came to the Feinsteins' for a meal, stayed a part of the afternoon. We didn't see her that night, but called in on her just before we left on Friday.' Joan stopped again.

'And?'

'I've talked to your father about this. We both had come to the conclusion that she wasn't pleased to see us.' Again the agony of search. 'I think I know Mary pretty well now. We used to talk a lot when she came up here to practise. She's had this great success. And it's in a strange place, with different habits and faces . . . Everybody's making a tremendous fuss of her, and rightly. She's being invited out here and there and everywhere. But she's a modest sort of girl. It won't turn her head.'

'Did she seem ill?' David had had enough of his mother's indirection.

'No. Not at all. She looked well. But we asked her about this. She felt a bit off in the morning, that's all. It was as if she resented our coming.'

'Wouldn't she talk to you?'

'Not easily. As if she'd forgotten all about you, and this house, and yours. I mean, I'm not saying she didn't ask any questions. She did. But she wasn't very interested in the answers. It didn't seem like her at all. I mean, she wasn't rude, or anything like that. If she'd had some terrible accident, or operation, or trauma, I could have understood it. She'd not lost trace of her life here, or us, or you, but it didn't concern her.'

'She'd be concentrated on the opera,' David objected.

'Well, yes. I can see that, but . . .'

'Nothing like that at all,' Horace interrupted.

'Of course she was interested in her work; we expected to find that.'

106

Horace drew in a lungful of breath, noisily, as a prologue, an announcement that he was about to speak.

'She did not want us there. That's the long and short of it. It took her all her time to talk to us.'

'She wasn't impolite,' Joan interrupted.

'She didn't show us the door, certainly. But her mind wasn't on us. I remember my father telling us once,' Horace's voice warmed, 'how he'd met some man, on a cruise, I think, he was a literary fellow, well known, a knight, a poet and magazine editor, something of the sort. They'd been very friendly, and this man pressed my dad to call in any time when he was in London. Well, he did. He phoned, was invited, but it didn't take him five minutes to see he wasn't wanted. He said the man wasn't busy, but he could hardly bring himself to remember the holiday. My dad had the photographs he'd taken, but he never got round to showing them. He upped and out. This man wasn't rude, but his interest in the holidays and the Blackwalls was minimal. It was embarrassing. My dad, well, you remember your granddad, wasn't exactly gushing, but he must have liked this chap or been impressed to have bothered to go round, and then, pooh, nothing. I've never forgotten him telling us this. It didn't exactly upset him, and he knew better than most that time's valuable, that if you're preoccupied or hard at work you don't want idiots in with their holiday snaps. This was different. And it embarrassed Dad, as Mary embarrassed us.'

Joan nodded. The anecdote had evidently already been tried out on her.

'We're not psychic, you know.' His mother trundled her hands apologetically in the air. 'Or at least your father's not.'

'Was she worrying about something?'

'She didn't say so. It was hard to pin down. We thought we might be at fault, that we'd got off on the wrong foot, and not recovered.'

'I don't understand you.'

'I'm not surprised. The nearest I can describe it, David, is this. It was as though we'd, we'd met her once in England, casually, after a performance, casually, I mean that, and then tried to presume on the acquaintance. She was preoccupied, and tired, I dare say, but she hardly asked us a thing, and sometimes didn't listen. It was hard work, I can tell you.'

'She gave me a kiss the first time we met,' Horace said, 'but you know how she used to pull my leg a bit. There was none of that. She didn't seem to want to talk about you, or music, or anything else. I couldn't understand it.' His father coughed his quandary away. 'Give him another cup, Joan.'

'I don't know what to make of it.' David, truculent, about to blame.

'We thought hard and long about this, David. We didn't know whether we ought to say anything. I wondered if it was me, until your dad asked, "What's gone wrong with Mary?" It may be nothing. The opera or a quarrel, a bad period. We saw it would worry you if we did come running back with tales. We didn't know what to do for the best.'

His mother's face wrinkled with pain, doubt.

'Has she been writing regularly?' Joan began again, tentatively.

'I had two long letters about auditions and first rehearsals on the Monday you left. They'd been written, oh, a week and a half before. And on the Sunday, the night after the first performance, she telephoned.'

'How did she seem?'

'Much as I expected.'

'That's good, then.'

'She talked mostly about how the opera had gone, and she seemed pleased. I didn't notice anything out of the way. She said she hadn't felt very well, but she didn't make a song and dance about it. I thought, guessed, if you like, that she was excited, but that didn't surprise me.'

'Well, that's not so bad, then, is it?' his mother asked. 'Perhaps it's our fault. We went with the wrong idea. We'd forgotten she'd been away from home a month, and working herself to death.' Joan smiled broadly, sat comfortably.

'Is that right?' David wheeled on his father.

'Don't ask me. Probably.' Horace irascibly cleared his throat. 'She didn't seem the same girl who'd left us here a month ago.'

'Thanks, anyway.'

'I'm sorry,' Joan said. 'It may be nothing, and it's bound to worry you, isn't it?'

'I can't let my wife go away and not feel it,' he answered, awkwardly.

'No.'

They talked, Joan leading, for the next ten minutes about Handel and about the Trent Quartet's plans, before the son left to mark essays. All three were apprehensive, blaming each other.

10

David heard nothing from Mary.

The promised letter with details of the extra week at New York State and the proposed Harvard performances did not arrive. Each morning before seven David lifted a corner of the bedroom curtain to follow the postman's flashlight along the street, and though the bills, the advertisements, the holiday brochures, interesting declarations from friends clapped through the letterbox, each day began with a disappointment that six days quickly taught him to expect.

There must have been some hold-up. If Mary said she had written to him, she was telling the truth. He fetched out the letters he had received, three airmail forms, two more substantial accounts of the audition and initial rehearsals. Five letters in five weeks; he must have sent ten. One only to the senior Blackwalls.

He reread the letters, not carefully because he could without trouble reconstruct the contents, but with an anger of speed, anger at his own weakness in returning to these pieces of paper which had now become more important than at their first glad arrival. Mary's writing was what it had always been; she used the little silver Parker, with two hearts on the clip, and the strokes were upright, well formed, bold, readable. She missed him, these notes claimed, she wished he was there; her sharp eye in the two long missives watched the vagaries of conductor, of fellow singers, of Red Gage, of academics or students she ran across. For all the change and excitement, she had her head screwed on straight. She represented the English Midlands, the shrewd shopkeeper class, the professionally trained craftsman out there in the welter of pretension, and cleverness, and kindness, and oddity. At the end of each letter she said, plainly, that she loved him; the third letter began with a three-word paragraph, 'I love you.'

The letters were kept behind the wedding photograph on the mantelpiece, but as each sad clack of the letterbox added its tithe of disappointment, David put the five into the drawer of his desk, at the back, out of sight, but safe.

He could not convince himself now that the postal services were responsible; he knew there was serious reason why his wife was not writing to him. He mentioned his unease to no one, for no one asked any questions, and oddly enough his parents maintained silence. Rehearsals with the Trent Quartet occupied him; when he played with them, he forgot his distress, as he did sometimes in his lessons, but always at the back of his mind this malaise nagged, rankled. He did not sleep badly, but woke half a dozen times each night uncomfortably, and though tiredness usually ensured he could drop off again, occasionally he prowled the upper floor of his home, staring out at darkened houses, the outlines of apple trees, hearing the wind, the scutter of rain.

Perhaps he was less disturbed than he ought to have been. Unreasoning optimism prompted, lifting his spirits. He remembered Mary's straight back as she marched off towards her plane. He remembered their first meeting.

He had been introduced to her at a party, where they had easily fallen into facetious talk. Neither had realized that the other was a student at the Royal College; when they did they compared notes about teachers, teachers' stand-ins, prospects, concerts. This dark striking girl from Derby had won two prizes in her first year, was highly regarded, was preparing to sing a leading role in the college concert, had taken principal parts in oratorios round London already, had been approached by the BBC for some schools' programme on the recommendation of her teacher and had acquired an agent on la Falconer's say-so, and he was on the lookout for operatic openings for her. David had seen her name about the college but had not set eyes on her before. She had never heard of him.

They laughed, drinking punch.

On the next evening she was due to sing a *Messiah* at a church in north London, and he offered to drive her over in his car.

'I have to be there for three for a rehearsal.'

'I can listen.'

'Well, if you're sure.'

She made no great show of refusal or gratitude, but quietly outlined arrangements for meeting. In a diffident, strong way she was sure of herself. Later she laid a hand on his arm, to say, 'You're drinking too much, if you're driving tonight.'

'I live here.'

'With Sue and Francis?'

'Yes. I knew him at Cambridge.'

Mary nodded gravely, impressed. She hardly drank, he noticed, and was in no hurry to quit his company. He explained why a comparatively rich man like Frank was willing to make houseroom for him. Mary listened; the friend with whom she had come, an oboist David knew slightly, left them to their tête-à-tête.

He was in love almost at once. When at eleven she said she must go, must have her beauty sleep, he offered to escort her.

'It isn't worth it. Two stops on the Underground. Iris will be ready.'

'Does she live with you?'

'The whole house is full of students.' She beckoned her friend over. 'Be on time tomorrow, there's a good boy.' She had drawn him a map earlier. She leaned forward, kissed him on the cheek, lightly, incredibly briefly, and had walked off. For the first time he saw that straight, retreating back.

He remembered that evening three years ago both sharply and vaguely. The poignancy of both expectation and surprise rang strongly still, though he could not exactly recall how Mary had done her hair, or what she was wearing. He had sat in his car ten minutes early, and had rung her doorbell two minutes only before the appointed time. When Mary appeared, she

111

seemed quite sober, pale and apprehensive, eyelids vivid blue. She carried an enormous portmanteau.

'Can you get it in your car?' she asked, laughing. Reassured she said, 'This is just right for my evening wear, but it's too big for carting round the Underground on Saturday afternoon.'

'You've acquired a porter.'

'It's not heavy,' she answered. 'Just awkward.'

She spoke quietly, but easily, with this confidence, not trying to impress. Of course she was beautiful, with the dark, neat head, the blue eyes, the flawless skin, the figure, her aristocratic carriage. She was somebody. At the rehearsal she made the same mark, knowing seemingly exactly what she could demand from the conductor, prepared to make it clear, but never hectoring, reasonably, without nerves. Again the power and beauty of her voice underwrote her certainty, seemed becoming, proper.

The young couple were invited to tea at the home of a local organist. The best china had been set, three sorts of bread, cheeses, ham and tongue, home-baked buns, a dark fruit cake.

'I come from Yorkshire,' the organist's wife said. 'I like tea as a real meal. It was always so when I was a girl before the war.'

They were treated as an engaged or a married couple, intriguingly, and accordingly offered family confidences. Mrs Banks's daughter had wed the son of a famous pianist; she had met him at an out-of-the-way training college. Another daughter had been a prizewinner at the FRCO examinations.

'You should see her play Bach trios,' her father enthused. 'She sits there as if she's buffing her fingernails. Hardly moves, and she doesn't make fluffs. "Allegro di molto." She loves it.'

'So do you.'

Mary was ushered upstairs to dress.

Then she astounded. Her dress, in azure and navy blue, was heavily skirted to suit her height, the pride of neck and shoulders, the tilt of the head. When they went out she wore a white fur stole she had borrowed. David wanted to express his admiration, could only gape, then say foolishly, 'That will lay them in the aisles.'

'That's not quite the idea.'

Her speaking voice, unchanged, suited the finery, was its

equivalent, lifted out of his class. She seemed unaware of her effect, not only on David but on their hosts, on everybody else, but her every move, sentence, glance strengthened it. This shopkeeper's daughter, not yet twenty, could assume regality, deserve it, carry it as a right.

The performance was good, he remembered, with a small, well-drilled amateur choir and a semi-professional orchestra. The youngish tenor and contralto soloists were at the beginnings of what would be, David decided, undistinguished but successful careers; the bass, a man of fifty odd, had been one of the best-known oratorio singers in the country and showed why, with each note in a run accurately placed, each accent perfect, each phrase shaped inside a pattern, though the compelling power of his voice had now gone. None rivalled Mary; she abode with shepherds, sang with angels, rejoiced, apostrophized the beauty of the messengers' feet, knew that her redeemer lived with a perfection of formality that left no room for doubt. Her interpretation had drama without rhetoric. 'And though worms destroy this body, yet in my flesh shall I see God.' She tuned the notes with a purity of conviction that brooked no denial; hearing her, only the fool now said in his heart that there was no God. At twenty, a student, she outstripped them all.

David driving her home past midnight, they had returned to the organist's house for a further celebration, tried to come out with something of this. He was sober on three glasses of tonic water, but drunk with the evening's revelation. Mary listened; she leaned on him slightly, there was contact, and said after consideration that she wouldn't mind a few lessons from Terence Duckworth, the bass.

She was pleased, and yet steady, recognizing limitations. This frightened David, in that anyone of her age ought to be knocked off balance by the success, the congratulations, the glasses of wine. She was not, and yet her balance seemed not unnatural, in itself part of her gift.

During the next few months they met regularly, but not frequently. He dropped Anna Monckton-Mason, later Talbot, without qualm. Mary Stiles worked hard at her course, her engagements, and encouraged him to do likewise. When they ran across each other in the college, not often, they would talk for no more than a few moments; they exchanged notes, they attended concerts together, went out once for a meal, spent a spring Saturday in the Regent's Park zoo amongst the packs and crocodiles of schoolchildren from the provinces.

There, standing on a path, near the aviary but looking at nothing, they had stopped in a daffodil burst of sunshine. Mary wore a ridiculous waterproof hat, matching her coat, but on her the garments looked impeccable above washed-out jeans, scuffed shoes. As usual, she appeared both pleased and preoccupied, glad to be released but still running over some tricky song, or emotional scenario.

'I hate to tell you,' David began. He had positioned himself behind, at her shoulder, felt emboldened. She turned her head, laughing.

'Well?'

'I love you,' he said.

'Is that all?' Her voice was flat; the large eyes did not discourage.

'It's enough to begin with, isn't it?'

'That's all right, then.'

He took her hand, which was warm. They stood close; he kissed her mouth. She returned the kiss, but quickly drew away, squeezing his hand violently, wrenching almost.

'Steady,' he said, 'you'll have my fingers off.'

'I think I love you,' she answered.

Joy jumped in him, like the sunshine, the dart of wind that blew sweet wrappers in scraping, wild somersaults. They began to walk.

They spoke of marriage, as a fairy tale. Mary, having a third year to complete, said that it was useless to discuss the date yet, and convinced him that she meant it. When at Easter he was appointed to his teaching post, he suggested again that they marry during the summer, but again she refused.

'But we're going to get married, aren't we?'

'In time. Yes.' Her answer did not discourage him; such common sense seemed second nature to her, overrode her passion. She was, he discovered, a virgin, and again that was typical. She guarded her career, totting pros and cons

114

as her mother and father counted pound notes, the nuts and bolts, the buckets and lightbulbs in their hardware store in Derby.

Once, in her final year, she came in her one free weekend before Christmas to stay with his parents. She had been, at first, shaken and suspicious that his people were so well-to-do, but now made herself a great favourite. It was at this period she had begun to practise with Joan, tentatively at first, but once she realized how good a pianist Mrs Blackwall was she made enthusiastic use of her. She and Horace had started to establish the jokey, loving, cautious relationship; in a way, and David laughed making the comparison because one could hardly envisage such a different pair of human beings as his dry father and this beautiful tall young woman, they were alike, both warily perched behind the counter, one eye on the till, the other on the customer.

Mary, on this occasion, had appeared uncertain, almost unhappy. She had taken the first audition for the German opera tour at her agent's importunity and had done, she was convinced, badly. David questioned her about the ordeal; she had had a slight cold, a bad period and nobody knew what she was supposed to sing. Her agent and her professor made suggestions widely at variance. She'd taken some Purcell, Handel, Bellini, Verdi, Smetana, Britten to a dusty studio at a music publisher's, where two men and a competent woman pianist had been waiting. One of the men, she thought she half recognized him, but they had made no attempt to introduce themselves, looked through her pile of songs showing no interest, and had picked out two at random, or desperation at the poverty of choice. She had been instructed to stand over by the piano and perform. The pianist, inquiring about tempi, had been the only one to demonstrate humanity, and that was grudging enough. The piano clanked like chain, but she sang to her judges, at them rather, from a distance in the dry air. Neither man watched her; both sat staring down in embarrassment at the floor. One had placed a brown trilby on the chair next to his; Mary offered the detail with no attempt at humour. When she had finished they asked her to choose a song for herself, and she had to walk over towards them, pick up her

115

pile, sort through it without any idea how to impress. In the end she chose Handel's 'Let the Bright Seraphim', announced this to them with an interrogative lift, but as they did not respond, she made a glum way back to the piano and waited until the accompanist was sure that the copy was complete.

'Did you feel angry?' David asked.

Mary shook her head. 'They didn't care.'

'At least they asked you to sing another song.'

She shrugged her despondency. He guessed that what had been a sad walk, scuffle among music, vacillation to her had seemed poised to the adjudicators, pulling them into their dull place with aristocratic detachment. They had thanked her without warmth, seemingly in a hurry for her performance of the 'Seraphim' had been interrupted by a knock and the nervous entrance of a young man with a music case, presumably the next for audition. She was asked to fill in a duplicated form, to give information they already possessed.

'You've got an agent?'

'Yes.'

'Who is it?' They knew that; the audition had come through him.

'Mark Wentmeyer.'

'Thank you.' Unimpressed.

Mary packed her case, had to return to the piano for her copies and there she expressed gratitude to her accompanist, who nodded nervously, afraid perhaps to spoil the dusty silence. The two men were already leafing through the copies the next client had provided. Mary wished them good afternoon, and both looked up in surprise. One cleared his throat, but the other, the man with the hat, raised a hand. She closed the door without noise.

David trying to cheer her wasted his time. It was the first time that he had ever known her in such despair. In a bout of violent kissing as they lay across his bed, she burst into tears.

'What is it?' he asked.

She could not reply, her cheeks drenched, her shoulders shaking. True, she quickly recovered, and even when she was crying the features under the tears were composed as if the bone structure did not allow her to express grief. As she apologized, she mended her face with a small crumple of tissue; her eyes were unswollen.

'We should get married,' he said.

'You're nice to me.' She put her arms round him, laid her head on his chest, but she was calmer than he, though now he began to sense the insecurity that fed her competitive spirit, drove her to excel. She would never explain.

Her parents loved her, she was the only child, had encouraged her to sing. When she as a schoolgirl had entered and won festivals, they had put her to lessons under the best teacher in the district. It was he, William Morton, who had trained her to the distinction in Grade 8, the scholarship at the Royal College, to her first engagements.

'He was the first real musician I'd met,' she told David.

'Were you in love with him?'

'Yes. I'd do anything for him.' She laughed. 'He was a nervy creature, lived with his mother. He kissed me once or twice, and blushed scarlet. And once he put his hands on my breasts.'

'What did you do?'

'Nothing. Let him. I was terrified and delighted. He seemed ancient.'

'How old?'

'I know for certain. He was thirty-eight. I looked him up. Thirty-eight on the day I had my third lesson with him.'

'Did you wish him many happy returns?'

'No.'

'Did he say anything?'

'He did not. I wonder if he'd remembered, himself.'

David, who was slightly acquainted with Morton, the head of music in a teacher-training department, thought that that sounded about right.

'He was marvellously good for me. He was scholarly, quick, and lent me his books. He helped me no end with my A-level music, got me an A. Miles better than anybody I have at the college. He educated me.'

David felt jealousy.

'Did he know anything about voice production?'

'He was sensible. And didn't bore me with exercises like Charles Trotter. And Liz was too fond of that sort of thing for my liking. But William showed me through songs how well I could do.'

'You didn't think you could before?'

'I liked singing. My first teacher was decent. But William taught me in those two years that it was an art.'

'Did you always want to beat other people?'

'I suppose so. I was always fierce. But mainly at running and high jumping. I was junior champion of Derby at a hundred and two hundred.'

It was during this weekend, not much later than the conversation about Morton, that he suggested, suddenly, to restore his spirits. 'Let's take our clothes off.'

She did not sit up, they lay still across his bed, but stared at him, levelly, as if he'd said something of real interest. He did not like the scrutiny; under it his suggestion appeared childish.

'We shan't make love,' she answered, steadily, condemnatory.

'Forget it.'

She stood, pulled him upright.

'Take your things off,' she ordered. Her blouse and skirt were already gaping from their previous exchanges. 'Beat you to it.'

The laughing, infantile challenge encouraged him, and they stripped.

He had never seen her stark naked before. Here in this not overwarm bedroom she stood at a short distance from him, slim, magnificently beautiful and yet not his. She did not appear embarrassed, rather more composed than he, but so different that he was taken aback. His fingertips knew this body, his eyes had learned it in parts, but now the completion caught at his throat. He clasped her to him; they tippled down to the bed again, staggering, because they could not bear to release the other even for a few steps. They touched, stroked, kissed but did not commit themselves to the final act, even briefly. He tried; she refused, fighting him off. When they had dressed, they were going that night to the theatre with the parents, he said, 'By God, I wanted you.' His voice withered in his throat.

'I wanted you.' Her answer had a baffling purity.

'Why didn't we then?'

She did not reply, but dabbed a very little unnecessary powder on her face.

He had not forgotten that day, when she stood in the middle of the room, the light of early winter behind her, straight, shoulders high, in a composition both perfect and submissive. Her nipples were proud, the navel exquisite in the belly's smoothness, the pubic triangle on the high mount of Venus of a different, electrical yet deader texture from the hair of her head, the legs shapely, powerful, yet nowhere disfigured by muscular bulges. And above, the blue eyes watched him, at judgement, a modest and strong intelligence playing there and about her mouth while the hands he knew so well from ordinary commerce, at a keyboard, or table, or stove, with a pen or a sheet of music, were perfect appendages to the naked length of arms, the breasts, the womanhood.

When he could divorce his powerful sexual urge from the memory, what remained, and it was a remnant compared with the shaking of his lust, was the girl he did not know, who had served behind the counter, won at local festivals, outrun athletes, in her dark blue shorts, white numbered singlet, spiked shoes, had loved, carefully against explosive uncertainty, the nervous music teacher putting his lips to hers, fingertipping her school blouse, drawing away.

After they had married, on a mad Saturday afternoon in London when she had almost immediately disappeared to sing in *Così*, the remembered figure touched and moved him, and on her return as they lived together, man and extraordinary wife, in their new house, 5 Station Road, it lost nothing as he learned more about her. He had married a woman who at her most naked and vulnerable could distance herself from him, assume her discrete self, take him in her arms to remind him that most of her life had been spent out of his company. Even their later sexual intimacy, their everyday exchanges, pleasures, their small quarrels at hearth or board only deepened for him the strength of the symbol. David realized that this was his fiction not her fact, but felt the power no less. I have married a beautiful, talented woman whom largely I do not know, who does not know me and who makes at present only minor

119

adjustments to alter this. He felt proud, both of achievement and conclusion, worked to alter it.

Now that she was silent in America, the remembrance, vivid again in the first few weeks of her absence, faded, dried, became nothing. Convinced that something between them was grievously wrong, he needed no specious boosts to imagination. When she had loved him, was close, he could bear to consider her separateness.

At this time he knew nothing else.

11

David waited each morning for the postman, hurried home in the lunch hour to see if the second delivery had broken drought, backed, dashed away from the door. He said nothing about his trouble, and his mother, oddly, where was she?, made no inquiries. Shostakovich occupied him, a new Haydn; one Friday evening the Trent had a savage play-through of Beethoven's op. 127, Britten's Third. Their second concert, in Northampton, same programme as the first, went well, though to a smaller audience.

The headmaster, on life's common way meeting him in the corridor, asked how Mary was shaping.

'Very well, so far as I know. I haven't heard for a bit.'

'You're lucky. When Dorothea's away she does nothing but ring up and issue orders.'

Both smiled, men who knew the world. The exchange between two liars had been easy.

One evening he left early for his quartet rehearsal to call in on his mother. She made him welcome, sat him down, sprang the brutal question early.

'How's Mary?' she asked.

'I haven't heard.'

'Not a phone call even?'

'No.'

'But it must be three weeks now. We've been back a fort-night.'

Awkward, uncouth silence stalked between them.

'It's a long time,' she said.

'I've not heard from you,' he ground out, 'for over a week.'

'We were away Friday to Monday. In Hereford, with the Wilders. I told you, I'm sure.'

'Who are they?'

'An old family friend. She is. We were at school together. We've kept in touch, intermittently. He's just retired from the Civil Service, and they've bought a house there. She's been pressing us to go, and your dad agreed.'

Old, vague acquaintances wrote letters, pressed. For the life of him he could neither recall any mention of these people nor of the visit. He had no grip; his own name would elude him next.

Again the damned silence, packed with unspoken openings.

'There must be something wrong,' he said at length. The words came out like phlegm cleared by an induced cough.

'David,' Joan asked, 'was there anything, er, amiss between you before she went off?'

'No. Not at all.'

'It's not my place to ask, but your marriage seemed, seemed all right?'

Yes. At least as far as I was concerned. We were on an edge about her going, but she was as bad as I was. She didn't want to go, with one part of her. She said as much, but we both knew she had to take her chance, and felt excited about it.'

'You're sure?'

'Yes. I suppose I'd lie about it if there had been a row. But there hadn't. That's what I can't understand. Mary's level-headed, much more so than I am.'

'What do you think has happened, then?' His mother made no bones about it.

'I just don't know. If there had been an accident or illness then my address would be about, in her bag, on her cases. They'd, surely somebody would let us know.'

'Have you tried ringing her?'

'Yes.'

'And did you get through?'

'To some office. They knew nothing. They tried to put me on to somebody connected with the opera, but couldn't. The opera was still playing there. At least, the woman, secretary whatever she was, thought it was. I said I hadn't heard and wondered if Mary was ill, and she promised to make inquiries. I rang again the next day, but it was a different voice, knew nothing about it, as usual, but this time she'd been to see *Semele* the night before, and Mary had sung beautifully. She promised she'd see to it that a note got through about my call.' He rubbed his head. 'I'm sure she meant it. Well, both of them. They seemed kind.'

'When was that?'

'Five days ago.'

'And you've heard nothing since?'

He did not answer that.

'Will you try again?' Joan continued.

'I suppose so.'

'Have you been writing all this while?'

'Not so much this last week or ten days.'

'Not at all?'

'I didn't say that. I posted a letter on the morning I first rang the university. An ordinary affair, everyday news. I don't know how to start now, except to ask what the bloody hell she's up to.'

'That might not be a bad thing.'

'I don't know,' David said. 'There's this business of not making you and Dad welcome. That worried me. It's not like her.'

'You'd had a call from her, you said, about that time, and she seemed normal.'

'She did. But this isn't normal, is it? Did she seem ill when you saw her?'

'Not really. But she made no attempt to accommodate us.'

'Was she guilty, do you think?'

'What do you mean?'

'Was she up to something she shouldn't have been? So that she wanted you out of the way?'

'That's not how I saw it,' Joan answered. 'She seemed not to know us. She knew who we were, but . . . It wasn't like her. I mean I spent a lot of time with her on *Dido*, and that Schumann, and *Semele*. And we used to talk.'

122

'You didn't get the impression then that there was something awry? Between us? Before she left?'

'No.'

'I thought perhaps she'd said something, and that's why you asked me.'

'No. She was happy. Excited about America, but worried about leaving you. Exactly as I'd have expected. We talked about it often, and I encouraged her, told her she was right to take the opportunity. Do you think Elizabeth Falconer will have heard from her?'

'I shouldn't imagine so, even if she were at home.'

'No.' His mother, face untroubled, sat still. 'Have you been in touch with Mary's parents?'

'No.'

'Don't you think it would be a good idea?'

'They were never very close. They'd go for weeks without phoning.'

'I'd try it.'

He left his mother, certain of the worst, whatever that was. She had made no attempt to disguise her unease, to offer spurious comfort. Even so, he wondered if she was hiding information.

He worked grimly at the rehearsal; at least that gave him occupation. The other three seemed not to notice anything out of the ordinary. Barton, in front of the violins, complimented him.

'If you go on like this,' he said, 'Knighty will have his work cut out to get his place.'

David nodded dourly.

'You're good for us,' Barton continued. 'Keep us on our toes.'

'How come?'

'We're not sure about you. You see, you're not just a fiddler. There's knowledge, scholarship behind what you say.'

'I hadn't noticed it.'

'You wouldn't. That's the beauty of it. You've acquired the knowledge and there it is for use. Second nature.'

'And you play as well as we do.' Wilkinson, surprisingly, topping it all.

123

'Only by practising, and then just by the skin of my teeth.'

'You don't get on any other way.' Payne, exaggerating nothing.

His colleagues' praise should have lifted him, for with the exception of Barton they were not men of words. They had talked amongst themselves, obviously, but however just their commendation, it skirted, touched only the outside of his life. By the time he had propped the cello in the back of his car, his mind raced, tumbling, uncontrolled over Mary's silence.

For three days he put off telephoning the Stileses, her parents. He would give her a further chance. He would make sure. He did not want to flash his anxiety around. He, he, he.

On Friday evening he rang New York. A third, unknown secretary answered, was kind, put him through to a Dr Anderson, who listened, said that the company were about to move to Boston after the weekend's performances, said that he had seen Mary, that she looked well. He disclaimed any close connection with the company, but said that the mail sometimes was unreliable; he offered a brief, illustrative anecdote, and then said he'd see if he had Mary's number, and then the switchboard could perhaps put him through. If David would excuse him, he would use another phone. He did so, returned, said that the operator would try, but in the event of a failure he would, he would in any case, write Mary a note to say her husband had telephoned. Back to the switchboard. A phone rang, disturbing the air in Mary's room, in the corridor outside, in some place that had known her presence that day. It rang unanswered. The secretary apologized, did not know what to suggest. All had tried; nobody had skimped on effort; consideration had been foremost, and the result, a blank. It was as if a conspiracy existed to lead him towards his wife and leave him staring at a prepared gap. He asked if she would let Dr Anderson know the result, and thanked her. She said he was welcome, she'd be glad to. He thanked her again.

For some minutes he sat.

He roused himself, looked at the clock, ten past seven, and decided that Mary's parents would have closed the shop and finished their evening meal. He reached for the address book;

most entries were in Mary's writing, this rather bold, slapdash hand that seemed unlike her.

'Hello.' Mr Stiles answered with one word. David announced himself, his father-in-law hesitantly asked him how he was, and said he'd hand the call over to his wife. Mrs Stiles inquired about his health, but was not free with conversation.

'I thought I'd ring to find out if you'd heard anything lately from Mary.'

'I see.'

'Have you?' He spoke rudely.

'We had a letter just this morning. I was going to ring you, but I thought you had an orchestral rehearsal on Friday nights. Haven't you heard anything from her?'

'Not for three weeks or more.'

'That's bad.'

There followed a silence, as if Mrs Stiles had disappeared. For the moment he thought she might have hung up, or been cut off; both would have been unsurprising.

'Hello,' he rapped. 'Are you still there?'

'Yes, David. I'm just thinking.'

He fought his anger down, imagining her standing by the living-room extension. She was tall, though not quite so tall as Mary, and she dressed soberly, blacks, dark blues, greys. She'd be energetically brushing at, touching, straightening her hair with her free hand.

'What did she say?' He could barely recognize his own voice.

'We only got it this morning. It wasn't very long. One of these airmail forms.' Again she halted.

'When was it written?'

'The seventh. That would be Monday, wouldn't it? Yes, it's Friday today. Monday.'

'And what did she say?'

'You've not heard anything from her?'

'Not for three weeks.' He could fling the phone at the wall.

'It was a funny letter. She said the opera was good. And then she said that she'd fallen in love with somebody.' She stopped; icy trembling raked his back. He had no strength; nausea snagged in him and his mouth gaped weakly. Why didn't the bloody woman talk? Was she waiting for a question? He heard

125

the rustle of paper. Mrs Stiles had gestured for her husband to bring the letter across, unless it had already been placed by the telephone in readiness and she had now opened it. 'His name is Redvers Gage, the producer. She doesn't say anything else about him. She says, "I don't know how to break this to David, but I have to tell somebody your side." '

'Is this like her?'

The question threw Mrs Stiles; she seemed unprepared.

'There's something else, David. She's pregnant.' The voice took on a wooden intonation. "I am pregnant. It's David's baby, and must have been conceived just before I left, though I don't know how. Red knows about this. We've talked it through." Then she says she'll have to write to you in the end, but she doesn't know how. "I keep getting messages from him. He rings up. I've always been out." ' Know, know, damned knowledge.

'Is that all?'

'Yes.' Mrs Stiles waited. 'I'm ever so sorry, David. We've been worrying ourselves about this on and off all day.'

'Did she ask you to contact me?'

'No. She just wondered if we'd been in touch with you. And then she tells us this lot.'

'She'd guess you'd . . .'

'Well, we talked about it. Today. Since we had it. We didn't know what we should do. Her dad wanted me to ring you up as soon as you got home from school. "It's only fair," he said. "Why don't you ring him, then?" I said, but he wouldn't. He leaves it to me.' She seemed pleased to lodge her own complaint.

'There's nothing else? In the letter?'

'No. Not really. She writes pretty large and she didn't use the back bit.' Mrs Stiles stopped, and at length broke into ensuing silence. 'I'm ever so sorry, David. I don't understand her, I honestly don't.' Break. 'Her dad's that upset. We can't make it out.' Comfortless hiatus. 'What are you going to do?'

'There's nothing much I can do, is there?'

'No. We shall write to her. We shall have to. She's our daughter, whatever she's done.' Breathing. 'Do you, should we mention that we've told you?'

126

'I leave that to you.'

'What will you do, David? Will you write?'

'I don't know. I'll need to think about it.'

'Yes. It's such a shock. There isn't any chance of going over, is there, David?'

'None at all.'

'Not in the Easter holidays?'

'No. I've two musical engagements. With the quartet.' Even his leaden distress, this seemed feeble, as if he'd thrown his hand in, given her up already. 'My parents went to hear her. They came back about a fortnight ago.'

'Did they say anything?'

'She wasn't pleased to see them, didn't make them welcome. I can understand why now.'

'But she never said anything to them?'

'No.'

Mrs Stiles continued steadily with her cross-examination, as if to keep him on the end of the line were important. She was shrewd; her questions probed; she was not unlike her daughter, and less kind than his mother. She meant to find out what had happened, and why, before she committed herself; he began to fathom a little of Mary's competitiveness.

In the end she confessed again she could not understand her daughter's behaviour.

'Our Mary goes her own road, and that's always been the case, but throwing over her marriage isn't like her. I mean, it's just as if she decided this other man was what she wanted, and she'd done wrong in choosing you.' The woman had as little idea as her daughter of her cruelty. 'Now that isn't like her.'

Mrs Stiles ordered her husband to the phone, where he delivered an untidy sentence or two, neither apposite nor well made. One could not guess where his sympathies lay, merely that this development embarrassed him. David had no difficulty in ending the exchange.

He walked away from the telephone frightened and numbed. He had promised to attend an orchestral rehearsal which would have already started, and even as he decided against appearing he rebuked himself. The life he and Mary had been building had gone. Absence, a necessary sacrifice, was declared absolute; what should have deepened the relationship had, within a matter of days, shredded it.

Now that certainty had been established, his grief assumed physical attributes. Slightly sick, he staggered; his limbs pained, lacking strength; his eyes defined badly, wetted themselves; the head lolled above a cricked neck; his hands and feet were cold. He put on the kettle to make a drink; as it shrilled he dragged his mind to the noise. He found he could not sit for any length of time but he leaped away from his chair and his twitching body only to find weakness as he stood. The television set played unnoticed. For some moments he held himself in front of a reproduction of Vermeer's *View of Delft*; his mouth dropped slightly open, and the picture was a dull patch on a dull wall.

He moved and scratched about the living room until past eleven, unaware of anything outside the turmoil in his head. Sometimes it took the form of a cinematograph show, bursts of film loop, untidy, repeated and inconsequential but all reiterating Mary's treachery. He saw their first quarrel, the honeymoon night, her laughter when once he had tripped with a tray of dishes, the decorating of the tree last Christmas, her entry to sing the *Frauenliebe und -leben*, a winter picnic in the car, gin on Boxing Day morning, a flashing series, unconnected except for her presence and all chained down, daubed with his perplexity, their feverish speed at odds with his corporal lethargy. Sometimes sentences, reiterated, interrupted, piling: her mother's, 'That isn't like her'; her father's, 'I don't know'; his mother's, 'We used to talk'; Mary's, 'Take care of yourself'; but not in their voices, in a mechanical squeak.

David had provided himself with a drink, heated the bathwater, turned on his electric blanket, but he could not say in what order. His life, if the clatter and shift could be so described, was contained somewhere in his skull, behind his eyes, between his temples. He could not sleep, tossed in his bed, blaming himself. He shoved the tousled bedclothes free and walked about the upper rooms, looking out into street or garden, at the black shape of houses where people lived without despair.

On Saturday he completed his errands, carefully prepared a

complicated lunch from a cookery book, inscribed, 'To Mary from Sandra and Syd', and spent the afternoon walking. Showers drenched him twice, but he did not turn back, determined to tire himself out. He had done nearly fifteen miles when he returned about seven o'clock. He practised, not competently, for the next day's rehearsal, took a bath, sat in his dressing gown limiting his grief with whisky. He opened, could not read his library books, but the pangs of his grief were masterable.

It surprised him that he found himself in tears. He had looked up, seen the mantelpiece and its photographs, and his stoicism was ripped away. He sobbed out loud, groaned and, dropping to his knees, swivelled to beat on his chair with fists. He could not check himself, then did not want to, but when he became calmer he stood, lifting the wedding photograph. Bride and groom smiled; he looked much at home under the porch, proud and sure of himself. Her image did not change; she raised her head, looked the world in the eye, her arm securely in his and this not two years ago. She had gained what she wanted. The tears dried on his face. He made his way upstairs and fell asleep almost at once.

On Sunday at rehearsal for minutes on end he lost his trouble. After lunch his mother rang him.

'Have you heard anything?' She wasted no time.

'Yes.'

'Is she all right?'

He gave her a dry, brief account of Mary's letter to Mrs Stiles. He did it grudgingly, but found himself capable.

'David. Oh, I am sorry,' she said. 'Come up here for a meal, this evening.'

'No, thanks.'

'Look, David, you've got to talk about this to somebody. It's no use bottling it up.'

'I'm talking to you, now.'

'The phone is different.' That bait disregarded, she continued. 'She's pregnant, do you say?'

'Yes.'

'By you?'

'According to the letter.'

'That might account for her being off-colour?'

'Yes. Suppose so.'

'You'd think that would have made a difference, wouldn't you? I don't know what your father's going to say. He's so fond of Mary. We both were. Come round, David.'

'No, thanks.'

'I don't like to think of you there all by yourself.'

'That's something I'll have to get used to,' he said.

'Don't talk like that, David. I'll come to see you.'

'No, you won't. Not today. Thanks very much, but I've plenty to occupy myself with. I shall be all right.'

'What did Mrs Stiles say, David?'

'That she couldn't understand it.'

'That's exactly how I feel. There's part of the puzzle missing. It doesn't seem like the Mary I knew.'

'It's happened,' he answered, and blushed, hotly.

'What will you do, David? Will you write?'

'When she writes to me.'

'Do you think she will? Now she's told her parents. She'll know they'll break it to you.'

'Perhaps.' His mind made no contact with the problem.

'There's no chance of going over there? At Easter?'

'No. The quartet has two concerts. And I'm playing in the *Matthew Passion* Good Friday.'

'Yes. I see. It's awkward, isn't it?'

'Not the word I'd choose.'

'David, I'll ring you again after I've talked to your father. May I?'

'Yes. Where is he?'

'He's gone to the hospital to visit Mr Frimley, the old head clerk at Blackwall and Small. He's dying.'

'That's not very like Dad, is it? Thought he couldn't stand hospitals. Did you nag him into it?'

'Yes. He knew he'd have to go.'

'What's wrong with Frimley?'

'He's old, David. And he's been living on his own since his wife died. He's neglected himself.'

'Um.' His mind drifted away from Frimley, in a tide of trouble.

'Is there anything I can do?' Joan asked.

130

'No, thank you.'

'It's awful, David. I don't know what to say.'

'Uh.'

'David, do you mind if I ring Mrs Stiles?'

'What for?' The question shot out of evil temper.

'I'd like to talk to her. It's as bad for her as it is for me. Worse. She may be able to throw some light.'

'She knows no more than I've told you.'

'Wouldn't she think of ringing up and talking to Mary?'

The thought had not crossed his mind, in that he'd imagined the Stileses would take the same view that he did, that Mary's decision was irrevocable. He made no answer.

'We don't know what pressure Mary has been under. In a new country, with the stress of the opera, and then this man Redvers Gage,' Joan said, each word emphasized.

'You've met him, haven't you?'

'Yes.'

'What's he like?'

'He didn't make much impression on me. They all praised him, said how marvellous he was, and what a dictator, but he was quiet. He dressed like an Englishman when I saw him, sports jacket with leather on the sleeves. His hair was beginning to recede. Very polite to us, but he wasn't a great physical presence.'

'So you were surprised that they all made such a god of him?'

'Not really. I never thought about it, or I took it for granted. They'd had a success nobody had anticipated. I mean, the thing was nothing, some little university event, and after two or three performances it was being praised all over the country. Gage is well known, I've heard of him, and I don't doubt he's a fair number of friends who are journalists or television critics, but *Semele*'s been done before, and nobody's gone overboard about it. No, it must have turned a few heads.'

'Mary's for instance?'

'It's possible. It doesn't seem likely, does it? I think Gage has some contacts with international opera. He's going to do something at the Metropolitan, isn't he?'

'The main roles will be settled.'

'I suppose so. They have to book so far ahead. But I wasn't

thinking in those terms about Mary.' Both ran out of energy; there was nothing to be said. 'You're sure you don't want to come round, David? I'll talk to your dad. He may have some ideas. And I will ring Mrs Stiles, if you don't mind.'

He had sat so still through the call that his limbs were stiff as he rose. The exchange had done him good; his mother did not think the last day on earth had come. Miserably, he marked essays, prepared himself for the morning's departure, listened fitfully to Janáček's first quartet which ended Radio Three's broadcasts, fortifying himself with some whisky. He did not sleep badly.

After assembly, where he sat gowned, theirs was an old-fashioned school, and where eight hundred boys rumbled through 'New every morning is the love/Our waking and uprising prove', and the headmaster read a collect without enthusiasm and left colleagues and pupils to find their own way in and out of the Lord's Prayer, but recovered élan at the weekend's rugby and cross-country results, David was surprised to find Kenneth Reeve hovering in the corridor outside the common-room door.

'Ah, Mr Blackwall.'

For a crucifying second David wondered if his mother had been in contact with the headmaster. Reeve ushered him into his study.

'Shan't keep you a minute. Dick Wilson's father died this weekend. Friday night.'

Black Friday for the history department.

'He's been up there all the weekend. Returned last night.'

'Was it unexpected?'

'No. I don't think so.'

'When I asked him about his father, he said it wasn't serious.'

Reeve looked over his shoulder. For eavesdroppers?

'He seems,' he said with quiet acidity, 'to be unable to accept the inevitable. That's not unusual. He would not take the doctor's word.'

'That's not like Dick.' He thought of the good suits, the black-sided reading glasses, the far-back voice, the air of authority.

'I don't know about that. He's the nervous type.' Reeve knew his way in the world. 'Keep your eye on him. Nothing spectacular.' He laughed. 'Let it be known in the staffroom. My impression is that he probably looks on his father's death as an embarrassment. It's often the case.' Reeve's voice was low, sympathetic, understanding, so that David felt suddenly that he should confess his own misfortune. He resisted the urge.

'That's all then. Thank you.'

Reeve, back to himself, had picked up a letter from his tray. David slipped out and into the staffroom where the PE master, in magenta tracksuit, complained loudly.

'He got the bloody things wrong again.' Obviously the head's announcements in hall. 'You write it all down for him, and then he cocks it up every time. I don't think he can read.'

'Perhaps it's your writing,' Dick Wilson said, passing on the way to his class.

'That's another such.' The PE man had waited, David noticed, until the door was closed.

'His father died on Friday,' David said.

'Have they told him yet?' But the PE man looked shifty, bounced out.

12

The Stileses came over from Derby.

Father made the arrangement on the telephone, under instruction from his wife, who kept her powder dry somewhere out of the way. The old man cleared his throat often, said David was not to make any special provision, though, yes, a cup of tea would be acceptable, cough, nervously strangled chuckle. David questioned him, but he was not forthcoming. Yes, Mrs Blackwall had spoken to Mrs Stiles, had dropped in. No, the three had just talked. No, they had not written to Mary yet; they wanted to speak to him first. No, they had heard no more from her. No, they didn't expect to. Well, yes, it was a bad job. George Stiles hung up with relief, but repeated the time and day of their visit, knowing quite well that if he had missed out some detail, he would be made to repeat the exercise.

David, without evidence, suspected that his mother-in-law had listened to the conversation on the shop extension. There was nothing vindictive or devious about Eva Stiles, but she knew her husband would back away from difficulty, given half a chance, and she was determined not to allow it. Mrs Stiles understood, if nothing else, man-management.

On the watch at the front-bedroom window David observed their car draw up. Mr Stiles checked the doors, while his wife stood a yard away disregarding the drill. Along the short garden path, she walked slightly ahead, entered the house first.

She grinned, the stiff baring of teeth could only be so described, while her husband shook hands with his son-in-law. George Stiles wore a decent off-the-peg suit, with herringbone stripes, and black shoes with ancient, polished toecaps; he hung grey trilby and raincoat in the hall. When David asked if they'd like him to make the cup of tea now, George said, 'Yes,' but Eva countermanded this. All three laughed, differently.

'Let's sit down and talk for a start,' she said. 'Then we can think about tea.'

David had the gas fire on in the front room, a place barely used since Mary's departure.

'It's warm here,' Eva began, choosing her own chair, pulling her hat clear. 'It's cold at night still.'

'There are signs of spring in the garden.' George occupying the settee. David settled opposite his mother-in-law. They had been afraid of him, he thought, because he represented wealth and education, but now they were sorry for him. The phrase 'in reduced circumstances' played in his head, foolishly like muzak.

'Have you heard any more from her?' he asked.

'No. We haven't.' Eva. 'I don't think we could expect to.'

'My mother came to see you?'

'Yes. She was very upset. She couldn't understand it. It didn't seem like the Mary she knew. It was, she said, as if some material evidence was missing. That was right. That was exactly how we saw it. I mean, Mary knows quite well what marriage is. People don't regard it as we do, these days, but at least she was brought up to know what we think.'

Eva leaned forward without aggression, trusting reason, not using her hands yet.

'We went over and over it. It must have been getting on for half past eleven when your mother left. And we were as puzzled as when we started. Perhaps we talked too much. I mean, you can, can't you?'

'So you didn't come to any conclusion?'

'No. Mary was always one for her own way. If she wanted anything, she'd make no bones about it. But she seemed happy. You let her do that opera tour in Germany, and then in London. I wondered at the time. I said so to George. She was a big admirer of Elizabeth Falconer, who's always off here, there and everywhere. She taught Mary a bit. And she lives up this way now at Plumpton Hall. I wondered if she wanted to be like her. Never at home. She's not been married ever so long, has she? Elizabeth?'

'About five years.'

'What's her husband called?'

'Fane. Sir Edward Brook-Fane.'

'What does he do?'

'He's a landowner, in a big way. And a financier.'

Mrs Stiles pulled a sour face, plucked at the dress over her knees. There was something of Mary's energy in her impatience with life, something unaccomplished to be complained of.

'Now there was one thing your mother said . . . She said, "Go and see David and ask him to tell you why Mary has acted as she has. It's better for you to do it than me." The more I thought about that, the more sensible it seemed.'

David waited, looking at the carpet between his feet.

'Go on, then.' Mrs Stiles stridently.

'I don't know.'

'Your mother said that's what you'd say. Well, make it up then.'

She dropped her eyes before his rude stare.

'This isn't a game,' he said.

'Will you try? It may not be the truth. Just make it up.'

'Invent something?'

135

'Try to account for it.'

That seemed good, honest, unshrinking. He saw his mother's influence here, saw the sense of it, that he might let something out. He knew too why his mother had not pressed him herself on the matter, for fear he'd be on the defensive, clam up. But she'd trusted Eva Stiles not only to do her dirty work, but to evaluate it, or at least report it properly. He smiled at his mother-in-law.

'I'm as much at a loss as you are,' he began. 'I don't know why Mary's done this. I thought you might be able to drag something out of her past that might give us a hint. But I'll make something up, as you put it.'

'Thank you.'

She spoke with firm politeness which touched him. This woman, stiff as she appeared, gave what little help she could. On the settee George Stiles nodded almost frantically, beside himself.

'She goes to America. It's new and strange. She's uncertain. She also feels unwell with morning sickness and anxiety about being pregnant.' He looked his parents-in-law over to judge the effect. They sat stock still, with faces to match. 'This man Gage is kind to her, helps her through the trauma and she comes to depend on him. Then on top of it all the opera becomes an unexpected success, and she finds herself fêted, and now she's grateful to him.'

'And it turned her head?' Mrs Stiles, sotto voce.

'In a new, strange place. Daily excitement. Praise, Parties. Drink. Yes, it's possible.'

'Would it have happened to you, David?'

'It might.'

That was not the answer she wanted. Mrs Stiles breathed in, a long, loud sniff not of displeasure, nor disbelief, but as a life-saving procedure for herself. She rallied herself to continue.

'I'm surprised you say that, David. Perhaps that explains it.'

'Perhaps.' Sarcastically.

'You might have taken up with some other woman?'

'In those circumstances.'

The three sat uncomfortably, not quite still.

'What do you say, Dad?' Mrs Stiles broke the silence.

'I don't know what I can . . .' George rolled uncomfortably.

'All I'm telling you,' David interrupted, in a flash of ill temper, 'is that most people might well have been tempted in those circumstances, and acted as she has.'

'Even though you knew it was wrong?'

'Yes. You may not begin with anything out of the ordinary. Or anticipate it.'

'One thing leads to another,' George Stiles said. 'That's so.' His wife looked neither surprised nor disapproving.

'That's how you think it started?' she asked, grinding away at him.

'You wanted me to suggest what had happened. "To make it up," was your expression. I've done so.'

'And is that how it was?'

'Probably.'

'You're prepared to say that about your wife?' Mrs Stiles accused.

'Something's happened that has to be accounted for. She's told you she's in love, and is presumably not coming back. Some pretty important change has taken place. What it is I'm as much in the dark as you are. But it's no use trying to make out nothing's happened.'

'I'm not doing that.'

'All right, then.'

'You're angry, David.'

He gave no answer and she quailed, shrivelling in on herself.

'This is the time for that cup of tea,' George Stiles said, almost cheerfully. When he went out David left doors open, but from the kitchen he could hear no conversation between the Stileses; they must have sat dumb as stones.

On his return with the tray they seemed not to have moved at all.

'Very welcome,' George said, sipping.

'It doesn't bring Mary back,' his wife snapped.

They champed biscuits, took second cups, George accepted a third, with barely a word exchanged. Mrs Stiles roused herself.

'What are you going to do?' Plain, businesslike, but lost.

'I shall wait until she writes to me, until I find out what she

137

has to say for herself.' David spoke flatly, pain singeing his words. His fingers seemed too large for his hands.

'I see. And should we write?'

'I'd think so.'

'Or would it be better if we telephoned?'

'Haven't they gone to Harvard? You won't know the number.'

'No, but New York might give it to me.'

'Yes.'

They sat glumly after he had collected the cups back on the tray.

'That's about it, then.' George Stiles, tentatively. He put his hands beside him as if to lift himself off the settee.

'I can't tell you,' Mrs Stiles interrupted, 'how ashamed I am. I would never have thought . . . She's had her head turned like a teenage girl.'

'She's twenty-four.' George.

'We shall write to her. I mean, I would have said there was always six of one to half a dozen of the other, that there was some fault in you. But since I've spoken to you, and to your mother, I'm not so sure. It's her.' This last was vehement.

'Life in this house isn't as glamorous as the stage over there,' he said bitterly enough.

'Glamour's not everything. I should have thought she'd have had more sense.'

'Now, Mother,' George spoke pacifically, without looking straight at her.

'What?' Fierce.

'Don't go upsetting yourself.'

'What would you feel like,' she asked, 'if you were in David's place? How many husbands would have agreed to let her go for a start?'

'It's done,' George answered.

'And the baby,' she continued, disregarding her husband. 'It's half David's, isn't it? She can't just deprive him of his share. As I shall tell her.' She thrashed about with her hands in the air very briefly, as if her language had become inadequate.

'She's not having an abortion?' David asked.

'I never thought . . . She never said so. I took it she was

138

keeping it, and this Red had agreed. That's what she meant when she said, "We've talked it through." She would never . . .' Mrs Stiles broke off. The idea of abortion had not occurred to her? That seemed unlikely. 'I don't know, David. It gets worse the more you think about it. Well, I'll write tomorrow. It's no use putting it off any longer. Perhaps I should have done it before. It's terrible.' Her mere position in the chair spelt out her distress; without moving she appeared to strain in all directions; the wrinkles, unnoticed before, were cut, deep, dirty. She stirred herself to jump upright. 'Come on, Dad. We've a busy day tomorrow what with one thing and another.' George struggled up. 'I can't tell you how sorry we are, David. To think it's our daughter acting like this.' She moved across, kissed him awkwardly, laid a claw on his arm, made for the door. 'Right, George Stiles.' The father put out a hand which David shook.

There was a second hiatus in the hall while George donned hat and coat, and then they were gone, without further words. Through the closed door, David heard the car start, and he walked back into the front room to turn out the fire, open the curtains.

He stood on the rug by the hearth, indecisive now the small chores were done. He could wash the dishes. The biting grief had dissipated itself; torpor asthenically blanketed him. There was nothing to be said in his favour. Anger had died, replaced by feebleness. The man of straw carried his tray out to the kitchen to stand by the sink staring at his reflection in the window.

Mrs Stiles was like her daughter in looks, but less finely fashioned. He recalled Mary who had fought him off her virginity until they were married, that Mary who had stood naked for the first time. She was nothing like this woman in temperament. And yet, Eva had kissed him, crudely expressing her concern, grabbing him by the sleeve. There was no way of telling what she felt, thought, suffered. She lacked the subtlety of language and experience. She must have known loss; both her parents were dead; Mary's determination, acquisition of a new accent and manners, the putting into her place of a mother who knew no better must have hurt, but she was unprepared for this. Her husband could do nothing for her but mouth clichés or put the kettle on, but she could not imagine herself deserting him on that account. She had given her old-fashioned word. David smiled, not sourly, wondering if ever Eva had been tempted beyond the business in nails and Cosywrap, the hard-working husband, the rising and beautiful daughter; they had been enough and now, when all should have been settled, this had felled her.

His mother, who seemed in on the plan of the Stileses' visit, made inquiries. When he had given his account, she asked, 'They're going to write, then, are they?'

'Mrs Stiles is.'

'Do you think she will?'

'Yes. She said so.'

'Well, as long as you're satisfied.'

'What are you getting at?'

'I wasn't altogether impressed,' Joan answered, 'when I went up there. The father will find excuses if she murders the President of the United States, but I can understand that. But she's a funny customer.'

'In what way?'

'Sly.' Joan waited for his comments and, receiving nothing, continued. 'She wouldn't say anything outright, but I had the impression that she thought you were to blame, that Mary wouldn't have acted like this unless you'd given her cause.'

He explained Mrs Stiles's present position about this, and Joan fell momentarily silent.

'Are you going to write?' she asked, recovering.

'When she writes to me.'

'Why wait? You know what's happening. Perhaps if Mary heard from you, it might make her realize what she's doing.'

'Don't you think she knows, then?'

His mother tried consolation, haltingly. He listened, without optimism.

'We'll wait and see,' he concluded.

Joan offered meals, advice; he said he'd survive. Both wished the conversation had not taken place.

13

A day or two later David crossing the schoolyard on the way to his car passed Dick Wilson, who was standing, overcoat unbuttoned, staring upwards, his case leaning against his legs.

'Going home?' David inquired.

'Yes.' Wilson dragged his attention earthwards with difficulty.

'Want a lift?'

'That's kind of you. My car's in for repair. But it's out of your way.'

'Not much. Not now I'm a bachelor.'

They spoke about the weather, wishing it was warmer. Wilson had to be told to fasten his seatbelt.

'Oh, yes, yes. I mustn't break the law.'

'I was sorry to hear about your father,' David muttered as they emerged through the gates. His occupation with busy traffic seemed to cover a risky interference.

'Yes.'

'Was it unexpected?'

'Yes and no.'

'He wasn't very old, was he?'

'Sixty-three. He was still at work. Wouldn't retire.'

Wilson's voice carried a heavy confidence; he laid down velleities or hesitations with the same strength as his certainties. His legs might twitch, his gaze drop uncertain, but his speech never lacked assurance.

'It's bad, really.' They were now on the main road, edging round buses. 'It's left my mother in an unenviable position.'

'I'm sorry.'

'The truth is that he was an inveterate gambler.' Wilson might have been making a judgement on some historical statesman. 'Horses. The stock exchange. The pinball machine. The casino. It all came alike.'

141

'Oh.' Wilson watched David skilfully manoeuvre his car across two traffic lanes.

'He got through a considerable fortune, one way or another. He always claimed that's why he had to stay at his teaching. I don't think that's exactly true, but it salved his conscience. My mother has a little private money, thank God.'

'I see.'

'She's thinking about going back to Sweden. She was born there.' David recalled Wilson's Christian names: Richard Henry Sellberg, pronounced Sell-berry.

'How long has she been in England?'

'She came over as a language student after the war, and met my father in Oxford. They were married in 1947.'

'And she's not been back since?'

'Only for holidays.'

'What does she think about it? Going back, I mean.'

'It's difficult to tell. She could have stayed where she is, or moved nearer to me, or to my sister. There are friends in Manchester, but not close enough to detain her. Janet wouldn't want her here at our place, and Eleanor moves about. I think she'd quite like to be Swedish again.'

David stopped outside Wilson's house, a Victorian semi-detached villa on a steep tree-lined avenue.

'It's worrying, though,' Wilson said, not hurrying. 'I've no idea what she really thinks. She's relieved now that my father has died. She knows where she is financially, and she realized that he'd only a year or so at most to live. The bad thing is that he wasted so much money. She ought to be well-to-do on his account now, and she isn't. On the other hand she thinks she'll be her own woman for the first time in thirty-five years. At the age of fifty-six.'

'She hasn't been happy?' David asked.

Wilson drew in a huge breath, shifted heavily in his seat.

'Who's to say?' he replied. 'She married a comparatively wealthy man, but then they have, or rather she has, never been certain where the next hundred pounds is coming from. She couldn't leave him. I believe she admired my father. He was an impressive man in some ways. And then there were the children. She couldn't desert us. By the time we were off her hands, it was too late.'

'Does she regret . . . ?'

'I shouldn't think so, for a minute. She kept the home together, saw to it that we had enough money while we were at school and university.'

'She doesn't think she's wasted her life?' Impudent and imprudent.

Wilson considered this, rasping his left hand over his throat, which was badly shaved compared with the chin.

'If she'd returned she'd have married some Swedish business-man or academic. No, her life wouldn't have been so markedly different.'

Still he didn't open the car door.

'Mary's thinking of staying in America.' David blurted it out. The sentence had been rolling in his head like a dried pea in a matchbox, but now he had said it he regretted the confidence, a more than just return for Wilson's confessions.

'To continue with her musical career?' Wilson asked, politely, distant.

'Yes. The opera's been a great success.'

'And she wants you to go over there to live?'

'Well. No. It's not been . . . I don't think it's possible.'

'No.' Wilson tapped the dashboard with a fingernail. He seemed incapable of sitting still. 'That's not good, is it?' He shook his head too vigorously, like a dog clearing its wet coat. 'Not good at all.' He blew breath out, noisily again, clasped the lapels of his overcoat, released them to pull his case to his chest. 'Well, must show my face. Thanks for the lift. Very good of you. Many thanks.'

He heaved himself out, crossed the pavement, pushed open his front gate but did not turn to wave. Already David guessed, he had forgotten about Mary. And now Mother Wilson knew she could return home, lose her Englishness, take up the rusty language of her childhood because her husband was dead and her children did not much mind what she did, provided she did nothing to impede them. That was her reward for thirty-five years of exile, fidelity to a gambler, making ends meet for respectable children. Put like that it almost seemed a

143

justification for Mary's decision to cut and run. Or a minatory parable.

Though he still slept badly and lacked energy David surprised himself by his perseverance at work, and the amount he got through. Depression, unrelenting as it was, could be beaten down by his teaching, his practice, his rehearsals. He found he began to resent his mother's daily telephone calls and her muted insistence that he contact America. The idea of writing before his . . . before Mary wrote angered him so that he would thump a fist incontinently down on his desk, and once scattered a pile of exercise books with a wild, back-handed blow. He rang the Stiles household on Sunday but they had heard nothing.

On Easter Saturday morning as he sat at coffee, having arranged cheap bunches of daffodils in the lounge, he was disturbed at the front door by a young man with music under his arm.

'David Blackwall?'

'Yes.'

'Are you free to play with us tonight?'

'You?' The man seemed afflicted with St Vitus' Dance.

'The London String Players.'

'Where did you get my name?'

'James Talbot.'

He invited the man, Barry Przeslawski, inside, poured coffee, listened. David had intended to go to the concert that evening; the London Players, an ad hoc professional group, were sometimes very good and their programme, Purcell, Elgar, Richard Strauss, Barber, Tchaikovsky and Britten would, he had thought, occupy him gainfully through a dead hour or two.

Przeslawski, the first cello, said that one of his group, a girl, had come up overnight to visit friends and had fallen at breakfast and now had her wrist in plaster. 'We might get away with playing one short, but Jim Talbot suggested you to Malcolm King, he's staying with them, and he dispatched me round here pronto.' Talbot had apparently rung earlier, but without answer. 'Will you do it for us?'

David agreed; Przeslawski lifted music from the settee beside him to the table, in triumph.

'Can I use your phone to let Malc know?' He dialled from a slip of paper, delivered David's agreement, rushed back, announced the rehearsal at two, said Heather would have conscientiously marked her copies if he'd like to look through them. They had had, it appeared, only one full rehearsal in London for this concert, but King could draw blood from stones, and they all had done these things often enough. Przeslawski gulped down his coffee, refused more, said he was grateful, leaped with flying arms and legs from the settee, grumbling he had hoped for a lie-in at his mother's in West Bridgford. He banged out, but before he left the front steps said, 'You've got an Amati, haven't you?'

'Yes.'

'Not thinking of selling it, are you?'

'No.'

'Don't blame you. Anyway, I couldn't afford to buy it.'

David enjoyed the rehearsal; it stimulated him to become one with these gifted young people, to learn from them. The evening's performance in the new concert hall was only adequately attended; he saw some of his sixth form, one of his colleagues from his place at the back desk of the cellos. King, the conductor, who would be fortyish, had this slightly old-fashioned, battered, contemporary face, a Mick Jagger, Julian Lloyd-Webber, a Martin Amis, and was good. A string man himself, he knew every part, and with short left-hand jabs, under finger extended, ruled entries while the right with baton swept the orchestra on. They played the Purcell G minor Chacony to open, then the Tchaikovsky Suite and ended the first part with an eloquent, plangently emotional reading of Richard Strauss's *Metamorphosen* for twenty-three solo strings, which arched, and reached, shouted, demanded, wept, compelled. King stood proud and Strauss's lament stretched their bow arms, fired vibrato, bounced the weaving sounds, the cliffs of grief heavily down from the ceiling. David had never felt so engaged; he had no time for show, even for emotion; he had to match his colleagues in attack, in rhythm, in sustained declamation, to make his instrument the conduit of Strauss's command. As King brought them to their feet for applause, David sweated.

145

In the orchestra room Przeslawski nodded approval at him, before David took a seat out of the way, in a corner, by the bull-fiddle cases. Anna Talbot looked round the door, made straight for him though greeting one or two on her way, found herself a chair, began congratulations. He had swilled hands and face and felt calmer, equal to the formality of his white cuffs. As Anna chattered her praise, he watched two of the violins carefully sharing out the contents of a thermos into plastic beakers. He felt at ease for the first time for weeks, and with a contentment which he had earned, and he leaned back to concentrate on Anna. One or two looked enviously at him.

'How's Mary?' she was asking.

'Well, as far as I know.'

'Where is she now?'

'Harvard, I think.'

James apparently had spent a year at Harvard, she said, after he'd finished at Oxford. He thought it marvellous. He hadn't been too keen on returning home.

'Mary's not coming back,' he said dully. Exhilaration deserted him; the decision to confide in her had left him drained, but he had spoken, clearly, on cue.

'You mean she's staying in America for good?'

'Yes.'

'She wants you to go over there to live?'

Exactly like Wilson she had not envisaged Mary's rejection of him. In their limited view Mary was his, belonged to him, whatever vagaries her artistic progress dictated.

'No.' He spoke so strongly that he seemed to himself to shout, but no one turned or took notice.

'What do you mean then, David?' Anna was trying to wrinkle her forehead into bewilderment.

'She says she's not coming back.'

'Ever?'

He shrugged.

'Did she write and tell you this?'

'No. She wrote to her parents.'

'And you've not heard from her?'

'Not for nearly two months.'

'Oh, hell.' He could smell her perfume; see her beautifully

146

tamed hair, her smoothness of face, lipstick, the flash of rings on her hands. Her mouth was slightly, attractively open; she breathed quickly, girding herself to say the right thing. She could manage nothing, sagged back into her chair, rallied. 'Oh, God, David. I'm so sorry. I'd no idea. It must have been awful for you.'

He looked around him. People moved about, or talked as the two bent forward in this corner whispering.

'You say she hasn't written?'

'No.'

'Not at all?'

'Not after the first few weeks.'

'That doesn't seem like her.' Anna struggled to speak. 'I kept thinking I ought to send her a line, but I hadn't got the address, and I never got round to phoning you for it. You know what I'm like. Don't do it if you can put it off.'

'She has fallen for the producer.' He spoke every banal word with sour clarity, and Anna drew back from him, silenced. She examined her fingernails or the backs of her hands.

'Up in three minutes,' the manager shouted from the door. 'Thank you.'

David and Anna faced one another, but their eyes did not meet.

'I shall have to go,' she said, making the effort. 'I'm so sorry, David.' She waited, fruitlessly. 'I'll be in touch.' She whirled towards the door, but one of the violinists detained her. David heard her laugh, loudly, socially. He lifted his cello from its case, and with the rest made his way outside. There was a temporary hold-up in the small foyer; from one platform entrance the manager jovially advised them to go easy because the audience was still drinking. King suddenly appeared, minus frock coat, shouting thanks. 'Great,' he said, 'great.' David stood there, in the mini-queue, noticing nothing, seeing nobody, his head heavy, not with pain but with vacancy, as if the ache had been removed but not the discomfort.

'Come on, come on,' the man next to him muttered to himself. David raised eyebrows. 'It'll be past midnight before I'm home.' The colleague grinned. 'Even if I drive like the clappers.'

147

They filed in eventually and David tuned, settled himself, checked his music, all by habit. He noticed nothing but the given A; when he looked out to the hall he had difficulty in focusing on or remembering the as yet restless audience. The buzz of undiminished conversation tangled with the unconstructed chaos in his brain. The partner, tapping the score, spoke.

'Sorry.' David had not caught the meaning.

'They're in no hurry.'

'No.' It did him good to speak the word.

'They never are. Nice instrument you have there.'

'Yes. An Amati.'

The young man, still prodding in front of him with his bow, slowly swivelled his head round the hall, in contemptuous surprise at what he saw.

'Could be anywhere,' he said.

'How's that?' David made himself speak.

'Same faces, same clothes, same noise, same smell.'

The audience transformed one noise to another to applaud the leader, and then King glided on to bow from the hips. He looked across his players, as if baffled by some last-minute question, opened his score, lifted the baton and as one they cut throbbingly deep into the first chord of Elgar's Introduction and Allegro. Playing at this intensity with such confrères left David no time for himself. Within minutes he was wholly occupied in the music, and by the end of the concert uplifted by the audience's enthusiasm. He could throw his shoulders back, but as soon as he reached his car fatigue numbed him. At home he sat downstairs catnapping over a television film, disregarding the whisky bottle at his elbow. On Sunday he woke at eleven, read the papers in bed without much interest in their spies, literary confrontations and inside reports on imminent elections or waste of public money. He shaved and dressed with care to lunch with his parents.

His mother had done him proud: marrowbone soup, roast beef, gooseberry fool, blue Stilton. Both David and his father refused second helpings of each course, making martyrs of themselves. The son carried the dishes out while his father loaded the washing-up machine, but Joan refused to allow

148

either near the coffee mill or percolator. David, awkward, would not accept either brandy or port.

They had questioned him whether he had heard anything from Mary or from the Stileses, seemed unsurprised by his answer. Now his father coughed, and asked, 'Have you written to her?'

'No.'

'Why not?'

'I'm waiting for her to get in touch with me.'

'We think you should write first.'

'I know you do.'

'But don't you see any sense in it?'

David waited, searching. Though he was certain that his mother had put Horace up to this catechism, he would give him, if he could, a fair answer.

'It's not so much a matter of seeing sense,' he began slowly, 'it's that I can't bring myself anywhere near doing it, emotionally.'

That quieted his father.

'We liked Mary very much,' Horace asserted, but without much conviction.

'I know.'

'And if anything could be done, I'm not saying it could, we'd like you to do it.'

'If you think writing letters is so effective, why don't you write to her yourself?'

'First,' his father cleared his throat, 'a letter from us is nothing like the same thing as one from you.' David marked that one up to the old man. 'Secondly, we have, or rather, your mother has. I added a postscript.'

'When was that?'

'In the week.'

'Tuesday evening, posted Wednesday,' Joan amplified.

'To New York or Harvard?'

'New York. We had no other address.'

'And what did you say?'

Joan looked at her husband, who signalled for her to reply.

'It wasn't all soft soap, David,' his mother began. 'I put it bluntly. Your father and I had gone over this all Tuesday

149

evening, over and over, point by point, and then I wrote it. I said how shocked and shaken you were, and how sorry we were. I also made it clear that we didn't think much of her roundabout way of letting you know, and that whatever happened out there, she owed you an explanation. That was about the length and breadth of it. Your dad wanted me to photocopy it to show you, but that didn't seem proper. I don't know why.'

'It was a very good letter, absolutely straight, and yet friendly.'

'It's no use getting on the high moral horse. She knows as well as I do that she's in the wrong.'

'Thanks,' David said. It sounded grudging enough, even to him.

'We don't say it will do any good,' Father interrupted.

'She may have taken legal advice, and been told not to write to me. That might commit her in some way. I don't know anything about American law. Or English for that matter.'

They exchanged a few more sentences before Horace nodded off.

'Serena Morley tells me you were in the London Players' concert last night. She phoned. I wish you'd have rung me: we'd have gone. We did think of it, anyway, but your father's been overdoing it again. His blood pressure's high.'

'I thought he was winding down?'

'It worries him. He doesn't like giving up responsibility.' She lowered her voice; her husband stirred, groaned, in his chair. 'We shall have to go on a cruise. There's nothing else for it. And it's the last thing I want.'

'I can hear every word,' Horace said from the depth of his chair, suddenly, not opening his eyes.

'That's why I'm saying them,' she answered, unperturbed.

David explained about the last-minute call to play before he too fell asleep. His rest was uneasy, lit by bad dreams, so that he woke after ten minutes with a crick in his neck. Horace dozed on, but Joan had left the room. David massaged his muscles, crept out.

He found his mother in the kitchen, baking.

'I'll have to go,' he said.

150

'I thought you'd both be out like lights all afternoon. I was making party buns and oatcakes for tea.'

'You should sit down.'

'I'm like you,' Joan answered. 'Fidgety. Will you write to her, David?'

'I don't know why you're making such a thing about it. She's made her mind up, and that's that. Any moaning on my part will only . . .' Speech tailed off.

'You won't moan. When your father and I were talking this over last Tuesday, he suddenly said, "Give me a bit of coggage, Joan, and I'll have a go." "What's coggage?" I asked him, and apparently it's the word the soldiers used in India for paper. And he put down what he thought I should say. I've never known him do anything like that before. It was good, really, his memorandum. "You write the letter," I told him, but he wouldn't. But it surprised me. He must have been upset. That's why I want you to write. Will you?'

'I'll think about it.'

She closed the oven door on two trays of buns.

'Then I suppose I shall have to be satisfied with that.'

His mother leaned towards him to be kissed; he was not sure that she was not mocking him. Outside there was a clatter. His father entered.

'That's where you are. Conspiring. I like to be the first to wake up.'

David left them almost at once though he could see their disappointment.

On the way home he stopped by a golf course, watching the players. The sandy place seemed crowded, mainly with men who had dressed for the game in tartan caps or rainproof trousers. Once he and Mary had stopped here as they returned from a visit to his parents, and she had been scathing.

'People ought to have better things to occupy themselves with.' Sometimes she came out with these unexpected denunciations as if from some source of puritanical savagery inside herself.

'Exercise,' he had said.

'Those stressful, competitive games do more harm than

151

good. I wouldn't mind if they were youngsters, but the majority are middle-aged men.'

'If they didn't come out here,' he countered, 'they'd be fast asleep in their armchairs.'

'That's what I'm saying. They don't know how to act sensibly.' She looked solemn. 'We shall be dead soon enough without wasting time chasing golf balls.' She had shifted in her seat. 'And don't you start about horsehair on wire.'

'I'd better drive home,' he had said.

'Why do I feel so angry?' she asked almost pathetically.

'Because many more people would sooner be Nicklaus than Heifetz.'

'It's awful, and the television encourages it. That's what's wrong with our civilization.'

'I suppose God would consider other matters more important. Whether these people were living moral lives, were good husbands or fathers or neighbours.'

'Sometimes I could slosh you.'

Mary had worked herself out of the spasm of anger, and by the time they had reached home had been laughing. As he sat now, watching two men trampling in the rough, he was uncertain whether these small irritations had been early, unconscious indications of her unhappiness. He decided against it. Mary now and again, like her mother, needed arguments, diatribes. For the rest, she was serene, busy, competent and competitive in her own field, even expectant. But her professional career had vanished with marriage, and to a serious musician, amateur recitals, even Falconer's *Dido*, were no replacement for a life dedicated to practice, achievement, public acknowledgement. That itself might well have palled, but she had not had long enough at it to know. Every artist is supported by anticipation of success as powerfully as by experience of it.

Red Gage, whatever his sexual or social attraction, offered her chances to make good as a musician. He would provide opportunities; he had valuable contacts. David could not bring himself to accuse Mary of deliberately thinking in this way, but it seemed almost moral, or justifiable for a gifted performer to choose thus. For every Elizabeth Falconer there were ten thousand decent wives-and-mothers.

152

He shook his head clear of these sophistries, which were self-induced, facets of an intelligence running wild, and he thought of his father asking for his piece of 'coggage'. Their minds had been employed as his in sifting the problem, but in love. He had felt the strength of their affection, for both, because his mother had turned to chocolate buns and letters to America and his father had left his afternoon nap to comfort him, to do the little they were capable of. Emotion surged, drenched him. He had never appreciated those decent people, not stepped aside once from his own devices to offer them an hour's peace of mind. As he sat, in a short line of cars, overlooking flowering gorse and crooked silver birches, his tears dribbled, and his mouth, rigidly stretched, emitted childish, soft cries. He made no attempt to check himself, but fiddled for his handkerchief to cover his face should any passing unoccupied pedestrian stare in.

The bout expired within seconds. He wiped his eyes clear of tears, feeling no relief. Already he condemned self-pity. His handkerchief was stiff, freshly ironed; he blew his nose vigorously. There was some gross fault in himself. He pocketed his handkerchief and drove off.

He would write to Mary, he decided, to please his mother and father.

14

The house struck cold, damp. Though he had washed the dishes, the unshaken cloth still covered the breakfast table. He turned on the heating, searched through a muddle of old letters to find that he had one airmail form. That evening the Trent Quartet were rehearsing from seven o'clock since Wilkinson had been away with his family and would not be back for the morning meeting. In the hour or two at his disposal he would write. He tore scrap paper from an exercise book for a first draft.

My dear Mary,

I write today because I've heard nothing from you. Your mother and father gave me a résumé of your letter to them. They did not show it to me, and as far as I could make out you did not give them any explanation except to say that you had fallen in love with your producer. Perhaps that is explanation enough. You can well imagine the effect on me; I was shattered. During the time of your long silence, I had imagined for myself all the bad reasons why you did not write, but that had not protected me from the blow when it landed. I don't want to make a performance of it here, because I can see whether I say little or much I shall seem feeble, but I can tell you that I felt as if life wasn't worth going on with. It's easy enough for someone to write that, but in this case it's the truth. I've done my best to make myself not give up, to keep busy.

When your parents told me, I expected some word from you, that, at least, you would let me know what you thought or felt. Instead the same cruel silence. I don't know why this is. I don't understand it at all. But the one or two people I've spoken to about your decision have said the same thing: 'It's not like Mary.'

I don't really know what to write because I don't know where or even who I am. It's as if all the rules I've worked by have been kicked away. Though I feel bitter, I hope you are happy in what you are doing. If you decide to return, I'm still here. [How was he to finish? With love? Yours? He wrote his name clearly, even on the rough copy.] David.

He looked it through, reading it with care, counting the alterations. There were sixteen. It did not say what he wanted, nor was it impressive. He walked into the kitchen to make a pot of tea, for this two hundred odd words with long blank pauses had taken an hour to write. Did his letter make it clear to her that she had acted meanly? He had not managed that, he thought, but the thing, ugh, said roughly all that was to be said. 'I am devastated; you owe me an explanation; I will take you back.' The last sentence of his letter was unclear, but again it reflected his own difficulties, ambivalence. He made the tea, sat sipping it scalding hot, both dull and desperate. He rose, washed out his fountain pen, filled it and copied the letter on to the airmail form, addressing it in block capitals. Snatching up his jacket he rushed along the street to the postbox, so that the message would be on its way by 7.30 tomorrow, Monday morning. On the slower walk back, he felt slightly relieved that the matter had been taken out of his hands, but indoors he had no inclination or energy to spend time on preparation for the evening's rehearsal.

Realizing that he had sat wasting half an hour, his mind a chaos of unfocused, unpleasant shifts, he rang his mother to tell her he had written the letter.

'I'm glad,' Joan answered. 'What did you say?'

'I've kept a copy.' He read it to her.

'That's good,' she said unenthusiastically. 'It's pretty much the same as we wrote.' She hummed to herself, perhaps preventing an interruption. 'Will you read those last two sentences again?' He complied. 'That means you'll have her back, if she wants it?'

'I suppose so.'

'It's not exactly clear.'

'No.' He spoke sharply. 'I'm not clear myself.'

'You don't mean it?'

'I don't expect her to come back. She's made up her mind. She'll be adamant.'

'David,' his mother spoke after a long gap, 'are you sure there was nothing wrong between you?'

'I'm not sure of anything now, I can tell you. But I hadn't noticed. Perhaps that's a judgement on me. Now I think back to it, and in view of what's happened, it's quite likely she was worried and frustrated when she thought she could have been travelling about the country from one engagement to another. But I'll say this for her, she didn't make a big thing of it. Of course, there was *Dido*; that meant going over to Falconer's and meeting Falconer's coach once or twice, and then she practised with you.' He blew his breath out histrionically. 'But as soon as she got to the States and among other professionals, it may have churned it all up again. I don't know. Did you ever feel deprived?'

'Often enough.'

'And didn't you want to get on with your career?'

'Yes.' He guessed his mother was smiling. 'I had depressions and fearful headaches.'

'But you didn't do anything about it?'

'No. I remember one offer I had from James Selkirk. He wanted me, or he and his agent did, to join him to play four hands, two pianos.'

'You turned it down?'

'Yes.'

'And he asked someone else?'

'I don't know. He made his own way as a solo pianist.'

'I've never heard of him. Where is he now?'

'He's professor or principal of some academy in Canada. I'm not sure.'

'And were you torn?'

'What do you think?'

'And what did Dad say? Or didn't he know anything about it?'

'He said,' each word fell separately, pearly clear, 'that I must make the decision and that he was willing to support me whichever way I chose.'

'Did he mean it?' David said sourly.

'As far as I know, yes. In fact, I'm certain he did.'

'But you didn't take him up on it?'

'No. Your father was very busy. He'd begun to expand the firm when he came out of the army and at that time he was making really large changes. He terrified his father, who was a good old-fashioned businessman, very very cautious. Your grandfather wasn't old, he'd be middle fifties at this time, but he was just aghast at what was happening. He could see every penny he'd made being lost. And he fought your father. "Horace is a gambler," he told me. "He's no sense of proportion." But Daddy didn't give in, and his father lived long enough to see himself very rich.'

'And so?'

'He needed me. I didn't understand it very clearly, I admit. He was out a great deal at all hours, and I was left on my own. I didn't like it. I felt I came a poor second to his work. It made me angry. I thought he was selfish. I used to knock hell out of my piano. And I made him buy me a big concert Steinway in addition to the Bechstein.'

'But don't you ever regret . . . ?'

'I did. Times without number. And it made me awkward and

156

ill tempered. But then you arrived and by the time you were ready for school it was too late.'

'Does it worry you now?'

'No. I'm fifty. I'm also pretty certain that I wouldn't have made it. One doesn't know, because luck plays a part, and I can name one or two people who weren't as good as I was who have done quite nicely, thank you. One other matter. Your father was a genius in his line, we tend to forget that, and he needed me at home with his apple pie or hot-water bottles. There you are.'

'Interesting,' he said in his dry, history-lesson voice. The use of the word 'genius' intrigued him. She had used it before of Gage.

'Just one thing before this phone bill ruins you.' Her tone darkened. 'What about the child?'

'What about it?'

'You didn't mention it in your letter.'

'I take it she has got rid of it.'

'I see.'

They did not speak for some little time, until David made his excuse and rang off. He found himself shivering, but took himself out to rehearsal.

Next day in school, as he crossed the yard from the music room to spend a busy free period, he felt a lightening of his spirits. He did not understand this, and it was not until the working day had finished and he sat over a cup of instant coffee in the common room half listening to two colleagues complaining about their mortgages that he realized why he was optimistic. The fact presented itself to him with a small jolt of pleasure that since he had now written to his wife he could expect an answer. He instructed himself warily that this was by no means certain and that the reply, if it came, might well be unacceptably disagreeable, but his brain or his body seemed immune to reason. He added his mite of contradictory information to the discussion, immediately staunching his colleagues' flow. When he had finished his coffee, he went out smiling.

He remembered an episode earlier this academic year.

It must have been in October, and during one of his few lessons with the sixth form specialists, he dealt with economic history, they had questioned him about inflation, during the Tudor period, then earlier, to throw light on what was happening now. He encouraged these digressions, feeling that Dick Wilson made narrow medievalists of his pupils, lively, learned even, but not prepared to venture out beyond what the facts told. One could deduce, certainly, but within strict limits; Wilson had been heard to declare that his subject was history not prophecy or crystal-gazing.

David had argued with his students but had been more positive than his knowledge allowed, and when he came back to check found that one or two of his salient facts were wrong. Immediately he made a close note of corrections to be offered, and prepared a recantation.

So far, so good.

He had completed his research that evening, found himself incapable of sleep, was in black despair by the next day. He could not account for the strength of the feeling. It was not that the boys might report his errors to Wilson, who'd have no qualms in quashing them there and then and probably in animadverting on his colleague's ignorance; the trouble rankled from the fact that he had been so badly wrong.

Mary, cheerful with the beginning of real rehearsal for *Dido*, and the first American hints, concerned herself with his gloom, probed so successfully that he, again out of character, confessed.

She was taken aback.

'But you just made a few mistakes,' she said mildly, 'which you'll put to rights.'

'Mistakes I oughtn't . . .'

'We can't know everything.'

'This is a subject I'm supposed to be teaching. And worse, I was convinced that what I told them was correct. I misled myself.'

'Yes. But you'll get it right next time. I can see you're a bit cross with yourself, and you'll be more careful in future, but you're taking it to heart as if you've ruined their careers or murdered their mothers.'

'You don't seem to see how . . .'

'No, I don't.' She spoke sympathetically. 'You've dropped a

little clanger. It's not the end of the world. Good God. When I think of some of the musical mayhem I've committed.'

'You knew as soon as you'd made your mistakes. I didn't. I thought I'd offered a logical case.'

'David. David.'

By the next day his gloom began to lift, so that he could barely recall his agitation. When he took the history sixth again, they accepted his self-castigation, began to argue from the new facts, seemed in no way put out, took it all in their easy stride. He walked out of the period much relieved, whistling Mozart. Over the evening meal he reported the outcome to Mary, who, serving lamb casserole, brought out a bottle of red wine.

'We'll drink to scholarship,' she said expansively.

'Don't know why I made such a fuss.' He felt ashamed.

It was a week or two later that she confessed how frightened she had been.

'I thought I kept these things to myself,' he answered.

'We know otherwise now.'

'I really am sorry.'

He saw that these two days had disturbed her, perhaps because his own depression had been so powerful, and yet he could have sworn he'd done his best to make civil conversation, to help with the chores, to cover the shocked sense of inadequacy that tore him.

'Let's put it down to artistic temperament,' she had said drily, dismissive, but he wondered now if the small episode had in some way altered her perspective on him, revealed that she had not married the steady helpmeet she had counted on.

The headmaster called him across the games field.

'How are things with you, then?' Reeve asked. The upper school, released for the last hour to watch athletic sports, milled round, scarfed against unseasonable cold. David, thanking him, murmured reassurance. 'And how's your wife? When is she due home?'

David shuddered, uncertain whether to confess. There would be no advantage; Reeve did not ask out of interest. The man vaguely recollected some fact, important or not, about a colleague, and made that the subject of his inquiries. He could as easily be asking about the purchase of a video machine or a set of golf clubs. David braced himself. The world would have to know, and before long; he'd make a start here.

'She's talking about not coming back,' he said. Reeve looked vague, as though the start of house relays had distracted him from the sentence.

'So Dick Wilson tells me.'

That jolted painfully. These two human shadows, interested only in their own small corner of unreality, had taken in information about him, remembered it, discussed it. David decided on silence.

'What will you do, then?'

'There's nothing much I can do, is there?'

Coated spectators, tracksuited competitors passed both ways.

'I don't suppose there is,' the headmaster whispered. 'I don't suppose there is.' Reeve stroked his chin; his fingers looked red, bitten by the cold. 'My wife was asking. Yes.' A member of the maths department hovered three yards away for a word. 'Sometimes I wonder what the world is coming too.' He waved the mathematician away. 'How can we account for an occurrence of this nature? It's not as if you had,' he fumbled for a word, 'deserved it. Of course, we don't know the devices and desires of the hearts of others. We never can. I'm sorry, sorry.' The head began to walk away, from David, from the maths man, from the races, from the human race. He turned again. 'Perhaps you'd like to call on my wife. She's a . . . woman.' The adjective had been snatched away by the wind. Reeve hitched at his collar and set a spanking pace across the field.

A week ahead David arranged to call on Mary's parents.

The Trent Quartet were to play that Sunday evening at a semi-private concert at the local polytechnic. One of the vice-principals was retiring and his wife had chosen to mark the occasion thus. She was a woman who knew her mind and had demanded a modern work. She felt that she had made enough concessions to the musicians by agreeing to this date, a Sunday, though in fact the friends she wished to invite seemed away at all other times. Barton, who had conducted the negotiations because he taught a few hours a week there, said he came away with the impression that the place was run by absentee administrators. Payne, unsure about its readiness, reluctantly agreed to play the Shostakovich 8. He could find no time for extra rehearsals, but they met as usual that Sunday morning and were to make a runthrough in the hall at six for the eight o'clock concert.

David, after an unsatisfactory morning when even Barton showed edginess, lunched with his mother, father again away, and had then driven over to Derby. A sharp walk would have done more good, but he felt a necessity to talk to the Stileses. They had heard nothing, phone calls had established that, but the sense of obligation, to them, to himself, had been strong.

He warred inside himself.

The disintegration of harmony at the rehearsal still marginally disturbed him. He himself had carefully prepared the piece, could play the notes without difficulty, but knew that the four together lacked cohesion.

'We've four separate ways of playing this,' Barton had grumbled.

'You fixed the bloody concert up,' Wilkinson answered, 'before we're ready.'

'It's the only possible date before Easter. I thought we'd be able to rehearse more often than we have.'

'Some of us have families and homes.' Wilkinson, who was mainly culpable.

'We're thinking of turning pro,' Fred Payne said, not pacifically, 'and here we are performing in public not half prepared. It won't do us any good.'

'Nobody'll notice,' Wilkinson muttered. 'Not in this damned thing.'

'Once you think like that, you're lost.' Barton, very quiet, senatorial.

'Look who's talking.'

They pressed on, hating the composer, each other, themselves.

David stayed behind for a word with Cyril Barton, after the other two had rushed off.

'Well, what do you think?'

'I feel depressed,' David answered. 'We've never been in such disarray before.'

161

'They tell me,' Barton began, 'that when the Borodin first played this to Shostakovich, he covered his face and wept. If he heard us, he'd sob his socks off.'

David looked up in surprise at the tone. Barton was not dispirited.

'You'll see,' Cyril Barton continued, 'when we meet at six for a runthrough. It'll come together. We can play the notes; we're over that hurdle. If we're going to be any good, it'll gel.'

He smiled at his slack language, the face thoughtful, rapt.

David, encouraged suddenly, explained in a brief sentence or two about Mary.

'I'm sorry,' Barton replied, placing a hand on his friend's sleeve. 'I didn't know anything about it. It must be hell. Our troubles are small beer compared to yours.' He plucked his sentences, divided each from each, out of the air into which he stared. 'I'm a bachelor. I never got married; I won't say I didn't think about it, but sex wasn't important. I'm not the other way inclined, like Fred. I'm not quite a eunuch, either. When I hear something like this, that you've just told me, I guess I'm lucky. And I begin to ask myself: "What use is Haydn and Shostakovich to this poor chap?" I can't answer it. I didn't suspect anything; you've worked like a Trojan with us. I don't know; I don't know.' He shook a bewildered head; his eyes were wet, and the intelligence seemed drained out of his face, as if after a fearful and unexpected physical attack. 'At times like this, I wish there was something that I could do, or even say. But there isn't.'

'Thanks, Cyril.'

'I feel angry. And that's not like me. I want to go and hit her.'

'You don't know her.'

'No.'

'It might be my fault.'

'You should know that.'

Cyril Barton had given the wrong answer, though he'd no idea. This decent man spoke his decent, limited heart.

'Would you like to stay and have some lunch with me? I've got plenty.'

David explained that he had arranged to go to his mother's and then to Derby.

'Yes. You don't expect to learn anything extra there, do you?' Barton put the question with extreme diffidence, edging it out word by word as if afraid to trespass on David's grief.

'No. I spoke to them on the phone yesterday. They'd heard no more.'

'I don't know how you've put up with it.' He hutched away, trying to end the conversation.

'I've worked hard. That's the value of Haydn and Shostakovich.'

'When my mother died, she lived here with me, this was her house, it paralysed me. I hadn't the strength to play or teach or do any shopping, even. She was old, and I'd had to look after her. But she died without warning. I went in with a cup of tea as I did usually, and she'd gone in the night. It was easy; must have been. That's the way to die. But I hadn't expected it. I just broke up. I'm a quiet, sensible middle-of-the-road man. Fred says that's why I swapped from violin to viola. But I was like a child who couldn't check his tears. It didn't matter who was there or where I was. I just broke down. And yet you . . .'

Barton had turned his face away from David to the wall.

'Thanks, Cyril.'

David swayed, battered, unstable as his companion. Two men, on the edge of tears, blocked the neat passage of bay-windowed, terraced house, 1905.

'See you at six, then,' David said, recovering.

'I wish I could tell you it would be all right. It isn't any use, is it?'

'No. I don't suppose so.'

'It's terrible, isn't it? And happening to a man like you.'

David looked into the open, rucked face of somebody who apparently believed that with a certain standard of education you disqualified yourself from vicissitude. He wanted to make a gesture towards Cyril; moved, he stood still.

His mother provided lunch, allowed him to help with manual dish washing so that talk could be extended for a quarter of an hour, then shoved him off towards Derby.

'I've heard nothing from them,' she said. 'Not that I expected anything.'

163

'Family failing.'

'I don't make them out, David.'

'She wears the trousers.'

'Mr Stiles doesn't say much, certainly.'

'He does as he's told because his wife's good at organizing, but he has his little reservations. He's a bit crafty.'

'Do you think he's upset by what's happened?'

'Yes. Because it's disturbed Eva and that means trouble for him. Otherwise, I don't think Mary can do any wrong where he's concerned.'

'Was he against her marrying you?'

'Not at all. But when she changes her mind, his changes with her.'

As he drove towards Derby he felt pleased that he could propound such views without doing violence to himself. Their truth was doubtful, but his mother was comforted to find him capable of laying down the law.

The Stileses hovered, ready for him, for anything.

Their lounge, upstairs over the shop, faced north and this afternoon seemed unusually dark under the piling clouds. The couple bustled offering hospitality, tea, coffee, sherry, a full biscuit tin, the electric light. They inquired after his health; he answered, at the same time refusing sustenance; the gas fire hissed to overwarm solemn furniture. Both parents-in-law had dressed for the occasion; the line of father's white shirt shone below the navy blue sleeves. He wore gold cufflinks.

David explained that he could not stay long, that he had to go home, collect his instrument and concert gear to be at the Poly for rehearsal at six. Eva Stiles asked intelligent questions about the programme, seemed interested in what he said about the difficulties of performing Shostakovich. Without embarrassment she recalled Mary's learning Alban Berg songs during one holiday from the college. Father constantly hitched his trousers to prevent bagging at the knees.

In the end, after a silence, Mrs Stiles sat a little straighter as if to announce that real business was at hand.

'After you rang yesterday dinnertime,' she began, and stopped. 'We were very busy. Rushed off our feet, and the two lads

164

we have in on Saturdays are no more use than ornament. But after I talked to you, it worried me all afternoon. It bothers me, I can tell you, most of the time, but I thought, there you were, ringing up, coming over the next day, and we'd heard not a thing. I mean we'd written, twice, and you, and your mother, and we'd tried to get in touch by phone and not a peep from her in reply, and it didn't seem good enough. It smarted with me all afternoon. I said as much to Dad, on the one occasion we had two minutes spare, but we were busy. When we closed at six, we didn't clear up as we usually do on week nights, I said we'd do it this morning, we plonked ourselves down in the dining room for a bit of a meal, we don't want much except a pot of tea, you're not hungry after a day like that . . .'

'We ought to go out for dinner,' Stiles said. 'Now and again.'

'You don't want it, and I don't. All I need is to get my shoes off and my slippers on and rest my hipbones. Any road, when we'd had our bit of a snack I said to Dad, it came to me suddenly, "I'm going to have a bath," we'd got the immersion on, "and while I do I want you to ring her up." ' Mrs Stiles stopped again. 'You should have seen his face. And heard the excuses. Wasn't it too late? "It's early afternoon there," I said. What should he say? I'd do it a lot better than he would. "George," I said, "just ask her what she thinks she's doing, and if she's not there leave a message for her to ring us. She'll know if it's you ringing it's serious." '

George Stiles wriggled.

'So I went off and George tried. It was Saturday afternoon. I hadn't thought of that. But in the end he got through to somebody who said he'd leave her a message.'

'They're back, are they?' David asked.

'I know no more than you do.'

'And you've heard nothing.'

'No, we have not. But at least we tried.'

'Who answered?' David asked, sorry for his father-in-law.

'Some man.' George sat straight. 'You can't tell from the way these Americans talk whether he's a professor or the caretaker. Eva should have done it. She'd have nailed him down. I was bemused what with the dialling and waiting.'

'Don't you dial straight through?'

'Yes. But there's a bit of a gap. And then I thought nobody was ever going to answer the thing once it started ringing their end. But I hung on. And then this man picked it up, in time, but he didn't say who he was. I explained who I was, and who she was. He seemed to get it, told me he'd leave the message. He didn't say whether the opera was there or not.' Stiles looked apologetically towards his wife.

'Thanks anyway,' David nodded, frowning.

'We don't know where she is, or what she's doing,' Mrs Stiles began angrily. 'It's like searching in a fog.' She continued in this vein, easing herself, alarming the men. Her spleen brought her no relief, nettled them. As if she felt bound to instruct them she recited what she knew of Mary's stay in America, looking now and again to David for additions or corrections that were not forthcoming. The men satisfied themselves with a silence as gloomy as the room.

At the conclusion of the performance, she went outside to the lavatory, and noisily returning pressed David to a cup of tea, a piece of cake baked that morning.

'You'll need it,' she said, 'if you're playing. I know what it's like. A mug of urn rubbish and two arrowroots.' She laughed vividly as David capitulated. He ate his way slowly through a slab of delicious fruit cake he did not want, and then fought off her attempts to cut him a second slice.

He rose as the clock struck four.

'I don't like to think of you there all on your own,' Eva said. 'I don't know how you've put up with it, all these weeks. You must have more patience than I have.'

'Not very hard,' Stiles said, back of hand.

'Listen to that. Swearing like a navvy this morning he was just because he dropped a bag of nails.' She laughed again, mirthlessly, hard and high.

'I didn't use any words you didn't know.'

'And I wouldn't be too sure about that.'

They were uncomfortable, this pair, distressed on his behalf, niggling at each other. She cut and wrapped him a slab of cake as he left.

'We'll be in touch,' Eva shouted, too loudly, on the pavement. One or two interested Sunday pedestrians dawdled past.

'We'll let you know if we hear anything. And ring us up if you're short of company.'

'You do that,' Stiles said, 'and don't forget.'

David shook hands with George, kissed Eva, who for a second in profile reminded him of Mary, a caricature perhaps, but her mother. The two fussed excitedly out here as if they'd done their duty; he guessed they'd be glad to be rid of him. In person he blighted their Sunday afternoon's peace, but once he'd disappeared he'd be an interesting topic of conversation. As he drove away the parents waved, making something of it, seeing him out of their lives, regretful, not unthankful for the entertainment. He dismissed his speculations, centred interest on Shostakovich.

He had not been in his house twenty minutes before the phone rang.

'I'm glad I've got you.' Frederick Payne. 'I've been trying since three. Can you pick Walter Wilkinson up about quarter to six tonight? His car's kaput again.' He gave the address. 'I'll see he gets back, but I'm supposed to go out to value a fiddle; I'll only just make it. If I hadn't caught you this time, I'd have had to cancel it.'

'You're busy on Sundays?'

'Somebody's always asking me to do something. I s'll be glad to go this afternoon, though. It'll take my mind off Shostakovich.'

'We shan't have much time on that.'

'Play it straight through. Hear what it sounds like in their hall. Glad I caught you. I thought you said you'd be home later.' He described the route. 'I'll tell Walt to be ready.'

Wilkinson opened the front door to David.

'Come on in,' he said. 'While I get my coat on.'

In front of a gas fire Wilkinson's wife sat with a small girl on her knee. The child, perhaps two or three years old, had been bathed, so that her golden, fine hair was still damp, with darker flat stripes on the soft halo. She wore a long nightgown and stared at the visitor with large eyes.

'Lorna, this is David Blackwall. You've heard me speak about him.'

Mrs Wilkinson smiled. She looked no older than Mary, in

167

jeans and a white blouse. She lowered the book of stories in greeting.

'Read it, Mummy,' the child whispered.

'In a minute, chick.'

'What is it?' David asked. 'A fairy tale?'

The girl quite violently buried her face in her mother's breast.

'That's Emma,' Wilkinson said.

'Hello, Emma.'

The child did not move, sat still enough to conceal breathing.

'She's shy,' Mrs Wilkinson said.

'Till you get to know her.' Proud father.

Mrs Wilkinson put an arm tighter about her daughter. She seemed an untidy young woman, fair hair loose, in shabby jeans, but smiling, much at home, showing large, even teeth. Her hands were red though the skin of her arms was pale, gold-furred.

'It's early upstairs tonight,' she said. 'We've been to Nana's. My dad had to bring us home. Walt's car broke down.'

'Is this the usual bedtime?' David asked.

'As long as she's in by seven.'

'And this is number two,' Wilkinson stood by the table on which lay a carrycot. David looked in. A very small bald baby slept under a ribboned quilt. 'That's Sarah Amelia.'

'How old is she?' David asked the mother.

'Seven weeks tomorrow.'

He noticed that Lorna's blouse was discoloured, splashed at both breasts. Emma had resumed her upright pose. Wilkinson had left the room. On the wall above the gas fire incongruously shone mounted crossed swords over a heraldic shield.

'They keep you busy, I expect,' David said.

'Between the three of them.'

'Yes.'

'He'll be calling out for a handkerchief in minute.' She smiled, easily, painlessly; she would know the answer.

'Read it, Mummy.' This time the child's voice had a small, forceful clarity.'

'When Daddy's gone. In a minute.'

'Do you get broken nights?'

168

'Yes. But we can't grumble. She's not too bad.'

Lorna Wilkinson crossed her legs, lifting her daughter. She leaned back, unembarrassed, seemingly very young. One could meet a dozen such in the cloakroom of any disco. She wore uneven mauve eyeshadow and her short fingernails were plum-dark red; her shoes had ridiculously crippling high heels.

'She's a good baby. They both are. Weren't you, chick?' She hugged Emma to her. Wilkinson returned in dark raincoat. 'You've found the hankie I put out for you?'

'Yes, thanks. We'll be off now. I shouldn't be late. We'll have it over for half past nine. You go to bed, if you want.'

He bent to kiss his daughter, wife, and then dipped into the cot.

'Right.' He rattled the 'r' for David, an adult. 'Bye-bye.'

In the car he complained about his banger, but without ferocity, as if his family had softened him. After a minute he jerked inside his seatbelt.

'Lorna's not keen on our turning professional,' Wilkinson said.

'What about you?'

'Starting kids on the fiddle bores me stiff. But travelling round wouldn't suit, either. That's if we made it. Still, you can't have everything.'

'What will you do?'

'I don't know. Wait. I'm putting it off until Bob Knight comes. I mean, if I stay the Education Committee's quite likely to cut down on peripatetic music teaching. They regard that as expendable. I'm in two minds. It'd be different if I were a bachelor.'

'Is your wife a musician?'

'Not professionally. She sang in the Harmonic and the Bach. She worked at the Central Library.'

Wilkinson sucked his cheeks in sombre reverie.

A caretaker led them into a hall where Payne and Barton were already occupied in discussion.

'Big place.' Wilkinson cocked a suspicious eye after greetings.

'And only a small audience,' Payne answered.

169

'The students have been invited,' Barton told them. 'Not that many will come.'

'Will you try the light?' The caretaker wore a suit. 'I stepped the bulb up, and put another by in case that one blows.' Payne fiddled for the switch.

'Can you raise it a couple of inches?' the leader asked. More time wasted.

'We'll try the Mozart for volume,' Payne said. 'Bit of the first movement, and anything else you want, and then we'll do the whole shebang of Shostakovich.' They removed their coats in no hurry, prepared to play.

'Have we got a room somewhere?' Payne quizzed the caretaker, and tiptoed round, unwilling to sit.

'Just through the door there. Not very spacious, but you won't have far to walk. Cloakroom just across the passage. Shall I show you?'

'Are you in a hurry? To go?'

'No. I might just as well sit here and listen to you.'

He took his seat in the middle of the front row, where he swelled his chest, crossing his arms, proprietorially.

They began the Mozart, confidently, stopping at the first double bar.

'Beautiful sound,' Payne said.

'And we can hear one another.'

'Let's do it again, so we aren't caught out.'

They completed the movement this time enjoying themselves.

'I'd like the Adagio,' Barton said. 'Or some of it.'

'How's the time?'

'Twenty-five past six.' David.

'Right. I want us out of here at half seven or soon after.'

They smiled, satisfied with the big sound of their Mozart.

'Now then. Shostakovich. As if this were the real thing. Blind on straight through. We'll pick up the bits and pieces when we've done that.'

They played cautiously at first, then, caught up, strongly, as if amazed at their progress. The concert performance two hours later touched, snarled, hung sobbing amongst the wide spaces, the empty seats, with a hundred or so spectators jolted, goaded, arm-broken into sympathy by the plangency of sound. True, the four told one another there were still too many mistakes, weak joints, awkwardnesses, but their fear furbished their skill and the composer's shattered art shouted his apprehension, his sorrow, his clawing for stars. Only when the Trent Quartet had finished their concert did they grasp quite what they had done; talent and terror had united.

'Some bloody good playing,' Payne congratulated them as they cased their instruments.

'We got somewhere near it.' Barton.

'How about it, David?' Wilkinson asked, as if the few minutes inside his home justified the intimacy of questioning.

'It was good,' David answered. 'And puzzling. As if we didn't quite make out what we were doing so well.'

'That's exactly right.' Barton, bemused.

A handful of the audience broke in on them garrulously. A bottle of champagne was opened for their benefit, but the effect was spoilt when they had to drink from teacups. The recipient of the concert, a stout man with untidy hair and insecure spectacles, thanked them but vaguely as if he had difficulty in recalling what they had done for him. His wife boomed out her pleasure. The principal of the place, grey hair smoothed down over his square white face, a trio of subordinates at his shoulder even on Sunday, arranged words into three banal sentences. A balding man, with a red, lively, Jewish face, touched Barton's arm.

'Great, Cyril,' he said, 'great. Thanks.'

'Shostakovich must have been a poor, lost sod.'

'You showed us how much. It was superb. I've never heard that better played, on record or off. You'd fathomed it.'

'Who was that?' David, who'd been close by, asked when the man darted away.

'Joe Horowitz. A mathematician. Family all killed in Auschwitz. They didn't know how he stayed alive. He'd be three or so at the time.' The age of Emma Wilkinson. 'Some English professor adopted him. I don't think he's got over whatever it was he saw.' Cyril watched the congratulatory antics with a guarded expression. 'It doesn't seem right that

171

Shostakovich is battered about and all the result is a retiring present for some stuffed shirt.'

' "Butchered to make a Roman holiday." '

Cyril's expression cleared, and he laughed out loud, committing himself with gusto. 'That's good,' he said. 'It really is.'

David guessed that Barton had worried himself that his colleague might be unable to bear Shostakovich's collateral grief, and was relieved to find himself wrong. Pleased with his knockabout psychologizing he offered to take Wilkinson back.

'I like Cyril Barton,' he said to Walter in the car.

'He's all right. Bit of an old woman.'

'How old is he?'

'Just a year or two older than Fred. Thirty-five, perhaps.'

'I thought he was more than that.'

'He's mean,' Wilkinson answered, at a tangent. 'Wouldn't give the parings of his fingernails away.'

'Was he an only child?'

'Yes. And his parents were getting on, from what he says. I was one of five.'

'Are the others musicians?'

'Two of my brothers are brass players like my dad. An uncle left us a fiddle in his will; that's why I started. How do you get on with Fred?'

'Payne? He's good.'

'He's a homo, you know.' A throwaway whisper.

'Does that make any difference?'

Wilkinson struggled largely in his seat.

'Can't help it, can he? Funny chap. I knew him a bit at the Royal Manchester. He was ahead of me. Bit of a big noise. Led the orchestra and so forth. He wants to drag the rest of us along with him and his ambitions.'

'And you don't approve?'

'I don't know about that. You're either one hundred per cent behind Fred, or you're out. He got rid of Jon Mahon. Oh, I know he left for Australia, and all the rest of it, but he knew Fred didn't want him, was fetching Knighty down. Jon tried to do it on him by nipping off without notice and saying nothing. That's why we're lucky with you. You don't think of taking it up, do you? As a career?'

'No.'

'Fred's weighing you up, I reckon. He's not sure about me, but keeps me on because I play well. He knows the sounds I make are as good as his, if not better. And that's what you need as number two. A bloody good player who practises and doesn't go in for ideas above his station. He'll out me if I don't fall in with his plans, I tell you. The reason I asked you was that when Bob Knight arrives there'll be ructions. Between him and Fred. Knighty can play, he's better than some fancy soloists, but he's aggressive and high-spirited, all for a barney. Fred'll let anybody argue; he'll listen to you for a bit, but he's got to be the leader.'

'Isn't that as it should be?'

Wilkinson looked across, considering.

'Yes, if he knows what he's on with. Somebody's got to make his mind up. He's also very good at organizing practices. He knows when to go over bad patches, and when to leave them. You don't waste much time at rehearsals; you'll have noticed that. But once old Jocko Knight appears there'll be bust-ups, I reckon. And that's why he's so pleased to have found you. He'll waft you in Knight's face; a Cambridge man who can play.'

'And is this good for the quartet?'

'There have to be stresses. There are bound to be, it stands to sense. But a good leader'll use them. He's made me feel uncomfortable these last few weeks because I wouldn't turn out every hour of the day and night to rehearse this Shostakovich. Oooh, yes. A hint there, a plain prod here. He's let me know.'

They had arrived outside Wilkinson's house.

'Are you coming in?' He consulted his watch. 'Nine twenty.'

'No, thanks.'

'What would you do if you were in my position?' Wilkinson asked.

'I can't answer that, because I don't know how successful you'll be. Presumably you have a mortgage. Would your wife mind your being away at nights?'

'Yes. She'd put up with it, especially if we were making money.'

'Which you won't be for a start?'

'That's the snag. We're starting late. It might be some years before we get recognized. I've some private pupils I'll be able to fit in. Jim Talbot'll find me casual work. I think Lorna wants me to give it a whirl. I'm the one dragging his feet. I thought I quite liked a flutter. What did you think about your wife going to America?'

'She would have regretted not taking the chance.'

'And you let her go. If she makes a success of it, you might never get her back. Not in the old sense. She'll be dodging about the world.'

'That's so.'

'And you still let her go?' Question and statement.

'The financial situation's different from yours.'

'I see that.'

David, suddenly reduced, debated whether to unburden himself to the man, decided against it.

'We did ourselves proud tonight,' he said, dredging the muddy sentence up.

'Ye'. Thanks for the lift, then. Seeing yer.'

Wilkinson had left the car, slammed the door and disappeared up the entry of his house, quick as a snake.

For the first time David saw the face of the street, a well-built terrace of workmen's cottages, each decorated differently with bright colours. One had white shutters; several flush doors. Curtains varied; pink lace to heavy yellow; one or two tenants had replaced the sash windows with black lengths of plate glass. Families lived here; made their mark. Fifty years ago, the doors would have been brown, varnished with artificial combed grain; only wear and tear marking off one from another. Now doors and windows, drainpipes and ledges had the garishness of a fairground.

That represented human effort. Men pleased their wives and established their egos with this free-for-all do-it-yourself.

He did not like it.

174

15

David spent the last Thursday and Friday of his Easter holiday with the Trent in Lincolnshire. They performed on Wednesday evening in Stamford; drove north early next morning to Cleethorpes where they demonstrated themselves about the district for two days in secondary schools, already launched into their summer term; and concluded with Haydn, Mozart and Beethoven, on the Saturday in Lincoln Cathedral. David drove back in the darkness, over flat roads, to Newark, along the Fosse, tired.

He had wasted his time; fatigue plagued his limbs; he yawned all the way.

Tomorrow, without a rehearsal, he would lounge about, preparing for the opening of term on Monday. He would see nobody, as his parents were holidaying in Cornwall; he would eat out of the fridge and since he had done no shopping would need to scout round for bread before he could have breakfast. He had not enjoyed the trip as he had expected; they had played together a good deal, had socialized with schoolteachers and culture-vultures while he had drunk more beer, precious little at that, than he had for months. The three nights in bedrooms in small hotels had not been uncomfortable, but the scratch nature of the school performances, nothing longer than a Mozart first movement, seemed unnecessarily unsatisfactory. The pupils looked interested enough, listening passively; even the final full concert in the cathedral had disappointed. The organizers blamed each other for lack of publicity, and certainly the audience was not large, seeming to crouch in dwarf rows round the quartet whose playing, good enough, precise, vibrant at the point of origin, long-bowed, dissipated itself into the huge darkening spaces of that great building. The prodigality of ordered stone about them diminished Mozart and Beethoven; he had never felt this before. It was as though the Lord God hovered and listened, a Jehovah compared to whom the divine sonorities of these gifted beings were as the lisping babble of a child learning to talk. He knew, and he regretted the knowledge, for the first time that music had limitations, that in eternity one would not listen to Mozart.

Perhps he was at fault. His colleagues were not displeased. This was to them the beginning of their professional career; some hundreds of people who had previously been ignorant of their existence now could name, remember the Trent Quartet. They had started, and saying little, keeping fingers crossed, went down to their houses, justified.

'Have you enjoyed it?' Barton in the windy darkness in Lincoln on the castle hill where they had parked. Payne and Wilkinson were staying behind in the Bell for a last drink.

'Yes. Very good.'

Barton pulled himself up from the boot where he was stowing away a portmanteau, took two or three steps over towards David, who stood as if uncertain of his next action.

'You'll have to put her out of your mind, David. Sooner or later.'

David Blackwall nodded; Barton might, like Cicero, have spoken Greek.

'There's plenty going for you, however it looks now.'

'I suppose so.'

'You can't let her ruin your life. I know that's what it seems like, but you'll get over it. I've been meaning to say this to you all week, but I could never find a minute when there wasn't somebody else about. But you looked so down in the mouth.' That surprised David, who had been sprightlier than usual, he flattered himself. 'You get over these things to a large extent. They might even bring good.'

'Thanks, Cyril.'

'I bet you wonder who I am to be poking my nose in. A bachelor. A mother's boy. But I think I know your,' he paused, 'desolation.' The word struck chilly in that place of thick shadows and stars. 'And you mustn't let it beat you.'

'No.'

'I like you, David. It's been a privilege for me to have dealings with you. And I won't have you cripped for life.' He backed away immediately and slammed down the open boot lid. He sniggered, a trivial, vulgar sound. 'Here endeth the lesson.' David saluted as Barton drove off.

Not three miles out of the town he passed Cyril, hooted, yawning, raised a hand. He could not make out whether the signal was returned.

'I won't have you crippled for life.' He examined the words, over, over again, but they had no relevance to his situation. He had not allowed this to maim him; he'd worked, occupied the corners of his soul, bent his will so that he believed he could live without Mary. These last three months had proved it. Driving fast, but without danger, he fought to check the squalls in his head. His pride had taken a thrashing; he could not yet easily confess to others that his wife had left him for another man. He could barely grasp that this was possible; the likelihood pained rawly. He turned off at Newark, still wrestling with himself; later he rounded the traffic island built above a Roman army camp at Margidunum, crossed the Trent, half closed his eyes against the dipped headlights of returning revellers. Bedroom windows in Burton Joyce were illuminated; people had had enough of the day, or stripped for the last rites, love.

By the time he had closed his garage doors he was almost asleep. The house smelt damply stale, the letters on the hall floor were uninteresting, three advertisements, one telling him that he had won a prize, and that if he claimed it by merely signing this form and posting it off at once he was in line for a Mini-Metro, a bill, the demand exactly as he had calculated, and a note from a university friend inviting him and Mary to a wedding. He poured out orange juice, swigged it down, decided he could wait neither for a bath, nor for his electric blanket to warm his bed, staggered upstairs, dragged his clothes off and was asleep inside five minutes.

The telephone disturbed him next morning.

Seven thirty. Nobody rang him at that time on Sunday. He ran downstairs in his pyjamas, expecting a wrong number.

'Hello, David Blackwall.'

At least they'd hung on.

'Hello, David. It's me. Mrs Stiles.' His mother-in-law had never quite known how to name herself in his presence.

177

'Ah, hello.

'David, we've heard from Mary.'

Why had the silly woman stopped? He had no inclination towards social prodding.

'She's coming home.'

The sentence stirred him, but strictly within the context of his lethargy. He felt improperly awake, yet, his father's expression, rousted about. Breathing became instantly difficult. He seemed to hold the telephone to his ear only by some long-acquired habit.

'She rang Friday. I've been trying to get you ever since. That's why I've rung early. I thought you might be going out again.'

'I've been in Lincolnshire.'

'That'll be the reason then. She rang about nine, our time, on Friday, to say she was coming back.'

'When?'

'She's not sure. Soon. This week perhaps.'

'What about the opera?'

'It's done, finished.'

Mrs Stiles was in no hurry. Why didn't she anticipate his questions, overflood him with information, instead of idling about with her snippets?'

'She didn't say a great deal, really.'

'Is she going back?' David asked.

'Going back? Where?'

'To America.'

'That's not my impression. She's coming home for good.'

Again they paused. These pitiful bits of sentences carried enormous weight, stress.

'Is she coming back here?' he began again. 'Home? To me?'

'No, David.' The voice mumbled, sluggish, miserable. 'To us. To Derby.'

'Did she say anything about me?'

'Well, when she told us this, I said, "Am I to tell David?" and she said I could please myself.'

'What about this Gage man?' He could only bear to name him in such terms.

'She hardly said anything. I took it that was over, though she

178

didn't say as much. She seemed very low. Not like her. It worried me.'

'And what did you say?'

'What could I? I said she'd be welcome.'

'What about the opera, then?'

'As far as I could make out, they came back to New York, went to Yale, would that be right?, and just finished. There were no more performances wanted. The conductor, Ulrich, had gone off somewhere else. It just finished.'

'And left her without work?'

'Well, yes. I should think so. She didn't say.'

'And she said nothing about coming back to me?'

'No. She didn't. She wasn't very talkative. And I was flabbergasted. She wasn't sure of anything, the air flight, the day, anything.'

'Did she seem worried? Or ill?'

'Well, yes. Listless. As if it was all too much trouble to bother. We've got her old bedroom ready for her, so it don't matter much when she arrives. We'll have to make her welcome, whether we like it or not. I said to her dad, "She's our child, whatever she's done." But I also told him, "We've got to keep David informed." '

'Thank you.'

'That's only your right. You let her go, and many husbands wouldn't, and then she acts as she has.' She stopped, staggered again into speech. 'Anyhow that's all I know, David; I ought to have asked her more questions, but I was so taken by surprise. I mean, afterwards you think of all the things you should have said. But as soon as I know anything else, I'll be in touch. I'm that relieved to get you. I just think if she'd come back and somebody had seen her, and said something to you, and you didn't know a blind thing about it. What would you have thought of us?'

'What does George say?'

'He's like me. Only this morning, when I told him I was going to have another go to get hold of you, he said, "You never get shot of 'em, however old they are." ' She paused. 'Will you pass the news on to your mother? I've been ringing her as well to try and find out where you were, but they were never in.'

179

'They're away on holiday.'

'That accounts for it.' Mrs Stiles hummed to herself, and David half-heartedly tried to make out her tune, failing. 'If she does say anything about coming back to you . . . ?'

'I've already written that if she wanted it, I'd take her.'

'That's good. O' course, that was when there didn't seem any chance of it happening, wasn't it?' The woman was either shrewd or malicious.

'I meant it.' He sounded pompous, portentous even to himself.

'I know you did. Well, I'll ring off now. Are you all right, David? I ought to have asked you before.'

'Yes. Thank you.'

Mrs Stiles advised him to keep eating. 'You've got to live, and it's no use doing other.' David prepared himself for a homily that did not materialize, for she breathed in, said, 'Goodbye,' and put the phone down.

He sat in rumpled pyjamas trying to make sense of the room about him.

After breakfast, he decided against even a token cooking of lunch, and lounged about with the Sunday newspapers which interested him less than usual. They seemed fit only to litter the floor. He had no excitement, merely a sense of grievance that just as he was about to come to terms with trouble, the situation radically altered itself. He bought a loaf, tomatoes and a packet of biscuits from a Pakistani shopkeeper who politely informed him that though the weather was unseasonably cool, he could do nothing about it. The smiling teeth, the dusky, pale-palmed, illustratively waving hand matched his own mood. He had flung down, not half-read, an article about starving children in Somalia not because it added to his discomfort, but because he lacked the mental energy to complete it. The world was heavy with death, avoidable tragedy; his present state rejected the conclusion placed it on a par with reports of politicians' rant or literary chitchat. He opened a tin of chopped pork and was about to sit down to that, tomatoes and pickles, when his mother rang from St Austell to find out about the Lincolnshire venture.

His brief résumé was interrupted by a gabble about a morn-

180

ing service the older Blackwalls had attended. The singing had been poor, the organ playing dull, the parson's sermon almost a caricature and yet Joan had been moved.

'Not until we came out,' she said. 'Then I realized that the place had been holy for generations. Don't you think there's something in that?'

'Yes. Larkin said as much.'

'You sound grumpy. Well, never mind.'

'There's been news of Mary.'

That put religion out of her mind.

He told her what he knew, parried her excitable questions from his lack of knowledge. At the end of ten minutes, she asked, 'What have you decided to do, then?'

'Nothing.'

'I can see I shall get no sense out of you.' She might have been laughing. 'Will you go to see her?'

'I expect so. When she arrives and I know a bit more.'

His mother was volatile with advice; his father was due, he guessed, for a lively afternoon.

When he rang off he wished he had been more cooperative with his mother. She meant well. She had vigorously promised to get in touch tomorrow and had ordered him to think positively.

'You sound like a politician.'

'You mustn't lose her for want of trying.'

'Are you sure I want her back?'

She didn't easily give up. He left the phone with his eardrums ringing, and ate with distaste. He could not think what he should do, but cautioned himself not to be surprised by this. He was emotionally bruised; pain, grief, uncertainty racked him. Mary had thrown him down. With some shame he remembered how one night soon after he was convinced she would not return, he had taken his car and driven out to Trent Bridge to stand on the embankment in the windy darkness at quarter to eleven. All the way there a voiceless fiat had scored itself on his body, not only in the aching head but in shoulders, chest, belly, backbone: Drown yourself, drown yourself. The diktat seemed forcibly sensible, but impersonal and in no way connected with black water, cold mud, a sodden corpse. At the same time he knew he would not do it.

181

He had stepped from his car.

The river flowed high, greasy with the reflected distant streetlights. Above, ripped clouds raced across the luminous patch round the moon. He could hear wind and water; his hair joined the disturbance; chill nibbled at his face.

All he had to do was walk forward from the road once he had stepped over the low fence, cross the grass and the pedestrian way, negotiate the steps, and head into the river. His distress urged him forward, fuelling mad resolve, but he knew he could not. In spite of loss, the total wreck of happiness, there seemed inbuilt inside him a common sense, an everyday rationality, a kind of formidable schoolmastery which had refused permission. When he had considered this later he had decided that his affliction, desperate as it seemed, earth-shattering, must have been weak, small, compared with that of men who hacked their throats open with cut-throat razors or drove headlong into brick walls. Perhaps he was pathologically incapable of such intensity of feeling. But if one way, why not at the other end of the scale? Was he capable of love? It felt so, but he would not die for its non-requital.

He had stood that night, injured on the road, flattening his jigging hair with a gloved limb, keeping it parted. With a shudder, he dared himself to lift his feet over the railings, to march the few paces across wet, wintry grass, smack down on the flat, tread the broad concrete steps where holidaying children sat in summer, to take a position at the bottom, on the concrete, within inches of the fast lapping of revelling floodwater. He did so and once there did not move, held himself still, testing himself.

Then he had nodded at the river, in formal acknowledgement, and made a firm way back to the car, jinking his keys. For the moment he had assuaged his grief, if not for good. Broken pride, longing, embarrassment, frustrated desire would rack him again, but inside, it seemed, a limit had been imposed on himself by himself. Next time he was in trouble, he would put it into words, he could 'do a Trent Bridge'. He remembered his father's mock use of an expression of surprise from his childhood, 'Well, I'll go to Trent Bridge.' He had been and standing there, had achieved something, a lowly place in the second division of love.

Baffled now, he decided he'd take himself out.

He drove once again through the city, past fading warehouses, duller clutters of modern housing complexes, but parked this side of the Trent. Though it was Sunday, a heavy drizzle kept people indoors. David, pulling up the hood of his anorak, walked down to the river again in the grey light. This wet spring the waters were high, threatening. He repeated some lines he had learned for A-level:

> The moving waters at their priest-like task
> Of pure ablution round earth's human shores,

picked with his toe end at the pattern scored on the concrete under his feet. The rain seemed both fine and heavy as he lifted his face. Keats's words meant nothing to him, mumbo-jumbo round one shell on the human shore, nor had this place any significance. Back to the road he walked hard under dripping trees; a pair of lovers kissed but they were in his eyes damp and disheartened. A woman clung on to the leash of a bull terrier; a smart, elderly man with a flat golfing cap and walking stick told him it wasn't pleasant.

'No,' David answered, half stopping.

'But my garden can do with any amount of this.'

He was away, the ferule of his stick tapping militarily.

David took a rapid tour of the memorial gardens where pruned rose bushes dripped, flowerless as yet. He tried a second circuit, equally unsatisfactory, before he stopped to read the names of the war dead. They meant nothing; his aesthetic judgement of the shape of the arches or the lettering meant more than the deaths these ordinary ranks, names, initials represented. What had happened to him in the last few months was as nothing compared with the grief splitting these hundreds of families caused by faceless governments and their decisions. Unenfranchised women mourned. The men who returned remembered bloody mud, stench, dirty fingernails on a headless corpse, trees and brickwork ripped to shreds. There were no Blackwalls commemorated. This piece of minor civic architecture pointed its lesson, they shall not grow old, in vain. 'They carry back bright to the coiner the mintage of man.' It was as nothing, but it was all that a silly city could do, and he, wifeless with wife returning, stared miserably at the polluted, wet marble or limestone, he did not know which. It represented the uselessness of the world, and his ignorance, gold letters and black on white, discolouring stone spelt out the message, 'We had back luck,' like a casual postcard from some foreign part.

It was raining more heavily; one could hear the rattle fall on the leaves of evergreens. His sinuses pained; his trousers below the anorak were damp. Dragging his mind together, he ran back to his car, arriving breathless. He had passed no one; the few pedestrians had disappeared from the face of the unsympathetic earth. He peeled off his anorak, thrust it to the floor, drove home.

He fell asleep in front of the gas fire, was woken by the telephone. Fred Payne.

'I'm glad I've caught you. Is June 18th free? A Saturday? We've been offered a double concert in Hull. Saturday and Sunday. They want the first Rasoumovsky.'

David dolefully filled in his diary.

'What if I hadn't been at liberty?' He felt awkward.

'We couldn't have done it.'

'The others are all right?'

'Yes. We haven't long, have we?'

'Do we play the same programme twice?'

'We'll need to think about it. Not very enterprising, is it, though?'

David stood condemned.

'I'll look the Beethoven over,' he said.

'Thanks.'

The word displeased him, and disgruntled he asked himself why he should exert himself to support the Trent, when they'd drop him in August on Robert Knight's advent without a qualm. He fell asleep unanswered.

Preparation for examinations, the school summer concert, a proposed trip to London occupied him in the next few days. On Thursday morning Mrs Stiles rang him at work to say her husband had driven down to Heathrow to collect Mary.

184

'What time are they due home?'

'About four o'clock.'

'Do you want me to do anything?'

'I don't think so.'

'Shall I come over?'

'No. We'll see how she is. I'll ask her what she thinks. That'll be the best. I've no idea what she'll be like. She just gave us the time of her plane. She sounded whacked.' The short sentences dropped like dominoes, spelling his defeat. 'You never know in any case, with these flights. They're often delayed. I'll ring you as soon as I know anything definite.'

'It's not very satisfactory.'

He took the call in the office of the head of the music department, surrounded by boxfiles and scores, records, cassettes, the classical repertoire meticulously neat. There was nobody about, but he expected any minute some lout would burst in for a book or an instrument.

'I think that's best, David. We none of us knows where we are.'

'Who's helping you in the shop today?'

'Mrs Thomas. You haven't met her.'

'Is this your half-day?'

'No.' He heard a second voice raised in query. 'I shall have to go.' Relief with exasperation. 'I'll ring you as soon as I can.'

She put down the phone; he went back, to ear tests for O-level.

Surprisingly his spirit lifted, so that he took rehearsals, practised that evening with élan as if on the edge of renewal. He refused a theatre ticket for Thursday evening, sat at home with his cello waiting for a telephone which stayed mute. Mrs Stiles did not get in touch with him until Saturday morning when she asked him over for a meal at eight that night.

'How does she seem?' he asked.

'Not too bad.'

'Has she said anything about returning?'

'I can't . . . Over the phone, y'know.'

Mary, presumably, had come into the room. Less than twenty miles away, with two nights in an English bed behind her, in the smell of the shop and kitchen she made an entrance at an

185

awkward moment. He hurried out of the place with his Saturday lists to preclude thought. The rest of the morning was wasted on household chores, on list-making and marking; he took lunch deliberately late, practised desultorily, weeded in the borders, gave up, watched television grudgingly, went back to Beethoven. Time would not move for him. He needed every few minutes to shift his haunches from one seat to another.

By six, he had bathed, dressed himself in slacks, an open-necked cream shirt, a new dark brown pullover. With shoes polished, hair schoolboyishly tidy he sat about his house shivering. He tried to imagine the Stileses' living room. By now the shop would have just closed, though George would probably be below there still, with his pocket calculator or his checklists keeping out of the way of the women upstairs. Eva would be sitting down to a cup of tea, shoes off, vigorously grousing about the stupidity of customers, travellers, the young men in to help, her husband. Before long she would make precise inquiries about the meal, soup, a salad with ham and tongue, a sherry trifle she had left to Mary to supervise. Once she was convinced that the preparations did her credit, she would shyly ask Mary what she intended towards David, Only the tone of voice would be diffident, not the form of questions. She feared her daughter, knew she had grown beyond her; it was highly probable that they barely shared a single, moral, social, political view, and yet she believed that the girl could be caught napping as earlier she had been certain that a crafty examiner could seize on the scale Mary played or sang most weakly, and damn her with it. She had worked in ignorance then, melodic or harmonic minor were merely names, but she knew once she had established a reasonable doubt Mary's own intelligence would do the rest.

'What are you going to say to him?' she'd be asking shortly.

David, even catching in his mind the exact intonation of the question, could not return the answer. Now, when weeks of his spare time had been painfully spent accounting to himself for his wife's behaviour, for he could easily imagine the raw temptation which had led her to fall for Red Gage and the opportunities he represented. To abort her child, to dump her marriage in order to achieve musical consequence seemed

186

understandable, hardly even reprehensible. In a new country, flattered and admired, he himself might have acted no differently. But to come back, creeping back, and to Derby, was incomprehensible. Perhaps her permit had run out; he did not know how long she had applied to stay. The hiatus of ignorance appalled; he had let his wife disappear from his life with no more inquiry than on a half-day trip to a stately home. Mary must have been battered. She'd not return if she could have prospered, survived, or marginally existed there. And *Semele*. That must have collapsed past devastation.

He used the last minutes before the starting time he had decided on so carelessly, so indecisively that he set off later than he expected, but found no trouble. The roads to Derby were relatively free of Saturday-night traffic. At two minutes to eight he had parked in the side street fifty yards from the shop. As he locked his car, he bluntly asked himself what he'd know next time he inserted his key. A clock chimed, eight, from the open door of a terraced house. A West Indian, well-dressed elderly man came into the small front garden and adjusted his trilby hat. Grey jacket, sky-blue shirt, multicoloured tie, trousers with turn-ups, suede shoes. He nodded at David, then turned back with a start into the still open door, closing it behind him. David gave himself a little time to wait for the re-emergence. Nothing happened.

He turned the corner. The rear of the shop was reached by an entry and then a passage behind four backyards with short gardens. In the first, the ground was piled high with cardboard boxes, litter prolific on an earth trodden bare. One could see nothing of the second; a dirty trellis perched high on the brick wall was backed by thujas. The gate, ramshackle yet solid, carried a notice, roughly painted on a square of hardboard: 'BeWARe of Dog AlsAtion' in a mixture of capitals and small letters without punctuation. The spelling mistake jarred, the secrecy, but no growl or bark warned. Upper windows were black. In the third a large ash tree tilted winter-naked, leaning away from the house; music sounded, unrecognizable with a thumping bass. He pushed open the Stileses' gate; it hung well, the hinges were oiled. A path of flagstones leading to the yard was flanked by two narrow stretches of lawn, two lengths of

187

privet hedge. Up three steps to the back door, on which he knocked, having failed in the darkness to find a bell. He hammered again. The switching on of lights rewarded him.

In this house Mary existed.

Waiting he could neither think nor notice thought, but his numbness fell short of comfort. He had braced himself, he concluded, to face a wooden door without a knocker. This world of backyards offered him little beyond shabbiness, neat or tidy according to effort. George Stiles would come out here on a summer evening to mow his lawns inside ten minutes, or whiningly plugged-in trim his hedge. The coal place housed his mower; the outside lavatory, white-painted, was unused; the row of dustbins and full plastic bags stood in strict lines. Mrs Stiles emerged on Mondays and Thursdays to hang out her washing. The back windows were stoutly barred. He could detect no movement inside; it was as if the bar lights had flickered on, beamed steadily now by chance, not in answer to his fist.

Bolts were finally drawn. George Stiles opened up.

'Thought we heard somebody. We didn't expect you this way,' he said. 'We left the shop door open for you.'

There was something, a credit mark, with these theft-conscious burghers. David wondered at what time, ten to eight, five to, one minute to, they had made the supreme sacrifice. He stepped past his father-in-law, who bent to rebolt.

'You go first,' David ordered. 'I'll turn the lights off.'

The younger man felt antagonistic.

'Not been a bad day,' Stiles ventured and went unanswered.

The downstairs behind the shop was shelved storeroom; new planks were piled in the middle, with two sawing horses. The smell reminded David of the workshops at school where he had hated the woodwork master.

'Careful with these stairs,' Stiles warned. 'They're awkward. We're getting near the age when I'll have to put a handrail up.'

At the top of the blatantly uncarpeted treads a white door faced them out. Across the whole of the square landing before it stretched a thick institutional rope doormat on which Stiles now cleansed his feet. He was wearing, David noticed, brand-new leather slippers.

188

'Go on in,' he said. 'I'll see to the last light.'

The door beautifully painted, Stiles had been apprenticed to a decorator, reflected the shadeless lamp in an atmosphere without dust. As soon as David stepped through on to a landing he knew rich change. The carpets were red and navy blue, two golden frames housed oils of high trees and lurid skies done by Eva's father, or was it grandfather?; and the space was illuminated from an elaborate candelabra and three shell wall-lights.

'Straight across,' Stiles shouted, as if his son-in-law were a stranger.

David knocked at the door, entered.

Curtains were drawn in this room which sparkled with an equality of brilliance. He remembered it by day when it was never properly lit, but now the place seemed to dazzle. They had imported standard lamps.

'Come in, David,' Eva said. She stood by the table, by a starched white cloth, by elaborate places laid, but aggressively, apprehensively welcoming. 'You're not late.'

'I am,' he answered.

'Only a few minutes then.'

Mary sat in a high-backed modern chair by the gas fire, upright, legs together, wearing a simple white dress with blue polka dots. Her hands rested on the arms of the chair, the position awkward as her mother's.

'What about a glass of sherry, then?' Stiles shouted from behind. 'It'll give us an appetite.' He bustled round, out of character. 'Mary?' She nodded. 'Evie?' – 'Yes, please.' 'David?' David refused; Stiles filled three of the largish glasses straight from the bottle on the sideboard.

'Hello.' David greeted his wife neutrally.

'Hello.' She lifted her eyes, stared him straight in the face, holding the scrutiny, wide-eyed, pale, unsmiling, neither one thing nor the other.

He moved towards her holding out his hand, which she took firmly but without rising. Her palm was clammy.

'Are you well?' he asked. It seemed preferable to 'How are you?', more friendly.

'Yes, thank you.'

'A good journey?'

189

'I suppose so.' That was grudging enough. Stiles bounced out, in front of David, with glasses for the ladies.

'Are you sure, David, you won't join us?' he said on his return. 'Good stuff. Best the beer-off could provide.' The man sounded jovial, excitable, savouring every minute, while his women were dumb. Perhaps he could not control his delight at his daughter's return, and nothing else mattered. 'The good health of all.' Up went his glass.

After the ritual wetting of the lips, there was silence which no one attempted to break. David at last in the presence of his wife felt embarrassment, nothing stronger, so that if anyone had invited him to leave he might have complied without compunction. He was sorry for Mary, in that her parents, her mother, had forced her into this situation, but she had thrown him over without excuse or word and it would do her no harm to make reparation for that. He had backed away, and stood by the door, as if to run. Hands in pockets, he tested his grievances without result. Mary wore plain blue shoes; he lifted his head no higher; little mattered very seriously. He could make his way through the evening without undue disturbance.

He realized that his jaw, his lips, his arms inside the sleeves of a well-cut dark sports jacket were stiff with tension, and he shrugged, smiled tentatively, limbering up. His mother-in-law watched him, glass in her hand, still by the table. She stood, a bundle of clothes, though her best, but crumpled by uncertainty, understanding nothing, expecting catastrophe. Perhaps, he thought, she would have imposed a vow of silence on them until they were used to each other, used to the idea that they could breathe the air of a room together, without consequent earthquake. He stole a glance at Mary who sullenly contemplated a curvetting bronze horse with pedestal which had been dumped, oddly, on the floor in the corner. Somebody had moved it, he decided, from its place of honour on the sideboard to make space for the sherry tray. Father Stiles was pouring himself a second.

'I think we should sit down,' he said, glass upraised.

'Right.' His wife found herself. 'You that end, David. Dad, that side. Mary, this.'

'Up to the scratch,' Stiles shouted.

Mrs Stiles made for the kitchen and the potato dish. George hummed to himself, imbibed alcohol already potent. The other two did not speak. David, keeping his eyes religiously away from his wife's profile, knew he acted ridiculously, but did nothing to thaw out his frozen social skills. The word 'frozen', it was presented to him, exactly described him; he could sit there, but he could not feel, either anger or disappointment or pity. It would have been better if he had swilled down a couple of George's big sherries, to loosen his tongue. He straightened his puritan back as Mrs Stiles returned.

The serving of the meal, and he had guessed correctly: ham, tongue, brawn, haslet, pork pie, salad, beetroot in a cut-glass dish, pickles, piccalilli, two styles of chutney, demanded question and answer. They spoke to each other, handed large gold-rimmed plates about, organized moves with the cruet so that for a few minutes friendliness managed a bogus appearance. Stiles and his wife both stood, both issuing orders or countermanding them, piling David's plate past reason.

'Nothing but lettuce,' Stiles said, forking up another segment of ham to drop without permission across David's meal. 'Off the bone.'

'You sit down, Dad, and see to yourself,' Eva said.

George laughed out loud, looking to others to join him, but obeyed only to leap up again.

'The wine,' he said. He knocked over his half-empty glass. 'Oh, Hanover.' His wife rounded the table, mopped successfully. 'You'll join us in a glass of red, David, now, won't you?' He seemed nowise abashed.

'No, thank you. If you don't mind.'

'No? Why not?'

'I have to drive back.'

'One glass won't stop you.'

'No, thank you.' He was determined on ungraciousness.

'Mary, then?'

'Not for me, thank you.'

'It's not worth opening the bottle for us,' Eva answered. 'It gives me indigestion, and you've had more than enough.'

Stiles subsided with a clown's ludicrous face.

Such conversation as there was crossed leadenly between the

191

parents. Stiles had been subdued. Plates were cleared of food; no second helpings were taken. Mrs Stiles brought in ice cream, tinned fruit salad; clearly Mary had taken no part in preparing the meal.

David refusing replenishment, thanked his mother-in-law.

'It wasn't really what I intended,' she said bluntly, voicing perhaps her disappointment with her daughter.

'It was delicious.'

'You could have prepared exactly the same for yourself, with no need to go out.'

'And when I do, what do I get? Limp lettuce, wet ham, bottled salad cream.' He felt sorry for the woman.

'Dad and I will clear away,' Eva continued grimly, ineluctably. 'And we'll wash up. I expect you and Mary have things to say to each other. We'll be outside for half an hour. Then we'll bring you a cup of coffee.'

'Or the first-aid box,' Stiles said, recovering. Eva sneered him down.

'Is that agreed?' she asked, irritably. It sounded like a game of forfeits.

Nobody spoke. All four rose to clear the table, and this was not forbidden. When the dishes were piled after procession into the scullery next door, Eva replaced the white cloth with a red, and pointed the young people to the chairs in front of the gas fire. She looked at the clock.

'I'll knock on that door at twenty-five past nine,' she said.

David could have smiled at her lugubriously determined goodwill. As the door clicked to, he turned to Mary for a lead. She hesitated, then gracefully took the chair she had occupied when he arrived. He did not sit down at once, but after a minute's fidgets and feeling disadvantaged on his feet made for the chair opposite.

She said nothing, appeared to muse.

'Welcome home,' he burst out, and wished at once he'd kept his mouth shut.

She looked at him, dartingly. In alarm?

'I had to make a start,' he said.

She did not answer that. He pulled at his chin, waiting. In the end she raised her head and in a perfectly normal voice said,

'Well, go on then. Say whatever it is you've got to say.'

'What do you mean?' He'd return unfriendliness with unfriendliness.

'My mother thinks I should see you, talk to you. I get the impression from her that you think so too.'

'And you don't?'

'It's too late, isn't it?'

'For what?'

'Talk.'

This was not good, but neither was it yet disastrous. They listened to each other testing out with something other than 'Would you pass the mustard, please?' Nervously awkward, his arms limp, David tried again.

'Have you considered coming home?' he asked.

'To Station Road?' That mildly encouraged.

'Where else?'

She held her breath, mouth open, head turned away from him, nose beaky.

'Is that what you want?'

'Yes.'

The word was immediate. He did not know whether it gave the truth, but it was, surprising himself, like the playing of a card over which one has hesitated, a relief.

Mary did not respond, held herself away. She struggled towards speech.

'Do you mean that?'

'Yes, I do.'

He would not vacillate. He'd committed himself, embarked.

'David,' she spoke without force. 'You don't seem to have any idea what I've done.'

The one passage of decent conversation during the meal, apart from requests and Stiles's frenetic dabs at drollery, had occurred when Eva had quizzed him about the Trent. They had gone through the history of his participation and he had understood, as he laid down his knife and fork to answer, that the interrogation was for Mary's benefit. She would know how he had spent his time, how he had occupied himself in the period of loss, and he had talked gratefully, even strongly, to Eva. Mary had not intervened, but continued picking ladylike at her

193

meal, but he had been convinced that she had listened, that this information had in some way united them. Perhaps he had been clutching at straws.

'No,' he said now. 'That's true.'

'I'm not the same woman who left here in January.'

'I realize that.'

'I doubt if you do. I really . . .' Her voice trailed off.

'You mean you met somebody you preferred to live with rather than with me.' His sentence rumbled pedantically on.

'You could say that. Yes. But that's not the half of it.'

He thought, and his confidence was fast disappearing, that he detected a faint Americanization of accent.

'Go on,' he said.

She did, said nothing; not giving even the impression of thought. She sat, in his eyes, a woman without will, bored out of her wits, prepared never again to open her mouth to him.

'What about the child?' he asked.

Mary glanced up, genuinely puzzled; he recognized the tiny frown.

'Our child,' he said.

She pulled the frock round her belly, ball-shaping it.

'You're still carrying it?'

'Yes.' Without interest, or with incomprehension at the stupidity of his question.

He had looked carefully, but had not noticed the signs of pregnancy. Why in hell hadn't that cracked, mischievous bitch, Eva, warned him?

'Do you still feel sick?'

'So-so.' She accompanied her words with hand movements.

Sedately she offered him a few sentences about her medical treatment in America, adding that she had visited her mother's doctor who had already fixed her a hospital place and relaxation classes. She appeared sombrely pleased, answered easily as he extended the interlude with questions.

They fell silent again.

'Will you consider coming back?'

'It wouldn't be fair to you.'

'Let me be the judge of that.'

She sat as if it were too much trouble to make the effort to reply. There was no distress, only accidie. He changed the topic, and these snap decisions came easily tonight, asking about the opera. This time she looked at him not believing her ears.

'I don't know what to say.'

'About *Semele*?'

'About you and me.'

'Leave it. Tell me about the opera. It's three or four months.'

'I didn't write to you, or phone, or anything.'

'No.'

'I meant to. The longer you put it off . . .'

'I think I understand that.'

Again silence groaned between them.

'*Semele*,' he persisted, 'was it good?'

'Oh, God. What does it matter what it was?' Anger spurted.

'You don't want to come back?' he asked.

'I don't know. I don't know.'

'Will you try it? Give it a run?' Why had he used the second, explanatory expression? Would a plain question attract an answer he did not want?

'Why should you take me back?' Her voice seemed stronger. 'After the way I behaved?'

'You mean you committed adultery?'

'Yes. That wasn't the important part. I mean, we did, yes. It isn't any use denying it.'

He managed to look at her, stifling anger, and found she was crying. Her voice had given no inkling of the rolling tears. He stood, walked across, bent by her, taking hand and arm. She ignored the squared handkerchief he held out. He closed his eyes, crouching uncomfortably, on his heel like a collier, waiting.

'Let me go.'

'What?' The rough monosyllable escaped his care.

'Let go of me.'

'No, Mary.'

She stood up but he still held on to her. When she dragged herself away, he freed her at once, rose, put his hands into his pockets.

'Sit down,' he said, at length, in disappointment.

195

She brushed with her left hand at the wrist he had been holding as if to rid herself of his presence. He could not have hurt her.

'Sit down, Mary.'

Immediately she obeyed, and he returned to his chair.

'You, we, need more time,' he began. 'So, if I may, I'll make a suggestion.'

She paid no attention.

'You know what I want,' he continued, 'so we'll leave it for now. Then perhaps you would come over to our house, when you've settled down, and we'll discuss it again.'

'That won't alter things.'

'Well, you may say so. I'm not so sure. Shall we leave it at that?'

She had dried her eyes, with a crumpled piece of paper, a habit he remembered. There had always been about her person two or three tissues, never new, tatty but unattractively handy.

'All right.'

'Thanks. I'll call for that cup of coffee now, shall I?'

'If you like.'

'We can talk to each other still. That's something.'

'I don't know what to say,' Mary replied. 'I'm in no position to talk about anything.'

He could see a slight eruption on the skin under her lips. Her face was bloodless, without health, blotched. Her neck was thin, and her arms.

'Do you sleep well?' he asked.

'Yes, since I've been home.'

'Have the doctors given you sleeping tablets?'

'Not with this.' She pointed at her belly. 'I won't have anything. I slept badly in America, especially this last month.'

'Your mother will look after you.' He'd no idea why he'd made the statement.

'She's too energetic. It makes me tired just to see her.'

They were having conversation, banalities, routine exchanges like the rest of the world.

'Your father's delighted to have you back.'

'I suppose he is.' Had she not noticed?

'Come and see me tomorrow.' He threw the mild command.

196

'I'm rehearsing with the quartet in the morning. So, afternoon or evening.'

'How shall I get there?'

'I'll come and fetch you. You suggest a time.'

'I don't know.' Back to the slough.

'Three thirty, then. That gives you time to stay in bed, have lunch and another nap. I shan't have much to feed you on. What my dad calls "bread and scrape".'

'David, I can't promise anything.'

'Yes.'

Perhaps he meant 'no', and they sat quietly, trying not to look at each other.

'How are your parents?' she asked suddenly.

As he began to explain, their Cornish holiday, his father's attempts at retirement, Joan's concerts, he realized that she had initiated the conversation, though she seemed less than animated at his answers. When he'd finished his bright paragraph she said, 'I don't think I can come back, David.'

He knew despair.

'Not tomorrow, you mean?'

'Yes, if you want me to. But I don't want to build your hopes up. I can't promise anything.'

David lacked the strength to answer her; he'd done well, and now the problem bested him. Some little time later he heard her say something about coffee, go to the door, call out to her parents.

The room seemed crowded with hundreds. Mrs Stiles poured into large, delicate cups, fluted edges perfect. The family talked, but incomprehensibly, with a garrulous friendliness in a language he did not understand. He heard Mary.

'David's coming to pick me up at three thirty tomorrow.'

'Where are you off to then?' Eva, facetious.

'Station Road.'

'For good?' Father, father.

'We'll see.'

David did not stay long. Heavy-eyed, he left through the shop. In the side street he leaned on the roof of his car, exhausted. Nobody came past to see him. On Saturday evening at 10.30 this part of Derby kept itself quietly to itself.

He gnawed at his knuckle.

197

16

David Blackwall slept soundly.

He shopped first thing Sunday morning to make sure he could feed his wife and arrived early at Barton's house for the Trent rehearsal, where he found Frederick Payne in expansive mood. Wilkinson had rung to say that he'd be a few minutes late, on account of a family crisis, but this did not, for once, perturb the leader, who, feet straight out, regaled Barton with gossip.

Payne had met the Talbots, and Anna had spoken to him about Elizabeth Falconer, now away preparing for a summer at Bayreuth and a recording schedule, having just jetted back from Australia.

'She's never at home, and, according to Anna, she won't allow her husband with her while she's at work.'

'Oh?' Barton looked sympathetically towards David.

'Nobody knows why she married him. She doesn't use the title.'

'Somewhere to settle in old age,' David suggested.

'Don't know, don't know. She's a mystery to everybody, herself included. There was that Colonel Tait, Holkham Tait, lives at Rathe Hall, he doted on her. Anna says he lives abroad now. His estate's in the hands of a manager. He's a millionaire, quite an elderly chap, but he lives in a bit of a poky place in the South of France, and on her account. Just has lost interest in life.'

'Why France?' Barton asked. 'She's never up this way.'

'Connections. Memories. She's a remarkable woman apart from her singing. You know her, don't you?' Payne to David.

'Not really.'

'Anna said she taught your wife.'

'Now and again.'

198

'I had one like that at the Academy,' Barton said. 'Eight out of ten of his lessons were given by substitutes.'

'It doesn't do to give women the power she's got. I know what you're going to say, Cyril, that men are just as bad, and women should have the opportunity if they're good enough. Well, I tell you straight. Women haven't got the mental equilibrium, the stability to bear the strain.'

Payne posted out his prejudices, good-humouredly, half humorously. David's mind ranged elsewhere, and Barton argued circumspectly, an eye all the time on Blackwall, in fear that one of Payne's sallies would hit home. Wilkinson arrived earlier than expected with a tale of a disturbed night, a call for the emergency doctor, the search for antibiotics. He looked cheerful enough, more so than usual, praising his wife's resolution, quick decision making, sturdy sense.

'And yet you say women haven't the stability,' Barton mocked Payne.

'What's he know about bloody women?' Wilkinson's eyebrows came angrily together.

'Brethren, let us play,' said Barton piously.

The rehearsal satisfied, quieted them all.

As they packed up, Wilkinson boasted, 'And I'm the only one of you who's going home to a cooked dinner.'

'Clever boy,' said Payne.

'None of your packets of frozen peas and a dried-up pork chop.'

'That's David,' Payne answered, laughing loudly, braying at nothing.

'Go on. Clear off, the lot of you,' Barton shouted, but he detained David, holding his elbow to ask, 'Everything all right with you?'

'Thanks, yes.'

He ought, he knew, to have stopped and spent five minutes explaining about Mary's return to that good man, Cyril Barton, but he dared not. He rushed out of doors, paying painfully for his silence as he clenched his steering wheel. Back home he deliberately looked out frozen peas, frozen chips, made no apple sauce, to accompany inexpensive belly pork. If he did not enjoy the meal, which he ate abstractedly, it seemed the careless, spartan preparation earned a little of his own back on somebody or something.

David was wasting the last few minutes before his departure when Anna Talbot rang. After her cheerful preliminaries, she said, 'How's Mary, then?'

'She's back.'

'I know. That's why I rang. Is she there?'

'No. She's staying with her parents in Derby.'

'Betty Braker, she was in *Dido*, saw her on Friday. They didn't speak. In a shop in Derby. She rang to ask me.'

Anna Talbot knew everything, everybody, Tait's despair, his wife's desertion. Why had he let it out to her of all people when he knew she couldn't keep her mouth shut?

'How does she seem?' The woman pressed on.

'Tired. Very tired.'

'Is she coming back here, to Beechnall, to live with you?'

'That remains to be seen.'

She did not desist, and he explained that he'd need to finish the conversation as he was about to fetch her. All through his tight-lipped sentences she yessed sympathetically.

'Will you let me know if there's anything I can do, David?'

'Thank you. Yes.'

'Be sure, now.'

'I will.'

He put the phone down neatly, but in anger. Curiosity would not kill that cat. He took a last look round his premises; he had rearranged photographs, removed dust and crumbs. Mary was not coming to judge his capabilities as a domestic servant. Constraint weakened muscles.

A thunder shower hindered him as he drove; the windscreen was splashed blind, so that he was forced to draw up in a parking place. The storm blew over within five minutes, but puddles lay deep on the road, were flung about by wheels. The streets of Derby, he noticed on arrival, were quite dry.

He went in through the shop, and upstairs the Stiles parents grew expansive, offering coffee, newly baked buns, excited talk. Mary was not to be seen.

'Are you in all day?' he asked.

'Yes. Why?' Eva.

200

'So I can give you a ring when to expect us back.'

George Stiles rubbed his chin.

'She won't be stopping the night, then?' he asked.

'Not from what she said yesterday.'

'She could change her mind.' Eva seemed to believe it.

'Has she said anything to you?'

'No. She's rested. Only got up just before dinner. And she slept most of the time.'

'That's what she needed,' George said. 'Whatever it is that's happened, it's knocked the stuffing out of her.'

They heard Mary outside; she made sure of that, even rattling the doorknob. She presented herself to them, incredibly neat, in a military-styled raincoat, sheer black tights, smart shoes. Though pale still, she looked composed, the dark hair tidy as a helmet; she could not surely have had it cut since yesterday. She carried a large, shiny handbag.

'Your chauffeur's here,' George said, too loudly.

'Will you take a few saffron buns for your tea?' Eva asked David.

The parents talked, ordered, delayed.

'I've never seen you in that suit before,' Eva said. 'Turn round. I like it.'

'I've had it at least two years.'

'I've had my best for fifteen.' George, affable.

'And it looks like it,' his wife answered.

The buns were packed while George expatiated on his wife's cooking. Now nothing stood in the way of their departure. Mary kissed her parents and the four trooped downstairs and outside the shop door to where he had parked.

'Enjoy yourselves,' Stiles shouted.

'Have you got some money?' Eva demanded.

'What do I want money for?' Mary raised a smile.

'You never know.'

David helped Mary with her seatbelt.

She said little for the first part of the journey, as he described the thunderstorm which had passed Derby by. Mary stared straight ahead, politely putting in a word to show she was listening. Smartly gloved hands were clasped on the handbag in her lap. Conversation was hard work, but he did his best. As he

201

drove slowly through the town, the streets empty, she did not look about her.

'Is there anything you'd like to do?' He ought to have asked before.

'Such as?'

'Well, drive somewhere. To Newstead, to one of the parks for a walk?'

'Is that what you want?'

'I'm at your service.'

'No, thanks. It doesn't look too promising.' Perhaps his facetious answer had riled her.

When he halted at the traffic lights where he turned off in the mornings for his school, she asked, 'Are you on first period tomorrow?'

'Yes. Why?'

'Nothing. I just wondered.'

He did not fall to silence, but commented on his timetable which was exactly as it was when she left.

At his front door, he stepped back to allow her to enter.

'You go first,' she ordered.

In the hall, he asked if he should take her coat. She slid it from her arms, and hung it herself, familiarly, on the pegs at the bottom of the stairs. Her dress, loosely falling, was of a striking claret red.

'I admire that,' he said. It sounded false, and she did not answer. This time, on his invitation, she led the way to the sitting room, where she headed for the chair he usually occupied. She made no obvious examination of the place.

'Would you like a cup of coffee? Tea?' he asked.

'Sit down, David,' she spoke without power. 'I don't want anything just now. Sit down.'

After an awkward interval, three minutes perhaps, seemingly unending, she became straighter.

'It hasn't changed much,' she began. 'Have you kept the garden tidy?'

He presented his account as she fidgeted in her chair, crossing one leg over the other, gripping or slapping the chair arms. David, watching, felt as uncomfortable as she.

'I'm glad you're back,' he said. 'It's good.'

202

She nodded, as if to acknowledge that she had heard.

'That you agreed to come over.'

Now she rose, walked to the window, looked out over yard or garden, motionless. With her back to him, she began to speak.

'I acted abominably in not writing to you.' It sounded prepared, without spontaneity.

'Let's forget it.'

'I can't. Neither can you. Nor should you.'

She did not face him; he made another effort in fear.

'Tell me about it.' No answer. 'About the opera.'

Mary began, but hesitatingly, in shards of sentences, to describe her arrival, her sense of disorientation, the first rehearsals. Soon she lost the flatness of voice, became animated, chose lively but succinct anecdotes, though still she did not leave the framing window. Her account was by no means detailed, but now it lacked a sense of guilt, acquired value on its own account, had interest.

She worked over the first days, the differences to her when it was decided she would sing Semele, how they had immediately changed her room. She touched on the cheerful, laconic kindness of an American girl called Kate Pastry from San Diego, her own realization that Red Gage, the unostentatious director, was a nationally pre-eminent, revered figure.

David questioned her; it seemed unarguably necessary for her to talk to him about Gage. By intervening constantly he dragged her back to the man, made him emerge.

Gage had softly said what he wanted, equally quietly made it clear when what they provided for him was not what he demanded, and why, and would insist then on their compliance. He never raised his voice, but his arguments were irresistible. He convinced them that the change of pace he deprecated or the misplacement of a prop or rostrum would, minute in itself, weaken the fundamental strength of his master plan. The conductor, Ulrich Fenster, a gifted musician, was as much dominated by Gage as the newest chorus contralto or ASM.

Only by assiduous questioning thrown into her back did David learn that Mary at first had not understood Gage's predominance. Certainly he was an intellectual, certainly he gave the impression that for every hour they had spent on the opera

203

he had given a day, but this hardly seemed a reason for the breathless drive that compelled the most egotistic into subservient silence. Only when, to her surprise, he showed a personal interest in her, he sat with her through a grand social evening and accompanied her back to her room, did people blurt out the stories of his success, in Italy, Australia, Japan, his influence, the dazzling performances he would mount at the Met, the Scala. Mary had mocked, 'What's he doing with a twopenny ha'penny university production then?'

They'd look slyly at her as if she were catching them out, or acted overly stupid, and then report his dictum: 'You learn more of stage drama from *Semele* than from *The Ring* or *Otello*, because in Handel it's implicit only.'

She acquired a nasal timbre as she quoted.

Gage had taken three weeks out of his high life to produce them, because he was interested, they said, in art, not in Gage. The world could wait for him. This unshowy extremist had earned, and he was not yet forty, the respect of the international circuit, could subdue divas, hand out patronage, recognize and promote the talented, and here he walked amongst them, a god on earth, blowing his nose, making a pass at this English singer, bringing in every New York critic to marvel at his first night.

The plaudits of the journalists were so lavish that it seemed momentarily certain that *Semele* could be sent unchanged out on a world circuit, but the total effect was lost inside a fortnight. Once the company went on tour, Gage had disappeared to his next engagement, the scenery did not travel well, began to disintegrate, there was illness in the cast, Fenster handed over to a deputy, the orchestra began to break up, arrangements were seen to be uncertain; even the funds ran out, in spite of rescue attempts. The university people in New York were great, fought to keep the company together, but they had their own concerns and too much effort and money had been spent earlier and a crack-up was inevitable. The girl's voice broke as she talked; from the stiff back David could learn nothing, but he heard her tragedy plainly.

He could understand why she would not move from the window. She had taken a stance there, in the first place, out of nervousness and once in situ found herself able to talk to him, express her failure. David wanted her back, in the chair, comfortably, but was afraid to make the proposal. His hesitation seemed ludicrous once she had begun to talk easily about the opera, once she had caught his interest without playing too blatantly on emotions, but now, as she spoke her disappointment, the faceless narration was only too proper. It kept him at a distance so that she was capable of confession.

Yet he hated the gap. When he knew all, they would still not have touched physically; the constraint between them would be greater because of what she said, her manner of saying it.

'Aren't you getting tired, standing there?'

'No, I'm all right.'

He had been surprised at his own quietude. It had appeared to him as she progressed with her narration that his professional interest had cooled his emotions. That could not be true; any next sentence might club him down, shred his carapace of disinterest. He asked his questions to keep her talking, that was important, but he could not, by thought at least, prise her away from that rectangle of light.

'Where was Gage, then?' he asked.

'He'd gone off to the West Coast.'

'Did he keep in touch with you?'

'No.'

'Not at all?'

'No.'

She had steadied her tone. He paused again, uncertain of the form his inquisition must assume, unwilling to dam the trickle finally.

'Was that the sort of man he was?'

For a second he thought she'd turn round, but she did not. Her obstinacy seemed ludicrous; he ought to walk across and spin her. He did not.

Without much difficulty she repeated the information she had already given. Gage was intense, but ungaudy, sombre. When he talked his voice, rarely raised, rapid, carried immense weight; he knew his mind, a wide universe. His reputation was enormous, but he refused to be diverted by publicity. He hardly slept. He crept round in his sneakers, black trousers, sweatshirt, small linen or velvet jacket, and altered every pre-

205

conception. An iconoclast, he revered each facet of tradition. Once he had made his decision, his certainty was so substantial that he saw no need to shout it from the housetops. Mary spoke of his patience, his galvanic effect, his huge conviction.

'And you were his mistress?'

The hiatus stretched, stretched; David's breath came short.

'We had sex,' she said, 'three times over three weeks. It didn't seem important to him. Or so it seems now.'

'When?' David snapped at her.

Again she described the brilliance of the first few performances. The low, shame-shocked voice sketched again preparations, parties, the enthusiasm of pundits, the intoxication of the professors, and her precious place in the centre of animation; stimulated beyond measure, delighted in herself, a cynosure, the scintillating stranger, she had known that the world bowed to her, envied her, was hers for picking.

Mary was no fool, David knew. She had experience of performance and achievement; her head would not have been turned without reason. These bits and pieces of sentences made him understand, even participate in, the bright solidity of success.

'And we fell into bed together.'

'You were not drunk?'

'Not with alcohol.' She filled her lungs. 'And he was strange. I don't think he liked women much, but he was taken out of himself. It was hard to tell. He wasn't on the same planet that I was.'

'But it was more than once?'

'Three times.'

'And then?' David could barely breathe.

'He switched off. I don't think he was particularly attached to women, but for a few days he did just consider marrying an English girl, pregnant by somebody else. But then he went on to his next thing.' The sentences seemed translated from a foreign idiom.

Zeus had become himself again, in divinity, in these sentences torn from her.

'And you?'

Now she turned round, came across the room, stood momentarily by the chair she had vacated, her right hand reaching down, touching nothing, and then sat. She lifted a blotched face.

'I wanted to marry him.'

David shuffled back, away from her, stationed himself behind the end of the table, crushed.

'He was overwhelming. He was a genius.' She seemed to plead for David's agreement. 'Perhaps the fact that I was having such a success turned my head.' Her fingers reached for reason in the air. 'Perhaps, I've gone over this afterwards, over and over, I thought he would put me in the way of a career. That wasn't deliberate at the time. I'm sure of that. It was just that he was so different. Remarkable. Powerful.'

'And physically?' He dragged the question up from his bitterness.

'Not very tall. Strong-looking. With this nice, curly hair.' She looked up, suddenly, eyes open blue. 'He wasn't as attractive as you really. I don't think so. Not in appearance.'

'But?'

She stared at him in dislike.

'And he just went away?'

'Yes.'

'Did you know he was going?'

'It was always understood that once we were established, he'd dash off for his jamboree, he called it, in San Francisco. But he went before I, before . . . I thought he'd . . .'

'He left you no note, no explanation?'

'No.'

'You expected to hear from him? When he arrived?'

'I hoped so. Yes.'

'And you did not?'

She did not answer; there was no need. She bowed her head, keeping herself to herself in humiliation.

'What about some tea?' he asked. It was 5.30; they had talked for over an hour.

'I was shattered. I couldn't eat. I felt sick all the time. It affected my singing. People were kind, especially Katie, promising me things, that he'd come back, that, that. It only took me a week to realize. I hoped he'd . . . I kept waiting.'

'And then you were stranded?'

'The schedule began to break, and that, that . . . There was no work for me there.'

'Liz Falconer's scheme didn't come to anything?'

'No. She never even appeared. Cancelled everything, they say. But you just imagine us, performing like hell so somebody somewhere would take us up. Nothing happened. We did no worse than when the critics were all over us. But it was Red they were praising. I understand that now. For all the effect we had, we might have been singing in the street.'

'Yes.'

'I rang my mother and told her I was coming home.'

'Why didn't you phone me, Mary?'

'How could I? After the way I'd treated . . .'

Subdued anger was directed away from him, towards the hearth.

'Tell you what,' he said. 'Come and help me get the tea ready.'

'You do it.'

He grasped it then, the extent of her effort. She was the husk of herself. This hour and a quarter had killed her beyond all politeness.

'You can have salmon sandwiches or ham,' he said.

'You choose.'

'I will.'

David felt glad to be in the kitchen, trembling, doing tasks not beyond him, cutting bread thin, making sure the best china was spotless. When he brought in the crockery, the cutlery, he noted she had not moved, that she sat, eyes wide open, in her chair, staid and stable. He arranged Mrs Stiles's saffron buns on a doyley on a plate. Twenty minutes had passed by the time he finally carried in the teapot.

'At long last,' he said. 'It's salmon. Made to your taste.' He carried over a stool which he placed in front of her, and lifted her feet on to it. She allowed the advance. Next he arranged a small table by her chair, handed her napkin, plate and knife, poured out her tea. She accepted a sandwich, moistened her lips, gave no thanks.

'Eat up,' he ordered.

She smiled, thin as water, across at him, tried a small bite. 'To your satisfaction?'

She nodded, incapable of speech. When she had masticated the sandwich, slowly, without appetite, in misery, he, watching her covertly, gave her a minute's grace before he carried the plate across. When she refused, he pressed her, and she yielded.

'We've got to build you up,' he said, and went unanswered.

Mary drank a second cup of tea, crumbled and ate one of her mother's cakes. David had lapsed into bleak, uncompanionable silence and was glad in the end to ask if she wanted more. She had removed her legs from the stool.

'No, thanks. That was lovely.'

Small victory sounded in the two sentences. While he was outside washing the dishes he heard her go upstairs, presumably to the lavatory, and then almost immediately come down. He had hoped she would look about, in and out of the bedrooms, but she disappointed him. Clearing the kitchen put off his return to the dining room.

He found her again at the window.

'Those bulbs have done well,' he said. 'Those you set in the tubs. Narcissi.'

She returned to her seat and he opposite.

'I've not asked you a word about yourself,' she said. 'It's been nothing but me and my foolery.' She skirmished with the last word.

'First things first.'

'Tell me.' Her voice lacked power, powerfully.

He described his time with the Trent Quartet, delineating the characters, making her smile at Barton's old womanliness, Wilkinson's domestic yoke, Fred's dignified homosexuality. From time to time she threw in a question as she would have done in the old days, and he relaxed, but she would then reassume the complicated stiffness of pose which kept him uncertain. He did not give up; he outlined technical difficulties in the Shostakovich, in Britten's Third, then sketched concert organizers, discomfort in dressing rooms, audiences, the chances of the Trent's becoming professional.

'How did you manage for white shirts for the concerts?' she

209

asked so feebly he wondered if he were inventing the conversation for himself.

'My mother bought me three, and kept them laundered.'

That seemed a confession of weakness.

'I did the rest. Honestly. Washing machine on every Wednesday and every weekend. I'm quite an expert with the iron.'

She dismissed the trivialities with a short sweep of the arm, violently energetic within the context of her immobility.

'How have you been?' she asked.

'Pretty healthy really. Usual coughs and colds.'

'I didn't mean like that.'

As soon as she had posed the first question he knew intensely how he had been. This afternoon he had hedged himself, disciplined himself to be her friend and host and now she came out with this demand. Depression winded him like a kick.

'Pretty bloody,' he answered.

'But you kept working?'

'To the best of my ability. I was lucky in that I had interesting things to do. If I'd been at a factory bench . . .' He rubbed his chin. 'Sometimes, even so, it was so painful it stopped me practising, but mostly I could stagger on, not very fast, not very straight.' He tried to keep his voice light. 'I wished sometimes I had an animal, a cat to sit on my knee, or a dog to take for a walk. Of course, for weeks I kept hoping, looking out for the postman, telling myself the transatlantic mail service had slipped up.'

'You must have . . .?' she faltered.

'In the end. Yes. I realized something was seriously wrong.'

'I'm sorry. It was awful, David.' She groped outwards. She was crying, soundlessly.

'Come back to me, Mary,' he said, off balance.

The imperative passed without effect. He had decided that she was not going to answer, that he must toss his cap again into the fearful ring, when she spoke.

'Do you mean that?'

He did not know; in his dizzy distress he had no landmarks except for this central pointer: he must take her.

'Yes. I wouldn't say it otherwise.' That sounded weakly, unconvincing even to him. 'I want you back.'

210

She said nothing, but her posture hinted of hope. She did not deny him, repel him with stiffness. She was listening.

'Come home,' he said. He remembered a catchword of his father's from some radio show. His all was subsumed under ham acting, comedians' foolery, half-forgotten ephemerality. The gaiety of nations.

'I have,' she said.

'For good?'

'You don't want me.' Silent crying began again; rolling of tears etched her grief into him.

'I do.'

'Why?'

'Because I love you.'

'But look what I've done to you.' Her voice was strong, letting him get away with nothing, checking his banalities.

'I want you here.'

'David.' She stopped, as if to make sure her argument was clear before she put it. 'You'll never be able to forget what I've done to you. It'll always be there, in your mind, whether you say anything or not. It will fester. I acted abominably. How can you say . . . ?'

'I've said it.' Strongly, upstanding.

'That's sentimental.'

The schoolmaster answered, on top of his class.

'Expressing more emotion than the situation warrants,' he said, mock-pedantically. 'Allow me to think otherwise.' He checked her with his hand. 'Argument is not going to change my mind. Do you want to come back?'

'Yes. If you'll . . . I think so.'

Her face, tear-stricken, was turned away from him. Was this wholehearted? He did not know, but he crouched, on his right heel like a miner again, by her chair.

'You won't be able to forget what I've done, will you?'

'I'm not perfect. No. I expect what you say is right enough, but it hardly seems worth wasting energy on just now.'

'It's no use starting off forgetting these things.'

'You'll be telling me next,' he said, flaring, 'that I only took you back because I didn't much care one way or the other about what had happened.'

211

'I didn't say that.'

'I know you didn't. But what you don't realize is how glad I am to see you sitting in this room, telling me you're going to stay.'

As soon as he established it in words it became the truth. A powerful sense of, at present, satisfaction rather than exhilaration gripped him, expressed by his monosyllable 'glad'. He could not define it, or defend it. Perhaps, these disclaimers darted, flitted at him sharp, resisted temptations, his pride had been temporarily bandaged, in so far that he had no longer to go about saying 'My wife has left me for another man.' It did not feel like this. He could not quite disturb the universe, even shake the street and his bent legs were beginning to hurt, but his conviction grew, strong, huge, deepening, not overwhelming yet, but near flood level. Dangerous, yes, all that. But right, right. Correct. Just.

The telephone shrilled. Both started.

For a moment he thought he should ignore its insistence, but could not. He smiled apologetically at his wife.

Anna Talbot asked how he had found Mary. Her impudence astounded, half angered him. He kept his voice low. 'She's here with me now.'

He could not listen to the welter of her answering, apologetic sentences. In the end she seemed to shout.

'You mean she's back for good?'

'I hope so.'

'Oh, David. That's marvellous.' A further flood of chatter penetrated no farther than his eardrums. Her talk took the guise of a ritual he could afford to ignore.

'Is she there now?' What did the damned woman mean? She knew quite well.

'Yes.'

'Would she, I mean, could I speak to her?'

'I'll see.'

He asked Mary, who had assumed the expression of one trying not to listen in. She rose without fuss, as to an inquiry from a shopkeeper, a telly-hire firm, the jobbing builder.

For a time she answered in monosyllables, so that he could only guess the direction of conversation. Mary's face was dry of

212

tears, but she did not smile, answered without facial expression as if she concentrated on a foreign language, afraid to miss the crucial word. David thought he detected in her stance something of that stiffness which had disfigured her earlier in the afternoon.

He listened, looking at his shoes. He had been convinced that Mary would stay with him, but he saw the possibility that Anna's impertinent intervention, person from Porlock, would give Mary the opportunity to draw back.

'Yes. – Oh, yes. – Um. – Is it? – Well. – Yes. Do they? – Oh. – I see. – No. – I don't think so.'

He tried to make sense of these separate dullnesses and the animated cackle between. He failed. He tensely took the arm of the chair.

'Oh, I expect so.'

Mary turned, looked at him. Suddenly he knew joy and certainty. God knows what she expected, perhaps to run across Anna some time, but the expectation was great. She would stay. She was his wife again. He would be a father. The sourness, the disappointments had not disappeared, but were in perspective. These would, she had said, and he knew for himself, savage him in the future, but for the moment he had made his proposal, only half understanding its nature and its commitments, and she had accepted. The act had remade them; they had begun, and already the pleasure of completion warmed him.

'Yes. I think that's likely.'

He was suspicious, and afraid. By God he was. Three months' hell is not wiped off the slate without trace. Smears blotch ugly.

'It's possible.'

What uplifted him now was the ease of his conviction. Once he had stepped up, like a sinner to the penitents' form, another of his father's childhood reminiscences, and declared himself he knew, without disclaimers, riders, ifs and buts that he had done right. It sang inside him. Father David and his anecdotes.

'There'll be snags.' Cackle, prestissimo, cackle, goose laughter. 'Aren't there always?'

It did not matter to him. He had taken a stance, almost against his nature, and the reward had been out of all proportion. Mary was talking now almost as fast as Anna Talbot about something Elizabeth Falconer had said or done, quite at home.

He remembered a sentence from his sixth form days, from *Cymbeline*, Posthumus to his restored Imogen:

> Hang there like fruit, my soul,
> Till the tree die.

David found his feet.

'No, no,' Mary was saying. 'Not at all. Must ring off, now. Thanks for the call. Yes. See you, Anna. Bye. Yes. Bye.'

She replaced the phone.

'I'll ring Derby,' she asked, 'shall I, to tell them I'll not be back tonight?'

She stretched a hand out to touch impossibility in an imperfect world.

Husband and father, he reached back.